SAVED WARRIORS

INTERGALACTIC ENOSIS: THE PYXIS SYSTEM

AURORA WELKIN

ALSO BY AURORA WELKIN

INTERGALACTIC ENOSIS: THE PYXIS SYSTEM

Fallen Warriors (Arana - Origin Story)

Saved Warriors (Arana, Rorc, Mes, & Kali)

Divided Warriors (Urien, Thora, & River)

Broken Warriors (Callibohr, Brarn, Hunter, & Lyra)

Healed Warriors (Callibohr, Brarn, Hunter, & Lyra)

INTERGALACTIC ENOSIS: THE SOLAR SYSTEM

My Destined Aliens (Kanurn, Kadohl, Kaer, & Sammie)

My Stubborn Aliens (Aux, Dagoner, Pirhanh, & Audrey)

SAVED WARRIORS

INTERGALACTIC ENOSIS: THE PYXIS SYSTEM

BOOK 2

AURORA WELKIN

This book is a work of fiction. Names, characters, businesses, places, events, locales, and incidents either are products of the author's imagination or are used fictitiously. Any resemblance to actual persons, living or dead, events, or actual events is entirely coincidental.

ISBN: 978-0-6489774-9-0

Cover design: Kasmit Covers

Editor: Stephanie Pretorius, Clause for Effect

❀ Created with Vellum

This book is dedicated to Lindsey and Stephanie.
The best critique partners I could have asked for.
You rock!

TRIGGER WARNINGS

This book is intended for mature audiences due to explicit language and sexual content. Contains steamy group scenes, but there are no M/M scenes. No cheating. Includes warfare and violence, as well as death. Reference to past sexual assault. **If you find this type of content triggering or offending, please do not read.** Books should offer an escape from our daily routines, not cause us extra nightmares.

Saved Warriors, book 2 in the Intergalactic Enosis: The Pyxis System series, is a science fiction alien warrior why choose romance featuring a human female and three aliens who are determined to claim their fated mate. Saved Warriors ends in a happily ever after!

MY WORST NIGHTMARE

KALI

"Entry points secured," Atlas reported.

"Bishop, Stallion, it's a go," I whispered.

We had eliminated all the men guarding Craden's sprawling estate, but I wasn't about to take any unnecessary risks with a paranoid terrorist. I'd rather be safe than sorry.

"Cobra, prepare for a quick exit," I ordered.

"Sure thing, Top."

"Target acquired." Bishop's voice rang clear through my earpiece.

"Target terminated," Stallion stated. His tone was somber, his usual mirth gone.

"All right, let's get out of here, boys," I said as I retreated to our vehicle.

In less than five seconds, Cobra had the JLTV's wheels spinning, throwing sand and gravel behind us.

"That was eas—"

"Don't jinx it, Stallion," Atlas grumbled as an SUV passed us from the opposite direction.

My gut had been churning since we got assigned this mission on the posh side of Afghanistan. But these were our orders, and we were one of the best black ops teams out there.

My eyes remained glued to the mirror. *Fuck*. It was heading straight to the mansion we'd just evacuated. "We're going to have company. Cobra, take us to base, yesterday."

Sooner than I'd anticipated, we had five open-top vehicles on our tail. Our Joint Light Tactical Vehicle was fast, but not fast enough. They were gaining on us, but at least with suicide armored doors, and a cabin wrapped in an armored shell, we could take fire and still make it out alive.

"Bishop track their positions; Atlas, get on the M2; Stallion, blow up those shitheads; Cobra, floor it." I barked orders, and the men jumped into action.

The vibrations from the machine-gun fire went straight through me; adrenaline-fueled electricity stimulated every muscle in my body. Turning the laptop my way, I sent out a distress signal and accessed the satellite feed. Surveying the surrounding areas, I searched for the least compromising route.

I needed to get my brothers in arms out of there safely. I'd never failed to protect them before and I wasn't planning to do so now.

"Take that moth—" The loud explosion of one of our pursuers' cars muffled Stallion's voice.

"Incoming vehicles on our east and west side," I yelled to our driver, "they're trying to surround us."

He shifted gears and pushed the JLTV to its limits. He was hoping to outrun them.

"Three remaining," Bishop reported as he took another jeep out.

"Shit! Four o'clock—they got RPGs," Atlas spun the M2 and released rapid-fire on the hostiles.

Cobra swerved left.

"Incoming," Stallion yelled.

For a second, time stood still as our vehicle was lifted off the ground.

My breath caught in my throat, and my heart stopped beating. I'd failed.

I saw Cobra's surprise, regret, and fear in that millisecond our eyes met, for as protective as I was of them, they were equally of me.

Then a tremendous blow rocked us—BOOSH! The awful sound of the blast drowned all others. An immense weight was thrown on me as the JLTV flipped forward and I was ejected out the windshield.

The impact forced my breath out of my lungs. Dust filled the air and slowly settled over and around me as I lay on the ground, too shocked to move.

Sand should be soft, not hard like concrete...I'm a hundred percent sure that I should be hurting right now, yet I don't feel any pain...where am I...?

Voices speaking Dari caught my attention, but for some reason I couldn't turn my head to look at them.

Why couldn't I turn my head, and why was the sun so bright?

Exhaustion threatened to pull me under, but I knew I was forgetting something important. My ears were ringing so loud that I heard nothing else. I closed my eyes, hoping to jog my memory. A few moments later my eyelids became too heavy, but I managed to open them again when I heard an animal's soft growls.

Oooh, what a beautiful kitty...

Was it hungry? I doubted I was tasty, but it kept prowling my way.

Oooh, what big teeth it has...

What I initially thought was a small kitten, turned out to be an enormous sabertooth who decided sitting on me was its best idea. Strangely, it didn't add to the weight pressing on my chest and leg, and the fact this species was extinct was of no importance at that moment.

No longer having the strength to keep my eyes open, I shut them. Everything went black one moment, and the next, sounds registered.

Chop-chop-chop—

The noise the helicopter blades made was growing louder when someone whispered, "Don't you travel to the Vaults of No Return! Hold on for us, we need you." His deep, raspy timbre breached the walls that safeguarded my heart and reached my soul.

"I'm not going anywhere," I said, but it came out as gurgles.

I wanted to look at him. To see who this stranger was, whose voice—so alien, yet so familiar—had touched my heart. Alas, exhaustion reared its ugly head, forcing me into a dark abyss.

Pain...excruciating pain brought me back to consciousness. I blinked repeatedly, trying to get something, anything, to focus. The sound of whirling rotors and the relatively smooth ride meant I was on the helicopter I'd heard earlier, but all was not well.

My thigh was on fire...

Fingers probed my leg...

Needles pierced my oversensitive skin...

Yellow-gold eyes focused solely on me…

The sight of a red-skinned man—no, not man, he was something else…

Was I dead?

"You will live."

His words were foreign to me, yet I understood their meaning.

Had he just decreed I'd live?

I wanted to laugh, but as he placed his huge hands on my chest, electricity zinged from his palms to my body. Searing heat emanated from his fingers, taking my breath and consciousness away.

Aliens didn't exist, yet the creatures running around me weren't human, and I was no longer on familiar ground.

Was my team playing a prank on me? *I swear if this is Stallion's doing, I'm killing him this time!*

I slapped my cheek. There was no feeling.

Nope, Stallion's safe. I'm hallucinating. There was no other explanation.

The craft we were in lurched sideways, throwing one of the beings on me. An involuntary scream escaped when the huge soldier passed through me.

Enemies didn't scare me easily, but having an alien—at least two feet taller than me—heading my way had me jumping out of my bones.

Okay, Kali, relax. You're dreaming, probably after watching one of your favorite sci-fi movies. You're safe. You can explore and look for the guys, just in case.

My pep talk worked. My breathing slowed, and my heart, only moments from escaping my chest, settled.

A purple-skinned soldier with emerald eyes caught my attention. He was barking orders to everyone else.

Mmm, sexy.

Where the hell had that come from? I needed to find a way to wake up, not lust after an alien. With limbs heavier than stones, I left the commotion—and the very alluring being—to go exploring.

You never know when you will need to navigate a spaceship. I snickered.

I was in a happy bubble, a tourist on vacation ambling around, when a ton of images flooded my mind's eye, bringing me to my knees.

Mere physical pain, I could endure. Emotional, though, was a whole other beast. I curled up into the fetal position, shivering, moaning, and sobbing as the knowledge of failing to protect my team returned to the forefront.

Why was I here? I needed to be with my men.

Suddenly, I was pulled from the spaceship and my wish was granted.

Someone threw ice-cold water on me. Or so I'd thought. I was back on Earth, but when I looked down I was dry, and…semitransparent, and…floating.

What the heck?

I whipped my head around. My body was on an operating table, two surgeons working in tandem, with five nurses helping them. The one removing a sizable piece of glass from my thigh was blond, whereas the other removing an equally big piece from my chest had hair the color of a raven's wings.

Great. More scars to add to my extensive collection. I floated closer.

I've never seen doctors operating on people. Oh...is that my heart? Gross!

I averted my eyes, but the truth was undeniable. They had blood and fluids going into my body and a tube through my mouth providing oxygen. I was in terrible shape.

Maybe it was time I let go; I felt tired, and I had no one to get back to anyway.

Your father, a voice whispered, and I hushed it.

There's a man for you out there, the voice insisted.

"Well, now there goes my chance of snatching a boyfriend," I replied, then mumbled, "as if the General—who shall not be named—hadn't ruined me already."

The voice quieted, and my eyes reverted to the sight in front of me. The doctors were doing everything in their power to save my life.

What was the point? I had been fighting for my country since I came of age, and I felt drained and empty. One of my worst nightmares had become reality. I'd failed to protect my team—my family by choice, the brothers I never had—and it might have cost them their lives. They were all I had, but maybe they'd be better off without me.

Having decided, I spun around, ready to leave the living behind. Tingling morphed into pins and needles, and then into sharp stabbing pains all over me, stealing my breath. The doctor working on my leg looked at the HRM, cursing.

The machine emitted a shrill sound when my heart started skipping beats.

"Hunter, her blood pressure is falling radically, we're losing her," the blond doc told his colleague.

"Let me die," I yelled, but no one heard me.

"Damn, the left coronary artery just ruptured," Dr. Hunter replied.

I didn't want to hear anything else. I could see the semitransparent figures waiting for me—outlined by a white light in the distance. My gut, which had never steered me wrong, insisted that in a little bit, there'd be no more pain. All I had to do was persevere until I reached the light.

Time to join them, I guess.

The moment the thought crossed my mind, I heard a guttural growl and words I couldn't understand coming from behind me.

The deep timbre of the owner intrigued me, and I turned toward the theater once again. What I saw made me gasp, and my body convulsed on the table. The doctors were yelling things at me, or maybe at the nurses—I didn't know.

No one seemed to notice the enormous purple alien approaching. Didn't they see the seven-foot-plus male?

His presence engulfed the room, but no one was paying attention to him. How could that be? His face was shrouded in mist, and I couldn't see his features clearly, but the rest of him was in high definition, and honestly…hard to miss.

But he was bleeding. Was he hurt? The thought alone caused my heart to constrict.

He headed straight toward my body; would he finish me off? Was he there to take me to the afterlife?

As if a whisper from a dream, I heard a doctor yell, *We're losing her!* Then the heart rate monitor's alarm went off. A flat line decorated the screen, and the sound propelled everyone into a frenzy.

The male, though, was calm. I saw his lips moving, but couldn't hear the words. When he placed his hand on my forehead, which was the only place on me that was not bloody or torn, it tickled.

I giggled, and my body convulsed once again.

At that exact moment, he spun his head and looked straight at me.

You're not dying on me, Colonel! You hear me? the raven-haired doc shouted.

So enthralled by the alien, I paid the doctor no mind.

"Come back now!" His voice carried the authority of someone who was used to being obeyed. I didn't understand his language, but I sensed he was furious with me for contemplating giving up.

When he realized I wasn't responding, he bent and kissed my forehead.

The sensation started as a light tingling, but then darkness abruptly engulfed me. The immense pain returned. All I heard before I lost consciousness was his sigh, and the steady beep-beep the HRM emitted.

The first week in the hospital after the operation passed by in a blur. Days ran into nights; time meant nothing, and I often found myself drifting away from reality. The times I was awake, I was either too numb, or drowning in guilt.

The nurses had told me that the members of my team were patients here. They were all recovering, although Atlas had lost part of his leg from the knee down, and Bishop had a spinal injury that kept him temporarily in a wheelchair.

I had cried at hearing the news because even though they might not all be whole, they were alive, and I was grateful for small blessings.

The nurses had also said that both them and my father visited often. Blurry images of the somber faces of my brothers swirled behind my eyes, but I didn't remember seeing him.

Today, though, was my lucky day. *Yay me. I can't wait to find out what he thinks about me now.*

A soft knock announced his arrival. A larger-than-life figure entered my room.

"Kalista, the nurses told me you're better today."

"Yes, General," I replied as he approached me, squeezed my hand, and let go to sit down on the chair next to the window.

Hell would freeze over before General Konnor Foster showed emotion.

Awkward silence ensued when neither of us initiated small talk.

Who'd break first?

I had all the time in the world. He'd have to return to his office at some point.

He gazed outside at the fountain that decorated the hospital's yard, before he turned his steely gaze on me.

Here we go.... The discussion I was dreading all week was about to take place.

"You and your team took a big hit. I know how much it hurts," he said.

I doubted my father, General Foster with the nearly perfect record knew the feeling, but I remained silent.

"Nonetheless, your mission was successful, and you were all awarded Purple Hearts. You'll receive yours once you return to duty."

"Purple Hearts," I echoed, stunned. My teammates were out of commission, and what did they get for it? A freaking medal. As if that'd be any consolation.

"I was also informed," he continued.

Oh great. What else is there?

"That you are getting promoted to Brigadier General. You will serve as a Deputy Commander to the commanding General of the First Armored Division." He smiled proudly.

My throat suddenly felt swollen, making breathing impossible. Sweat beaded all over my body.

My father jumped from the chair and came to my side. "Should I call the nurse, Kalista?" he asked, at the same time said nurse burst into the room.

"Honey, what's wrong? Your readings skyrocketed. Are you in pain?" She talked while pressing buttons, measuring my temperature, and checking the tubes connected to my body.

General Foster furrowed his brows.

I was certain he was annoyed with her for coddling me. I managed to swallow and take a deep breath.

"I'm okay. Just got some exciting news, that's all. No pain," I croaked.

"Congratulations, hon. Call me if you need anything," she said, and left the room.

Getting a promotion was what I had been working so hard for. Working under Lieutenant General Jonas Spencer—the one who should not be named—would be like opening a Pandora's box tailor-made for me. But I was no longer the naive and helpless girl I'd once been.

I could deal with whatever he threw at me.

I would.

IF ONLY I HAD AN RPG

KALI

Eight months later.

LTG wants you in his office in ten, General Foster. I'm off for the day, see you tomorrow.

I couldn't avert my eyes from my secretary's message on the computer's screen. Bile burned in the back of my throat. An uncontrollable shudder swept through my body.

Slamming my palm on the desk, I shot up, my chair falling backward.

The bastard. He wanted me to meet him in his office after the rest of the staff departed.

Six months had passed since I resumed duty. During the first couple of weeks, he had been here, and we had many meetings. His behavior remained cordial the whole time. He acted as if he cared about what his best friend's daughter had been through. Then he left on a classified operation. That gave me the opportunity to get acquainted with my colleagues and settle into my new role stress-free.

Well, until now.

I could feel the headache forming in the back of my head. It took conscious effort to relax my shoulders, and then stretch my neck muscles.

'If you tell a soul about this, I will destroy your father's career and put this little video we just created, online. You don't want that, do you?' His disgusting threat, delivered in a sugary sweet voice from all those years ago, reverberated in my head.

His words had crushed me then, had made me feel helpless… weak…trapped. And they still had the same effect.

I would give up my career in a heartbeat if it meant punishment for his actions, but I couldn't destroy my father's life.

"Deep breath in, Kali, deep breath in…. He is your commanding General, you'll have to work together. Let the past stay buried in the past. He probably wants your report."

Talking to myself was a habit I picked up after the fiasco that was the last mission. The nights during the first few weeks had been brutal. Whenever I closed my eyes, it would happen all over again.

I tried meditation; it didn't help.

I tried therapy; it didn't help either.

Pushing my body to its limits until exhaustion put me under, was what ended up working.

I used my ten minutes to regain my composure, then I walked, chin lifted, toward his office. I knocked on the door and waited.

"Come in."

I entered and formally saluted him. "Lieutenant General."

Out of habit, my brain registered everything in the room, the exits, the window, and his weapons.

Although many years had passed since that fateful day, his appearance was forever engraved in my mind. His brown hair was now gray, his face was a bit thinner than before—making the rest of his features look even sharper—and he still kept himself in great shape.

"At ease, Foster. Sit down," he said while typing on his computer.

The ensuing silence was uncomfortable. Whether it was on purpose, I didn't know, but I wouldn't give him the pleasure of seeing me fidget.

He finished whatever he was doing and turned his brown eyes to me. "Thomas informed me that you've settled into the office. Has anybody given you grief?"

What the hell? Was he keeping tabs on me?

"I've been here for six months. More than enough time to acclimate, and get to know everybody, sir," I deadpanned.

Had he called me in to chitchat?

"Good, good," he mumbled, and got up.

I lost sight of him. Eying the exits, I debated whether I should get up and leave when his palm landed on my throat. I jumped up, hoping he'd let go. He didn't—instead, he tightened his hold while wrapping his other arm around my waist and pulling me backward.

Something hard poked me in the ass. Did he seriously have an erection right now?

"You've grown, Kalista. You've filled out," he said, nipping the bud of my ear. "I thought having you once would quench my thirst, but you are an addiction I plan to indulge in." His voice dropped as his fingers squeezed tighter, cutting off my airway. "Inquiring minds want to know, did you let your men touch you like this?" He grabbed my breast and pinched it.

Hell no!

I leaned forward, then in the next instant backward head-butted him. He cursed when I threw my weight to the side, making him lose balance and loosen his grip on me. Elbowing him in the stomach, I wrenched myself free.

"Did you think I'd ever let you do that to me again?" I said, fighting the urge to take one of his guns and shoot him point blank.

"You cunt," he spat, and lunged at me.

Just before his fist connected with my jaw, I stepped backward. I retaliated with a left jab, which he deflected, but caught him with my right hook under the chin. His head snapped back, and he fell on his ass.

"I'll leave and pretend that this never happened." My voice never wavered, but inside I was a trembling mess.

He got up and straightened his uniform, as if he didn't have a care in the world, before piercing me with his beady brown eyes. "Oh, it'll happen, and you'll accept it, unless you want me to destroy your career and bring down your father in the process too."

"Try touching me again, and I'll fucking kill you."

Without waiting for a reply, I spun around and stalked out of his office.

"We'll see about that." He chuckled but didn't follow.

Grabbing my bag, I raced outside to my car, entered it, and locked the doors. I had every intention of driving home fast, but all I managed was to grab the wheel and freeze. The leather crinkled under my clenched fists, and I squeezed my eyes shut.

I can't believe this is happening again.

A heavy feeling settled in my stomach with the realization that as long as I was there, he'd never stop. Tears welled up, and I wiped them away angrily before pressing the start button and driving to my house.

Nightmares kept me rolling and sweating. Around five I gave up on sleep, got dressed, and went for my morning run.

Today would suck big time, but I'd put my big-girl panties on and face whatever challenge my slimy boss threw my way.

It was during my secretary's lunch break that shit hit the fan. A knock pulled my attention from the report I was writing.

"Come in," I called out.

Gratification filled me at seeing the bruise under Spencer's jaw when he walked in, but the triumphant smirk decorating his lips bothered me.

"Hello, Kalista." The familiar deep timbre sounded from the door. He never called me by my first name at work, which meant this wouldn't bode well for me.

I rose to my feet. "General Foster, I wasn't informed you were visiting today." I gestured toward the chairs. "General Spencer," I added as an afterthought.

What was my father doing here? He had been recently transferred to the new Space Force branch in D.C..

"I received a worrisome phone call last night." Straight to the point, as always. "Jonas told me about your episode. Why didn't you tell me it was getting this serious?" Was it disappointment coloring my father's voice?

As usual with my father, my mouth was faster than my mind. "Excuse me?" But then his words registered.

Episode? What the fuck!

"Are you going to play dumb with me, daughter?" the General growled.

"I called your father to let him know about your post-traumatic stress disorder, about how I found you in your office spaced out," the monster in disguise interjected smoothly, "and when I tried to bring you out of it, you punched me. The bruise will heal, but what if I'm not there the next time? It's getting worse—you could hurt someone, Kalista."

My mouth fell open, but otherwise I was completely still.

"We're looking out for you, kiddo." Spencer's voice was patronizing. I wanted to throttle him.

"I don't have PTSD." As the words escaped from my lips, I heard the lie.

The pointed look Konnor Foster gave me would have stopped me in my tracks when I was younger.

Okay, I had it, but punching the scumbag across from me had nothing to do with PTSD. I briefly considered my options. Telling the truth to my father was the most obvious one, but of course I wasn't planning to make the same mistake as before. He wouldn't believe me anyway. This knowledge left a bitter taste in my mouth. Should I dig into Spencer's past? Were there more women he had abused? My father's voice pulled me out of my reverie.

"I won't allow my daughter to waste away." He dropped the papers he had been holding onto my desk. "You're taking personal leave, and you're expected to be in therapy in Washington in seven days. Everything's been arranged, so it's not up for debate."

"Washington?" I echoed.

"Yes, you'll be staying with me as I'll be overseeing your progress."

Crossing my arms across my chest, I said, “I can’t just quit and come at the drop of a hat.”

“We’ve taken care of everything already.” Spencer’s smug tone grated on my ears. “Kalista, you’re like a daughter to me, take this opportunity to heal.”

I threw up a little in my mouth.

The sorry excuse for a human being who was currently my superior had set me up, and my father had gone along with it, but more importantly, I could do nothing about it.

“And it’s also time to think about your future. I’m sure your last mission showed you life is short. You have to consider leaving field work behind, and finding a good man to marry and have kids with,” my father added.

Nope. I wasn’t touching that subject. Not now, not ever. I would never be able to have a normal relationship. I was broken. I had tried to tell my father once, and he hadn’t believed me. Now it was too late. So when I stubbornly remained silent, the two friends went on about issues that were none of my concern. I tuned them out and studied the papers in front of me.

My leave would start the following day, but I didn’t have to be in Washington until next Monday. Seven days would be enough for preliminary research. I would expose Jonas Spencer’s true nature to the world. With a plan in place, I felt in control again.

Half an hour later, my father and my boss left to attend another meeting.

To say I was a mess on the inside would be the understatement of the century. I had underestimated the Lieutenant General’s cunningness. It was time I reached out to the Captain I’d replaced. Her retirement circumstances had raised many eyebrows. She had moved on though claiming life in the army had been too demanding and she couldn't keep up with it, so people had dropped the matter. I wasn't so sure that was the case, and only a face-to-face discussion would suffice.

A simple online search revealed her current location.

Making the necessary calls, I set everything in motion. So after a restless night, a short drive to El Paso airport, a five and a half hour flight, and an Uber ride, I had reached my destination.

The huge rectangular sign—with a depiction of some canyon—sitting at the entrance announced my arrival at Yosemite National Park. I had booked a cabin for the week and my driver dropped me off right outside.

It took me a few minutes to enter, put my stuff away, and get out the door again. I had only brought a duffel bag with me, with a few civilian clothes, since I wasn't planning to socialize or attend a military establishment. There were signs everywhere, making navigation easy in this part of the park. I found the place I was looking for in no time.

"Hello ma'am, I'd like to talk to Melinda Rose," I said to the old lady at the reception.

"Hi, my dear. She is on patrol today. Do you want to leave a message?" Her motherly tone was foreign to me.

"No ma'am, I'd like to meet her in person."

"She will be at her desk tomorrow afternoon." The landline rang, and she lifted her forefinger, indicating she needed a minute —"Rangers' office, hello?"—She nodded her head to whoever was talking to her before covering the handset with her palm and addressing me, "You can come by anytime between twelve and two and you'll catch her."

"Thank you," I replied, but she had already diverted her attention back to the person on the other end of the line.

Walking out of there, I contemplated my next steps. I had a full day at my disposal and nothing else scheduled. Maybe going for a hike would help clear my mind and lower my stress levels. I grabbed a sandwich and two water bottles from the nearby cafe before examining the hiking difficulty options. My muscles could use a good stretch, and a workout would be beneficial, so I started on a moderately strenuous path.

Three miles into the trail, my body fell into a comfortable rhythm. The stillness of the trees and their vibrant colors were a sight for sore eyes. Nature's calmness slowly slipped into my pores. I picked up my pace; the pull in my quads and the slight strain on my lungs showed me I had let myself fall out of shape. The chirps of the birds got quieter the farther I went, and the intense pine scent overpowered all others. The loudest sound was coming from my feet hitting the gravel and soil. The part of myself I thought had been irreparably damaged in my last mission, began rejuvenating. It was the first time in eight months that I had exercised outside, and although shame and pain were my constant companion, it felt good.

Up until the moment guilt for being the one making it out alive in one piece, when not all of my teammates did, overwhelmed me. My steps faltered, and I almost lost my balance. Breathing became impossible when my throat tightened shut. Chills ran through my body and I sat abruptly on the ground. I could no longer hear the birds or the wind, just the wild pounding of my heart. I placed my head between my knees.

"It's only a panic attack, Kali, breathe through it," I mumbled to myself, but it didn't help.

A woman's scream penetrated the haze in my brain, and my

reaction was instinctive. She sounded close. When she screamed again, I followed the sound into the forest.

Fuck, I didn't have my cell with me. One problem at a time, though, because the woman's yells were cut abruptly, and the absence of sound scared me more than anything else. My gut was screaming at me to turn around, to run away, but I couldn't abandon a person in need.

There was a clearing up ahead, and I was eighty percent certain her voice was coming from that direction. As I broke through the trees and into the grass area, I froze in my tracks.

The woman was floating midair, bathed in a yellowish light, and she looked like the one I had come here looking for—Melinda Rose. Above her, suspended in the air, was an unidentified flying object. What could I possibly do to help her? I couldn't just jump, reach her, and pull her down; she was too high. It wasn't as if throwing rocks at the craft would bring it down. What other weapon did I have at my disposal? *Think, Kali, think.*

If only I had an RPG, that might have made a difference.

While I was debating the best course of action, a yellowish light encircled me too. Startled, I looked up, and there was another UFO above me.

Oh shit!

One moment my eyes were open and my feet were on the ground, the next I was sinking into oblivion.

I WOULD NEVER SUBMIT WILLINGLY

KALI

There was someone petting my cheek and speaking a foreign language. On second thought, it didn't sound like words at all. It was a struggle to pry my eyelids open, and when I finally did, everything was blurry. Closing them again, I tried to remember what had happened. I was running on the trail and had a panic attack, then my mind went blank. Currently, my back was too cold for how nice the day had been in the forest.

Did I faint?

I moved my palms around me, trying to get a feel for my surroundings. Steel…and scaly, bony flesh?

My eyes snapped open and I tried to sit up, only to find my world tilting on its axis. I would have hit the floor again if it weren't for the cool, slimy arm supporting my back. I would not be so ungrateful as to point out to this stranger that he or she needed a bath.

Am I hallucinating?

Pinching myself hard, I yelped. Damn, this was real. I tried to gather my wits about me and blinked rapidly to bring everything into focus. I was on a floor, surrounded by people. The one holding me up was speaking to me, but instead of words there was hissing with a few vowels thrown in. Taking in the green skin and the definitely-not-human appearance of the good Samaritan, I barely held myself from screaming. I focused on the others in the barred cage and gasped.

Someone must have been playing tricks on me. Aliens didn't exist, right?

Then another alarming detail registered. I could see what could pass for breasts and other private bits on many of them. Actually, on all of them, so they were female. They didn't seem to mind the temperature—

Wait a minute. Why were these beings naked? Was I too?

My eyes drifted down of their own accord.

Well, that explains the cold drift I've been feeling since I regained consciousness.

I was sure I flushed a bright red, and oh my God, the one by my side was still stroking my cheek. I focused on her.

She was a child, maybe four feet tall, and she was murmuring to me. Dark-green scales covered her sides and her back, whereas a lighter color decorated her front. A tail that should belong to an alligator rested next to her legs, and an almost humanoid face that reminded me of a mix between a crocodile and a snake—with no visible ears or hair, and big slitted eyes—was looking straight at me.

"Hi, I'm Kali." I doubted she understood me, but manners kicked in, and being under pressure was an environment I thrived in.

My training overrode the terror that was trying to engulf me.

The one still propping up my back said something, and I turned toward her. She was a carbon copy of the other one, only bigger. It would be safe to assume they were related, mother and daughter, or sisters.

"Thank you. I'm good now," I informed her as if she'd comprehend me. She realized, though, what I wanted to do and helped me get on my feet.

Time to take stock of the situation.

Judging from our naked condition, our numbers, and the surrounding bars, we had been abducted, and seeing as weird looking creatures surrounded me, by aliens nonetheless. That was something I would've never imagined happening to me.

Melinda was nowhere in sight. Shit, she had been taken by the other spaceship.

"Are we even still on Earth?" The question slipped, and the woman I decided to call Croco, answered. I didn't understand the hiss she emitted.

All of us were huddled in the middle of the cage. Most of them were at least a head taller than me and obstructing my view. I needed to check if escape was possible, so I stepped out of the throng. There were four guards in the room. Judging by their ripped physiques and sizes, they were male. Their skin was dark blue, and black uniforms molded to their bodies, covering everything, but leaving little to the imagination.

My gaze remained on them more than it should, and one of them caught me watching. Having his hungry eyes focused on me was unnerving. I covered my lady parts and tried to pay him no mind. I only needed a few more seconds to evaluate. He stepped toward me, and would have come closer if another hadn't grabbed his arm and mumbled something unintelligible.

To my utter displeasure, they all aimed their attention at me. The one that had taken a step forward earlier was now holding his crotch and making lewd gestures that seemed to have a universal meaning, no matter which planet you were from.

Calling a spade a spade, their appearance was appealing. Coloring and sharp angles on their faces aside, they were pretty similar to human men on the outside, albeit a lot larger and in great shape. But piquing their curiosity was not good at all.

I slid easily between the larger females and retreated to the center of the group, mentally slapping myself because wondering what they looked like under their armor was not in my best interests. Plus, I never thought about men that way. Something was seriously wrong with me if I had such musings regarding the four alien creeps.

Think, Kali, think.

The room was barren, except for a table that sat on the opposite side of the entrance. There was only one door leading in and out of here. Would it open if someone approached, or did it need some kind of key?

The situation looked grim, but what gave me hope was a sense of déjà vu and the space between the bars. There was a possibility it was just wide enough that I could squeeze through. Seeing as all the other females were at least a foot taller and broader than me, it made sense that they wouldn't think of making the aperture narrower. It would be a tight fit, but once I'd escaped this room, I had a feeling everything would click into place. Now, if only the guards left us alone, because I wasn't going anywhere near them if I could avoid it.

I was already in the middle of our group, with my back toward the door, when it opened. An earthy celestial aroma tickled my nostrils, thrusting the image of a starry sky above the ocean in my mind's eye. The deep, sensual voice thrilled my senses next; my nipples instantly hardened, and the heat gathering in my core had me clenching my legs. I pinched my eyes shut and inhaled through my mouth to avoid taking in any more of the scent wreaking havoc on my body.

I was freaking turned on, and on display for everyone to see.

Why did my body have such a visceral reaction, when it'd never had one in the past?

The other females were affected too. Some of them jutted their multiple breasts outward, displaying the goods. My jaw dropped when I spotted one who had started playing with herself. Who was this guy who had such an effect on others? I inched closer to the bars to steal a glance.

He had his back turned to us. His broad shoulders were well-defined and formed a v that led to shapely buttocks. His legs were like two tree trunks. Damn, he was built. Judging from his sharp movements, and all the yelling, he was also furious.

The other aliens lowered their gazes to the floor.

This was some weird shit, but it offered the distraction I needed. Pushing with all my might, I slipped between the bars, freeing myself. I tiptoed toward the exit; the newcomer had left the door open and had gathered the others near the table for what appeared to be a heated conversation.

I felt, more than heard, Croco and her child following me. Their steps were silent. They wouldn't hinder my way, and if I could free them too, that'd be a win. But how had she fit through the bars? She was bigger than me. Could she shrink at will? I'd ask her later when I got us out of here and on a craft.

The beginning of a plan forming made me grin. It was a shame, though, that I didn't get a good look at the newbie.

The commotion he caused…the way some females almost threw

themselves on the bars to grab his attention…he must have been a stud.

There my mind went again, straight into the gutter. Something was seriously wrong with me, but I had no time to linger on that thought. I peered into the corridor and, finding it empty, hurried to put distance between the room and me, still mindful of the tiniest sound. I had to reach their Docking Bay with no one the wiser, and then I had to steal a craft. Preferably a pilot too, but I doubted that'd be an option.

I had never been on a spaceship in my life, yet I felt like I had been on this one in the past. Had I dreamed it? Sending a quick prayer, I hoped my instincts led me true this time too.

Since I could remember, I'd had sharp senses and a sixth sense that, for the most part, had kept me and my team safe from harm during tours and missions. At the moment it was telling me there was a guard ahead. I raised my fist and both my companions stopped in their tracks.

Hm. Maybe military signs were universal.

Lips tight, I suppressed my chuckle. There was no reason to alert the alien to our presence. The others I saw were huge, and in a one-on-one fight, the outcome wouldn't be in my favor. Surprise, though, would give me a much-needed edge, and a better chance at winning.

Different scenarios ran through my mind as we stood out of sight. The guards I'd seen earlier wore armor that covered their entire bodies. They didn't wear helmets, but given the fact they were at least a foot taller than me, head-butting was out of the equation. So that left only one vulnerable spot I could take advantage of. Their throats.

I turned to Croco and used hand signals to convey that they

should stay there. Her curt nod was all I needed. Exhaling slowly, I sneaked a peek. There was only one guard. He had a holster on his hip, with a knife on the one side and some kind of weapon on the other. My gut screamed at me not to kill him, that he was a good guy. Damn it. Sometimes knowing things was a pain in the butt.

Okay, Kali, change of plans. You'll only get one chance to knock him out. Use it wisely.

Creeping toward the alien's back, I exploded into action when he was within arm's reach. Putting all my weight behind my kick, I knocked his feet from under him while I simultaneously grabbed his gun. As if in slow motion, I saw him open his mouth to yell. Not wasting a second, I circled him and punched his trachea, then raised the weapon and brought it down on the side of his head. It hit the floor with a thud, and his body relaxed. Blood trickled from the point of contact, and I averted my eyes.

Although he couldn't hear me, I still whispered my apology.

I placed his gun a safe distance from him and out of the way; it was too heavy for me, and difficult to conceal in my current naked state. The knife, though, was a better option, so I took it.

Croco started when she saw me. I giggled. She was bigger than me, and if her muscles were any indication, she'd be able to squeeze me like a bug. I put my hand on her shoulder, hoping to reassure her. She closed her eyes and pulled her daughter into a tight hug. I gave them a moment, but then shook her gently because we needed to get moving.

We passed the guard and kept walking, hopefully toward the Docking Bay. The silence in the maze-like corridors was disconcerting. Shouldn't a craft this size make noise? I was lost in thought when my sixth sense warned me the newcomer was closing in on us. Had he noticed we were missing?

There was a door to our right that opened when we stood in front of it. I ushered Croco and her daughter in.

It was dark, but the metal glint on the countertops, and the stack of plates on one of them meant this was a kitchen. We each hid in a semi-empty cupboard and waited with bated breath.

In previous missions, during extremely stressful situations, there had been a few times I'd managed to influence our enemies into doing or not doing something. It was worth it to give it a shot. I breathed in through my nose and out through my mouth. Finding my center, I focused on it, then mentally nudged the newcomer to keep walking past our hiding place. But no such luck.

Whoosh. The entrance slid open.

Another whoosh, and it closed.

I'd left the cabinet door ajar when I hid so I could see anyone coming my way.

His comms beeped, and some kind of screen on his wrist lit up, outlining his body and confirming my suspicion he was in the room with us, before he turned it off. Oh my God, he was enormous, with broad shoulders and nothing but rippling muscles. What were they feeding him? And how could he be so freakishly silent for such a huge male? He was getting closer.

Think fast, Kali.

I needed to guide him away from my two new friends. Inwardly, I snickered. 'New friends' was the exaggeration of the century.

Still, though, I was trained to fight, and I wasn't so certain Croco and her daughter could handle themselves if it came to that. I decided to wait until the last second to jump on him, hoping that the element of surprise would work in my favor. Butterflies took flight in my stomach, but I didn't have time to ponder this unusual sensation because he was almost on me.

I sprang at him from my hiding spot, knife concealed.

He didn't draw a gun; instead, he spoke in a language I didn't understand. When he made a move to grab me, I threw a quick jab at him with my left hand and, as expected, he easily deflected, but in doing so, he missed my right one coming at him. I sliced across his left pectoral and the knife cut through his armor like butter. I saw red drops of blood pooling around the wound. Why would he wear armor that wouldn't protect him, and why did the sight of the injury bother me?

He stood there frozen, predatory emerald-green eyes focused on me, instead of defending himself.

"You ass. Did you just smirk at me?" I didn't know what I was waiting for; there was no way he'd answer me, but I definitely wasn't expecting the smile that broke across his face.

I doubted it boded well for me, so I ducked, slid between his legs—God, they were almost the size of my torso—and ran like I was on fire. If I was lucky enough, he'd follow and forget all about Croco and her daughter. As I increased the distance between us, the high of adrenaline began fading, a burn across my left breast making itself known. What the fuck? Did I accidentally cut myself? Slowing my pace, I looked down. There was nothing, not even a scratch, but where was this burning sensation coming from?

Lost in thought, I didn't see the two guards until I was on them.

Not noticing the knife in my palm, they both tried to grab my arms. I took the first one by surprise when its hilt connected to his temple, knocking him out cold. The other's eyes bulged, and I would laugh at how comical he looked when he witnessed what he thought was a helpless female taking out his partner, if my situation weren't so dire. Then he spoke to his wrist and lunged at me.

My size was in my favor as I slid on the floor and stabbed his thigh. I needed to incapacitate him without causing permanent damage. So I turned the knife before pulling it out. He screamed as he fell to his knees. With his head at almost the same height as mine, I took the easy way out, using the weapon's hilt to knock him out too.

I stepped to his right and slipped, but managed to stay upright.

What did I step on?

There was a small pool increasing in size at an alarming rate under his leg. I must have hit an artery. I didn't have the time for this, but unless I stopped the bleeding, he'd bleed to death. Being extra careful not to injure him while he was unconscious, I tried to cut a strip from his uniform. Even though the alien material felt like fabric to the touch, when I pulled to separate the ribbon, its fibers stretched as if they were made of some gooey substance. I had to tug extra hard until they finally snapped, solidified again, and I was able to tie a tourniquet above his wound to stem the flow.

Running footsteps echoed in the hall behind me, so my flimsy attempt to provide first aid would have to do. The steps getting louder spurred me into a full-blown run. Staying silent wasn't as important as escaping anymore.

Ahead of me there was another door, and I just knew it led to the hangar. As I approached, it opened automatically. The sight of the spacecrafts almost brought happy tears to my eyes. Then I noted the seventy or so soldiers milling around, and my hopes were crushed to smithereens.

I had been lucky to best three troopers. There was no chance in hell that I'd make it out of here alive, with so many of them.

Utilizing what my training and experience had taught me, I walked stealthily toward the closest aircraft. I had a pilot's license on Earth. I prayed these were not that different. I just needed them to have a cyclic or a yoke, and I would figure out the rest.

Now that newcomer seemed to have quite a stick!

Gee! Kalista, get your mind out of the gutter!

General Spencer killed my libido the night he took by force what hadn't belonged to him.

Why were they returning now? I didn't know how to deal with them.

Lost in my musings again, it took me a second to comprehend that I was compromised. General Spencer would bring about my end, and he wasn't even here. And damn it, I was only thirty feet away from my target.

Someone addressed me, but I could not make out a word being said.

The others heard him and instantly formed a circle around me, blocking my exit. I saw a couple speaking to their wrists, and everyone heard the booming voice replying through their comms.

Weird fact, though—no one was closing in on me. They outnumbered me, so fight or pick my battles? I still had a knife, and that allowed me a third option. If I used it on myself, maybe I would be doing myself a favor, compared to what these aliens might have in store for me.

The moment that thought entered my mind I heard a deep roar, followed by the loud crash of a door.

Everyone turned to the source of the sound, momentarily forgetting about me, as the finest male specimen in the universe walked in.

In the kitchen earlier, the darkness had concealed features that were now on display in the well-lit area. Short dark-green hair framed a face very similar to a human's. A Roman nose and sharp cheekbones emphasized his masculinity. Strange markings decorated his purple skin from the neck down. Annoyance flared because his uniform was blocking my view, yet teased my senses with the way it molded to his body, showcasing every valley and bulge. Broad shoulders, a muscular chest, and a torso that led to a tapered waist had me salivating.

Shaking my head, I tried to break the spell he'd cast on me. When my eyes traveled lower to the thick bulge between his long, strong legs, my jaw hit the floor, causing me to bite my lip hard.

The sudden pain helped clear the haze in my mind. I rolled my shoulders and relaxed my rigid muscles. Taking a defensive stance, I waited.

He prowled purposefully toward me while barking orders at his men.

Like the red sea, they parted to let him pass. If the others' reaction to his presence and the five stripes on his uniform were anything to go by, it'd be safe to assume he was their Captain.

He stopped a couple of feet away from me, and I focused on his face once again. He was mad; no, that word was inadequate. He was furious with me.

Well, color me baffled.

Surely he would understand my point of view and my actions. He was a soldier. How would he like it if he were the one kidnapped? No matter, this was my last chance. Defense wouldn't work, whereas I had a shot if I chose offense. I wasn't fooled; he wouldn't be easy to defeat. I wasn't sure this would be a battle I could win either. What I knew with certainty was…I would never submit willingly.

SHE ESCAPED

RORC

We had just blasted a second Crootan spacecraft to smithereens in the same circle, and yet I derived no joy from the act.

The fight with the first smugglers had been intense but had ended quickly. Such a cruel race to treat males without mercy and females with no regard for the reverence they deserved. When these pirates attacked, their method of operation was to kill the former and capture the latter. Then they'd either sell them to the highest bidder, or use them to satisfy their deprived needs before dumping them into one of their dungeons, so others could take advantage of the poor captives that'd manage to survive. These abominations would exploit even their own mothers for a few credits, and I had dedicated my career to finding and destroying them and their operations.

So I should have been used to the state we often found their captives in. But I wasn't, and this time the condition of the dying females—their bodies having been assaulted to their last breath—shook me to my core. I lost it and killed most of them with my bare hands. I pulverized the captain's head, and if my men hadn't pulled me away by force, telling me they had discovered other prisoners that required our help, I'd still be there.

We hadn't been in time for some, but at least we managed to save the rest. And then we stumbled upon the Saberian. Unanswered questions were running around my brain. I'd have to wait for the warrior to wake up, but until then we had the captain of the Crootan ship we just blew to pieces under custody.

First things first, though, we'd have to return the females to their planets. I needed to visit the Bay where we had teleported their cage and explain the next steps before we assigned them to their temporary quarters. It was the usual procedure, yet the compulsion to see these females rode me hard.

"Cubjornh, did Toctoll send you the file with the destinations?" I asked my Second in Command.

"Yes, Admiral, I've coordinated with Barianh. We are heading to Chondeirm first," he stated, then furrowed his brows. "We identified almost all of the females. There is one of unknown origin in the group. The Crootans didn't catalog their catch this time." His voice vibrated with the anger we all felt.

"I've been scouring the Intergalactic Enosis database, and I can't find a species that matches her characteristics," Toctoll added.

My curiosity was piqued. I needed to see this female with my eyes. "Take over the Bridge. I'm heading to the Holding Bay," I ordered, and left the ship in Cubjornh's capable hands.

The urgency to go to those we rescued increased. I usually felt this way before an attack. So why now? I had destroyed the two in the Aquar System, and there weren't any other enemies near. We hadn't entered Pyxis yet, where we'd be safe, but Barianh, the ship's AI, would warn us if any hostiles approached.

Was the unidentified female the cause of my unease? I quickened my steps. As I neared the Bay, I heard Khan and Maleoh's raised voices and my hackles rose.

What the fuck are they doing?

I stepped inside to find Khan focused on reaching the females and Maleoh holding the other warrior back. Movement in the cage caught my attention, but I only saw her back and her delectable rear-side retreating into the middle of the group. Such round, perky cheeks. Images of her sprawled over my knees and on my bed swam behind my eyes. Blood pooled low and my cock hardened, making me groan. I had to deal with my soldier first, but she was next on my list. It wasn't like she had anywhere to go.

"Khan! Back to your station and report now!" I barked at him.

Was the idiot trying to terrify the females? They were to be praised and adored. Such delicate and fragile beings. The carriers of life. He had no business talking to them as if they were a dungeon's menu offering.

Even though he was young and hadn't been in my fleet for long, he knew not to challenge me. He'd witnessed in training what happened to those who did.

"I'm sorry, Admiral." He averted his eyes to the floor and hunched his shoulders.

His submissive stance appeased the side of me that craved to confront and dominate.

"I don't know what's come over me," he stuttered, "the moment I saw her, all reason flew out the window…"

Pinning him with my stare, I said, "We do not treat females that way. We are not one with those we hunt! Tonight in the ring, I'll make sure you remember it."

Having arranged the manners lesson, the need to see her rode me harder than ever before. No female had captured my attention like that. Turning around, I perused them. It was quite a catch this time, they would have brought the pirates over a million in credits. Especially that exotic one.

She was smaller than the rest; her long hair was the blue-black color of a starless night, her skin the palest shade of ivory. Her body was lithe but still very appealing.

Where is she?

There were many Cajolisans. These females were very sexual, with a submissive disposition. Their males were weak and unable to adequately protect them, so they quite often became the target of traffickers.

"Where is the small female?" I asked, notes of alpha command woven unintentionally into my voice.

Instantly, some of them fell on their knees, and others started offering their bodies to me. There were Wravukians that preferred their company due to their obedience, and I demanded it in my quarters too—my nature too dominant to tolerate anything else—but I couldn't stand a meek mate.

None of them answered. I approached the cage and growled the question one more time, my patience running thin.

"She es…escaped," a Trinar female replied.

I went completely still. The ringing in my ears muffled all other sounds. She'd pulled such a stunt, with three Wravukians in the room and none noticing her escape. I let my senses expand in search of her. Locating the position of others was one of my least powerful gifts, yet it was worth it to try. I gasped, disoriented, when her life force shone as bright as a beacon and called me toward her. She amplified my power. That could only mean one thing. I basked in her light as the realization washed over me.

She was nearing Kasmir. He'd stop her for me.

Fuck, she's naked! Kynthelig hasn't brought garments for them yet.

Racing out the door, I was on them in a few clicks, but I had to rub my eyes and blink a few times to comprehend what I was seeing.

Kasmir was lying on the floor, and she was nowhere to be found. I knelt and checked his pulse. He was unconscious.

How had she incapacitated him?

I instructed one of the Healers through my comms, "Fiacre, come over to Kasmir's post."

"On my way," he replied.

Having taken care of that, I let my senses flare outward again.

Got you, clever female.

She was in the kitchen, where there were many hiding spots, but she wasn't alone—there were two more with her. So they knew I was after them and hid.

Now Kasmir's state made more sense.

Is she leading them or following? Will she take well to orders, or is she the disobedient type?

Burning questions swirled in my mind on my way to them, and I looked forward to getting the answers.

The noise of the door sliding opening would announce my entrance, and that'd be the only warning I'd give her. Light on my feet, and aware of their positions, I stalked into the room.

I hadn't expected her to jump almost on top of me as soon as I reached the center of the kitchen. Seeing her up close for the first time froze me in my tracks. She was the female from my vision. The spark that had ignited when I dreamed of her, turned into an inferno in her presence. Her exotic beauty rooted me in place and stole my breath.

"Mate," I whispered, "I've found you. You're safe with me. Come."

Shoulders back and chest out, she exuded calmness. There was no fear in her light-gray eyes, only resolve. I was glad she recognized me as her mate. My worry that belonging to different species would be an obstacle, vanished, and all kinds of sensual thoughts caused by her luscious lips swirled in my head, with them wrapped around my cock being the most prominent one.

Unable to resist the temptation her soft alabaster skin presented, I reached out to touch her cheek. Suddenly, I felt a burn on my pectoral. A flash of adrenaline tingled through my body. I looked down at the blood slowly staining my uniform, then smirked at her.

Well…maybe she didn't know I was her mate. I would find great pleasure in earning her submission and making her mine.

Logic pierced my lustfilled haze, and I remembered that when the bond between mates was strong, they could experience each other's sensations.

A snarl rumbled in my chest. Wravukians learned to compartmentalize at a young age in order to become formidable warriors. The wound she'd inflicted was only a slight annoyance at the back of my mind, but she'd be feeling the pain.

No one was allowed to hurt my female.

Not even her.

"Give me the knife," I ordered.

Instead of handing it over, she bolted.

"It is pointless to run, little one. I will catch you," I told her, before following after her.

The scent of the other two indicated their species.

I turned on my comms. "Mavjerik, we have a pair of Mardonians in the kitchen. Extract them and return them to their temporary quarters."

"A female is on the run. She's hostile and armed." Uluiru used the common channel to alert everyone.

Fuck. She was fighting my soldiers. No warrior worth his salt hurt females, but she had a knife, and they would defend themselves. A blow by one of them could kill her. She was so small in comparison, and more fragile.

"Do not harm her!" I barked, and raced to her location.

Once again, though, I'd underestimated her. I had to stop midstride to avoid stepping on Quirkam. A minor cut decorated his temple. Uluiru had a big puddle of blood under his leg, but it seemed she had suspended the flow of blood with part of his uniform. Both of them lay unconscious.

The air in my lungs left in a whoosh. She had attacked them. She was nimble and could function under pressure. What were the males of her species thinking, permitting their females to fight?

That would change immediately. No female of mine was allowed to endanger her life.

"Mes, you're needed outside the Cargo Bay. Uluiru has a leg injury, and he's bleeding." The irritation settling in the pit of my stomach made my voice gruffer than usual.

"You couldn't resist, could you?" was his prompt reply.

I ignored him.

As I was nearing the Docking Bay, her thoughts invaded my mind and rocked me to my core. She was thinking of ending her life, to avoid being recaptured. A roar was wrenched from the depths of my soul. Didn't she understand we were the rescuers?

I put on a burst of speed and barged into the room, faintly hearing the door breaking from my momentum.

My troops surrounding her made me see red.

Her jumbled emotions threw me off-kilter. The swirl between trepidation, resignation, and defeat gave me whiplash, sending an icy chill down my spine.

My own emotions wreaked havoc. The sight of her naked body was like a punch to the gut. Her tempting curves pulled my focus from seeing targets over her weak spots, to seeing images of this alien female undulating under me. They made desire blast through me. I pushed it back. It wasn't the time nor the place to notice how delectable she looked while prowling toward them.

"Move away from my mate!" I yelled at my soldiers, who all turned their curious eyes on me. They'd never seen me lose control, and I was very close to doing exactly that.

As I neared, they moved aside so I could enter the circle they had created around her.

"Has anyone harmed her?"

Silence followed my question.

"Has anyone harmed her?" I demanded, more furious than ever.

"No, Admiral. We just asked her if she was hurt." I didn't know who answered because I could only focus on her; scanning her body for visible injuries.

"You put yourself in harm's way, Mate. You're not allowed to do so," I growled, anger turning my voice gravelly.

She couldn't understand my words yet, but she went from eyes darting for an escape, tendons standing out in the neck, and elbows pressing into the sides, to making eye contact with me, correcting her posture by spreading her legs slightly, and raising the knife—ready to take me on in a fight.

Any lingering doubts about her being a soldier evaporated in a puff of smoke. Such a neglectful species to put their females in harm's way instead of cherishing them for the treasures they were. I sighed.

She wasn't concealing her weapon anymore, and her eyes were following my every move. A challenge if I ever saw one. Maybe she needed her male to conquer her, but did she actually believe she could win in a fight with me? Well, if she wanted to play, I would indulge her.

I pretended to charge her. Two of my strides and I was on her. At the last minute, she evaded me, going as far away from me as possible. A laugh escaped my lips. She was magnificent.

Taking her agility into consideration, I feigned an attack on her left side, and when I was almost on top of her, I spun to the right. She slipped from my grasp, nicking my arm in the process.

Murmurs and gasps followed. I stopped to address them. I didn't need anyone hurting her, thinking I was in danger.

"How many of you have cowered when fighting against me? My mate has a fiery soul. She knows she can't win, but she persists. Do not intervene," I said, letting my dominant nature show.

My praise, unfortunately, had a different result than I'd intended. Their testosterone permeated the air, and I saw the heated looks they sent her way.

They thought they could challenge me for her.

I spread my arms and roared.

They stumbled backward while averting their eyes to the floor.

"She is mine," I yelled at them, then turned to her and said, "Time to end this game, Mate."

The vein at the base of her neck was pulsing rapidly. My display had scared her. I cursed myself and approached her slowly, praying she'd come willingly. I reached for the knife, hoping she'd understand my intentions.

She didn't—instead, she thrust it low. I deflected her attempt to stab me, and we kept dancing around each other.

How is she anticipating my moves? Is she that good, or is our bond stronger than I thought?

Picturing the endless void in space, I emptied my thoughts and charged her head-on, bending just before our bodies collided. Triumph warmed me from the inside when I threw her over my shoulder, but then her hand holding the knife found a target in my left shoulder. She stabbed me and screamed. To everyone else it sounded like defiance, but I knew she felt my pain.

I strode out of the Bay and headed straight toward the Healers. She was silent, her body rigid. She hadn't fainted, but she was trying to control her breathing.

How experienced a fighter was she? Besides the initial scream, which I was certain was only because the pain had caught her by surprise, she didn't make another sound. I had a few choice words to say to her and questions that she needed to answer. Communication was key. If I was lucky, Mes would have a translator for her.

I scowled. The Arch-healer was one of the best Healers across the Pyxis System, and quite resourceful. Always calm and prepared to face the worst. Despite the darkness lingering under the surface, which I sometimes sensed through our bond, I often pushed to see what it'd take to ruffle his feathers.

As Admiral, I had access to every area of my ship. Barianh, the ship's AI, opened the door the moment I approached. A scanner-droid circled us, measuring our vitals and checking for abnormalities.

"Sit, Rorc, I'll be there as soon as I'm done with Uluiru," Mes informed me. He, along with Cubjornh—the Vice Admiral—were the only ones who called me by name. Of course Mes, being the

Second Son of the King, did not need to be here at all, but it was his choice. One night after we'd had a few glasses of kupna, he had confided in me, saying he was too much of an empath, and his healing abilities would never let him settle in a role that had no use for them. His father hadn't been happy with his son's decision.

I placed my precious package on the operating table, the strain on my shoulder making me wince. Her swift intake of breath told me she felt it too. Our eyes locked, and I saw fear. She didn't know why she was feeling my pain. I moved a few paces away to give her some breathing room, and to show her I meant no harm, before I returned to sit on the table opposite hers.

Her gaze traveled everywhere but on me. That gave me the chance to take a good look at her and study her body. Her torso was full of faded silver lines, her legs had fewer shiny ridges, and her arms none. Was she born like this, or were these battle scars? The way she'd handled herself earlier was proof she was trained. The why, though, was still a mystery. She was slender, with lean muscles. I loved that her two breasts were exactly the right size for my palms. Her pussy was bare and a beautiful shade of pink. Saliva filled my mouth, and drops of pre-cum beaded on my cock, which was currently straining against my uniform.

I'm not sure if it was my elevated breathing or heartbeats that made her notice, but she turned her steely-gray eyes at me, then snatched the sheet that was next to her and tied it around herself, covering the temptation.

What a pity.

Mes would have a field day with me when he joined us.

The moment she heard footsteps, she turned toward the sound and gasped.

I knew Mes was an imposing figure and quite an attractive male.

Momentarily, I wanted to throttle him.

What the fuck! That had never happened before, not even while sharing the same female.

Tantalizing images started dancing behind my eyelids—me pounding her sweet pussy while she sucked Mes; Mes reddening her delectable firm bottom and me watching, waiting for my turn; both of us taking her at the same time—and I groaned, then doused the desire. She was mine alone, and she'd soon realize it too.

Returning my attention to the present, I noticed Mes had frozen in his tracks.

Well...well....

I finally found something that ruffled his feathers.

Smirking, I called out to him, "Are you going to stand there gawking, or are you going to save your Admiral, who's bleeding all over your floor?"

EXPECTING CARNAGE

MES

Why was I on a spacecraft again?

Helping others was the reason for my existence, and much to my father's dismay, I'd chosen to follow Rorc's steps and join the Wravukian Space Force—because his goals always aligned with my own. At times like this, though, I regretted being in an enclosure where I was deprived of my solitude day in and day out.

Why couldn't I be strong like my father and my brother? They never let their struggles overpower their will, whereas I was approaching my limits—the headaches were getting worse, the nightmares kept me from resting, and the darkness threatened to consume me. It didn't help that since rescuing the females from the Arkad, I couldn't shake this feeling of frustration and despair. It was impossible to concentrate on my work.

Was the emotion mine or someone else's?

With a huff, I got up and decided to re-examine the unfamiliar blood sample Maleoh obtained from one of the females. Maybe I would run a few tests to try to define her species. But first, I needed to meditate to clear my mind—otherwise, I'd be of no help to anyone. Lying on one of the examination beds, I closed my eyes and focused on regulating my breathing.

Imagining that I was standing near the edge of the Great Suprhal—the biggest lake from my homeland—helped as well. The water's surface was smooth and its crystal-clear green color reflected the frozen mountain tops surrounding it. Fish were playing underneath the surface, and there was a slight wind softly caressing me. The sky was a beautiful lilac, and our two suns warmed the clean atmosphere.

"Mes, you're needed outside the Cargo Bay. Uluiru has a leg injury, and he's bleeding."

Rorc's booming voice through the comms shattered the carefully constructed image in my head, and the emotions I was trying to escape from returned with a vengeance. I pressed my thumbs on my temples to stave off the upcoming headache.

"You couldn't resist, could you?" I replied.

What had the fool done? Didn't Uluiru know that no one messed with the Admiral when he was in a mood?

I grabbed the stretcher and headed toward the injured soldier.

Quirkam and Kasmir were standing next to him.

'What happened?' I demanded.

They both hung their heads. Waves of shame rippled out of them, engulfing me. Mental shields in place, I deflected their intense emotions.

Curious...

Then Kasmir replied, "One of the females escaped. She knocked us out and stabbed Uluiru."

My eyebrows shot up and my mouth gaped open before I remembered to close it.

"A female?"

They both nodded, and it took me a second to shake the shock of this revelation. That had never happened before.

"All right, help me put him on the stretcher and take him back to the infirmary," I ordered.

I was fixing Uluiru's leg, admiring the quick mind this female possessed—she'd managed to staunch the bleeding successfully—when I heard the whoosh of the Bay's door.

Barianh allowed only one person in without asking me—the Admiral, who immediately called my name.

"Sit, Rorc, I'll be there as soon as I'm done with Uluiru," I snickered. It wouldn't take long, but usually he was very impatient when he wanted something.

Uluiru was still unconscious, and the nanites kept him in that condition.

I preferred it that way. My empathic abilities gave me access to other beings' feelings—at times a blessing, and at others a curse. For the most part, I could control what I allowed in me. I'd learned to build walls in my brain, so that I could function. Still, strong emotions sometimes slipped through the cracks, and it was never a pleasant experience.

I used the micro-laser beam to seal the artery that was nicked, while thoughts of the female that caused this occupied my thoughts. Kasmir said she'd knocked out all three of them in a matter of seconds. What species was she? Was it a superior one? My people were gifted, but their powers always manifested differently.

But for a being of the opposite sex to overpower a Wravukian—it's unheard of! Astounding.

As I covered the wound, I dropped my shields and let my senses flare, so I'd get a feel for anything else that might be wrong with the soldier on my table. What drew my attention, though, was the low, rhythmic ba-bump coming from where Rorc was waiting. His heartbeats almost drowned out the feathery sound of the single slow one.

Who's with him? Is it a female?

Then it hit me. I wasn't feeling their emotions.

How's that possible?

I had to see this person. I disinfected my hands and strode into the other room, only to falter and stop, zeroing in on her.

Time froze and everything stood still.

The female I saved in the vision is...here.

She clutched a sheet around herself as if it were her lifeline. She was magnificent, her presence a magnet designed to pull me in. She was also quite smaller than us. How had she incapacitated three soldiers?

My life force contracted, stretched, and enveloped both of them. The moment she was wrapped in the cocoon, her gaze jumped to me. She felt it too.

Her emotions rushed at me all at once. Their intensity was ferocious and almost forced me to my knees. She was furious, embarrassed, frustrated, and in pain. Still, her defiant eyes shot daggers at me before she turned her head away.

"Are you going to stand there gawking, or are you going to save your Admiral, who's bleeding all over your floor?" Rorc's voice brought me out of the trance she'd thrown me into.

"I can always clean the floor." I snorted, but hurried to check the knife protruding from his shoulder. "Who dared stab you? Haven't they learned their lesson by now?"

He laughed, and I furrowed my brows.

He rarely laughed.

"Did you have one too many glasses of kupna?" I asked as I went about gathering the tools I'd need for his wound.

"She did," he mirthfully said. "She stabbed and nicked me too. Twice."

I chuckled. "Good for her."

"It's her." His tone turned sober and serious. "My mate. The one I saw in my vision."

Rorc was like a brother to me, and I was glad for him. But I couldn't stop my chest from caving in, or the pain from showing on my face—at least it was shielded from their view.

My life force had never embraced anyone else before, so apparently she wasn't just any female.

Composing myself, I returned to them.

"It was time you found her," I said, then sprayed the nanite-carrying anesthetic around the wound.

How did she manage to stab him? She is smaller than us, yet the knife is indisputably protruding from his left shoulder.

I started pulling it out slowly when she gasped and clasped her left shoulder. Immense pain radiated from her and rolled over me.

"Raise your mental shields, Rorc! She's in fucking pain," I ordered gruffly, and he complied immediately.

Her silence didn't go unnoticed, nor the fact that she was taking everything in. Her gaze was calculative. She was trained, but for what I had no clue.

Experiencing the emotions running through her was fascinating. The need to escape was fighting for first place against confusion.

"I'm sorry," he told her, even though she wouldn't understand. "I'm ready. Go ahead, Mes."

"I don't think I've ever heard you apologizing," I teased while proceeding slowly with the knife's removal, paying special attention to her breathing.

The rhythm remained the same, which meant she wasn't feeling Rorc's pain anymore. I scanned the area to see if anything important got cut by the blade. When I was satisfied all was well, I applied an antibacterial paste before using the sealant. The female gasped and leaned forward, watching as the new layers of tissue and muscle, and then finally the outer layer of skin, formed. I treated the minor abrasions too. Her eyes never left my hands.

"You're good as new, Admiral." I turned and looked at her, searching for injuries I might have missed earlier. "Is she hurt?"

"No, at least I don't think so," he stated meekly.

"For the love of the Creator, Rorc!" How could he be so negligent with our mate!

The thought stopped me short. Our mate? Where had that come from? My brother had laid his claim first, and I would never get in his way, no matter what that cost me.

"What is it?" He hopped down from the examination table, his posture tense, and his sharp eyes focused on me.

Sometimes the bond between us was disconcerting. "We're all right. I'll check her and we'll talk afterward," I replied, hoping he'd let it go.

I picked up the scanner again and turned toward her, only to find gray, turbulent eyes fixed on me.

"She needs a translator. Do you have any that will fit her?" Rorc asked, his voice lighter than I'd ever heard it.

"The only one that won't damage her hearing—as I don't know her species yet—has to be injected. Do you think she'll understand that we mean her no harm? Since I picked up the scanner, she's been eying me suspiciously. How will she react when she sees the injector?" The last thing I wanted was to scare her even more. But admittedly, we needed to communicate.

He thought about it and nodded, coming to a decision. "It needs to be done. I'll hold her down and you inject her."

Even though I was a Prince, and Second to Wravuk's Throne, I had chosen to serve under Rorc as the Arch-healer. So technically, he was my superior. We would try it his way.

As I retrieved the needed instruments from a side compartment, I noticed Rorc approaching her slowly. He lifted her gently and placed her on his lap.

Lucky bastard.

She gasped, her eyes glued to the Admiral. It seemed as if she'd forgotten all about me.

I ground my teeth and went back to them with the injector in hand.

The moment she noticed what I was holding, though, she started struggling against Rorc.

He wrapped his arms around her tight, restricting any movement.

She stopped fighting, and I let a sigh escape my lips. I did not want her in distress.

The next tick, though, she became a wild cat, writhing, biting, and clawing Rorc like there was no tomorrow. Her terror gripped me. It was so intense and all-encompassing that it immobilized me.

What's causing this?

The doctor in me wanted to solve the mystery; the empath was dying to soothe and take away her pain.

As if from afar, other sounds slowly started registering. Muted thuds were coming from the Saberian's chamber. Fuck. He was wounded pretty badly when we found him, he'd make his situation worse with all this exertion, and would undo all the healing I had done. He needed to recuperate, not try to bring down the door. The room was sealed with no way out from within. Did he think he was a prisoner?

Why is he acting like this now, though, and not earlier?

"The female's heartbeat is elevated to dangerous levels. Heading into shock in less than sixty ticks." Barianh's voice brought me out of my reverie.

"Let her go," I ordered.

The Admiral gave me a pointed look before releasing her and standing by my side.

I dropped the instruments on the nearest table—she wouldn't know how to use them anyway—and raised my hands. "We mean you no harm. We'll leave you for a while so you can calm yourself," I told her, hoping the soothing tone of my voice would calm her somewhat.

We retreated to my lab, and I closed the door, giving her some privacy, and us a little reprieve. She couldn't go anywhere. The exit would open only if I or Rorc commanded it.

He was too quiet and was rubbing his eyebrow back and forth. His mind far away from here.

I rubbed my neck and massaged my temples. Even though I was used to being the punching bag for others' emotions, I could usually build walls high enough to stop them from affecting me. But not this time. I couldn't block her terror out. "What just happened?" I growled at Rorc, who was leaning forward in my chair, with his hands draped limply over his knees.

"Fuck if I know! One moment I'm holding her, and the next she turns into a wild beast," he responded through gritted teeth.

"There must have been a trigger..." I mused, "Was it the injector...or you restricting her?"

"I'd never hurt her. We need to communicate," he said, dejected.

"I'm aware of that, but she isn't. In an instant, her emotions became a tangled mess. It was impossible to discern one from the other, but all of them were laced with terror."

"I could fucking smell it, Mes."

The sudden need to connect with her was overwhelming. I let my senses flare. The Bay she was in was awfully quiet. I couldn't sense her emotions or her presence there.

I shot up, slammed my hand on the palm scanner and the door opened with a whoosh. Rorc was right at my heels.

What I saw terrified me. She wasn't where we'd left her, and the Saberian's door was open.

Tremors racked my body and my pulse raced. I wanted to crumple to the ground.

Next to me, Rorc was shaking his head.

The Saberian was volatile, dangerous—a predator like no other. We picked up two swords and inched toward the quarantine chamber.

We were expecting carnage, but what we saw instead stunned us.

She was sitting on the floor, pushing playfully at the head of the powerful shifter who was...sniffing and licking her.

Isn't she afraid? For all she knew, he was preparing to eat her. Yet I didn't detect fear—only joy—radiating from her.

Suddenly, he pushed her against the wall with his solid mass, then turned toward us. He curled his lips, snarled his warning, and lowered his body to the floor, bracing for an attack.

Saberians were formidable fighters; their sabertooths were equipped with some kind of armor underneath their fur that protected them from most weapons—if not all. Up until the moment a virus claimed their females, and almost decimated the entire species, they'd never lost in a battle.

The situation we were in had disaster written all over it, yet even knowing that we'd lose in a fight against this warrior, Rorc would never abandon his mate, and I'd never leave his side in a time of need.

"Easy, Rorc, I'm not sure if he's turned feral or not," I warned.

The Admiral tensed, raised his sword slightly and took a step toward them. Beast's answering snarl was an indication he didn't like being challenged.

"Get away from my mate, Saberian! You are overstepping your welcome," Rorc ordered.

The shifter's reply was a deafening roar.

The whole time of the stare-down, the female had lowered herself to the ground and was skulking toward the door. The ear-splitting roar stopped her progress and made her hunch over herself; then, right as Rorc stepped forward, she squared her shoulders and jumped in the middle, between the sabertooth and the Admiral.

"Stop," she said, and irrevocably changed all of our destinies.

I TRULY BELONGED

KALI

Utter humiliation! He had thrown me over his shoulder like a sack of potatoes!

I pounded my fists into his back until I realized where they were landing.

My God.

His ass was as hard as marble—the round globes muscular, without an ounce of fat.

I froze. If I continued, I would end up hurting myself more than him. The pain still radiating through my shoulder was unexplainable. The moment I'd stabbed him, I felt the tip of the knife tearing through the soft tissue under my collarbone. How was that possible? What did it mean? Was he a telepath projecting his feelings?

He hadn't even grunted when I stabbed him. Did he even feel it?

The many questions running through my mind, and all the blood gathering in my head from being upside down, made me dizzy. I hadn't been paying attention to which way we were going until he said something and gently deposited me on a bed.

My lips couldn't stay sealed when another current of pain radiated through my shoulder, and a moan escaped. The power he had over my body scared me.

Kali, you need your wits about you. Focus, plan, escape.

Obviously he was the one injured, not I. What I was feeling was only in my head. I had endured worse—I could get through this too. Looking around me, I discovered he'd brought me to the infirmary.

In the dream I'd had a while ago, I hadn't been able to enter this room. So, as nonchalantly as possible, I perused the place and located possible escape points. On the right side of each door, there was a small screen, and none of them had locks besides one that I felt positive I could open. There were no medical instruments around that would come in handy, and the knife was still lodged in the alien's shoulder. I didn't think he would appreciate it if I tried to take it back.

Damn, his uniform leaves nothing to the imagination, I snickered. I might have sworn off men, but technically he wasn't one, and I wasn't dead, yet.

In the next few minutes, no matter how hard I tried to avoid looking at him, I could not help it. He had the body of a Greek god. His skin was purple, and he had beautiful markings that went up the sides of his neck and stopped under his ears, which were slightly pointy. I could not discern a pattern, and I wondered whether aliens got tattoos. His face was more angular than a man's, but it only enhanced his looks. His eyes were a startling emerald color and his eyebrows were slightly arched.

I barely held my giggle back. *Maybe they are elves and Legolas will appear any minute now!*

Then my eyes dropped to his plump lips; on anyone else they

might have looked feminine, but the only picture that popped into my mind was of him between my legs, doing things to me that no one had ever done.

Fucking snap out of it!

Being on a ship in outer space had definitely messed with my sanity. And then another presence drew my attention. I turned my head his way—major mistake!

The other guy—who was probably the doctor, based on the robe he had on—was even more breathtaking. My captor's looks were more rugged than traditionally handsome. This guy, though…I almost raised my hand to fan my face.

What was wrong with me! I was kidnapped by aliens and all my mind could think of was sex?

I furrowed my brows and shot daggers at him. It was their fault. That was the only explanation that made sense.

The doctor was probably the same height, and just as bulky as the purple one. What did they feed them here? His skin was as red as fire and his blond hair was a bit longer than my captor's. His high cheekbones and straight nose were the most prominent features, along with his yellow-gold eyes.

The moment our gazes met I felt a wave of energy wrap around me. Security and calm enveloped me like a cozy blanket. I got tingly in places that had been in hibernation up until I'd set foot on their ship.

Did all of them have telepathic powers?

Would it even work if I raised mental walls to protect myself? I did it anyway, and broke eye contact for good measure too.

The purple guy said something to the red one, and with a sinking heart I realized that even their voices had a soothing effect on me. I had to get a grip on myself. If I lowered my defenses in this enemy territory, it would be the end of me, and I wasn't ready to go just yet.

Suddenly a searing pain burned my shoulder.

Even though I was trained to withstand most forms of torture, the first wave always took my breath away.

My gasp sounded loud in the room, and all eyes focused on me.

The doctor chastised the newbie, and I smirked. The next time he wrapped his fingers around the hilt of the knife, I tensed. But they must have done something because I didn't feel anything that I wasn't supposed to. Intrigued, I leaned forward. The doc applied a paste, and then poured a gel-like liquid in the gaping wound. Right before my eyes, the skin mended itself.

This would save millions of lives back home. I had to find a way to grab some of it. In my peripheral vision I noticed the red-skinned one picking up a thick wand; then, the soldier picked me up, like I weighed nothing, and sat me on his lap.

Shocked, I held still. Then I saw the needle protruding from the instrument.

Shit, it's huge!

Were they planning to stick it in me? I twisted to get myself free. Under my bum I felt the barrel of a gun. *Perfect!* If I could get it, I'd have the upper hand. I looked down between us.

Huge mistake—as huge as his erection.

Hell no!

It was one thing thinking about sex on an intellectual level, and another being held against my will on top of his hard-on with only a sheet covering me.

I elbowed his side and backward head-butted him. His hold loosened for a second, and I bucked wildly, hoping to free myself.

Instead, he tightened his arms around me, sufficiently immobilizing me.

The second I felt confined, my mind took a dive into the past. Images of that evening started flooding in, and I lost reality.

I was looking at General Spencer.

"You'll pay for the tease you've been," he sneered.

Fear raced down my spine. I tried to run, but I couldn't. Why were my feet not moving?

I looked at him again, pleading, but his leering expression raised all kinds of warning bells right before he punched my right side. The pain was intense, but nothing compared to what I knew would soon follow.

It took me a few minutes to realize I was sitting on the table by myself, and the strange sound—as if a wounded animal was near—was coming from me. Blinking a few times to clear my vision, I noticed that both males had moved away from me.

The doc said something and raised his hands in what was apparently the universal gesture of surrender. He wasn't holding that thing with the huge needle anymore.

My breathing was still erratic, and images of that night kept swirling behind my eyelids as I slowly, but steadily, managed to push them behind a locked door.

I must have scared them because they left the room. Not knowing how much time I'd have, I needed to take advantage of every second I had at my disposal. I jumped down from the table and raced to the door with the lock.

The mechanism looked simple enough.

Here goes nothing...

While working on it, I made plans. I'd leave this room and rush to where they stored their spaceships. I would get on one, and lie in wait for a pilot. Once he took off, I'd ambush him.

Click.

Perfect.

In my excitement, I stepped into the room without thoroughly checking it first.

Big mistake. It seemed I couldn't stop making them.

I heard the snarl before I saw a creature that reminded me of the pictures of sabertooths I had seen when I was a kid. Only, it was at least three times bigger than what we were told. It had black stripes and spots all over its gray-silver fur. Its head—with the knifelike canines, around fifteen inches long—reached my chest. It had a thick neck and a broad chest, along with well-muscled legs.

Shit! I did not want it pouncing on me.

Its calculating eyes—an intense electric-blue color—drew me in. There was blood on his black nose and upper lip. Weird.

During my panic attack earlier, banging-on-the-door sounds had registered. I dared to break contact to look around the room.

I could see claw marks and a couple of dents on the walls. The door, from this side, was pretty banged up. Drops of blood decorated the place.

Was it a prisoner too? Would it understand if I told it that I would free it?

"Easy, big kitty," I purred, "I can free you."

Locked on me, it approached with intent.

I had worked with animals in the military for a while, so my training kicked in instinctively.

Do not show fear. Let it smell me—not that I have much choice in the matter, but at least it hasn't attacked so far.

It put its head under my hand. The strands tickled my palm.

Maybe it was more bark than bite after all, and it wouldn't eat me because it kept pressing its head under my hand. So I started petting it and talking nonsense. It rested on its laurels and purred in return. Its fur was surprisingly fluffy and silky, but underneath, where the skin was supposed to be soft, it was hard like it had armor underneath. It was weird, and I wanted to take a better look.

Lost in my musings, I suddenly felt a sting on my neck, and I realized a tad too late that its tail had a stinger.

I staggered and fell on my knees.

"Well, curiosity killed the cat. What did you expect, Kali?" I murmured.

Oh the irony of being eaten by an animal in outer space. It brought its huge teeth next to me, and my feeble attempt to push it away did nothing. I was thinking, *this is it,* when I felt his hot, raspy tongue licking the side of my neck.

The dizziness soon passed, and I felt normal. Actually, that wasn't accurate—something felt different, but not in a bad way.

The predator moved in front of me, put his head on my lap, and sniffed.

Did he just sniff my private parts?

I tried to knock his head away, but all he did was lick my hand,

and I could swear I heard him laugh. I could also feel joy spreading through me, and I was certain it was not my emotion.

Wait a second! How do I know it's a he? What the heck?

Those happy feelings running through me disappeared in a heartbeat. Fury and murderous intent replaced them as the animal stuck his head under my arm, lifted me, and pushed me toward the wall. Then he turned around, lowered his body to the floor, and started snarling. His tail was swishing, and I was pretty sure he was preparing for an attack. He sensed the others before I did, and protecting his mate took precedence over everything else.

How did I know that? That was not my thought…and mate? My head had started hurting again. I closed my eyes and took a deep breath, trying to find my inner strength to deal with everything. When I opened my eyes, I noticed the aliens outside the door, talking and looking intently at us. My captor had drawn a sword.

A fight was imminent, and it would offer a second chance to escape. I could not miss it this time—I did not know how many chances I'd get. I had to go. I started inching toward the door, but when I heard the sabertooth's snarl, something in me wouldn't let me leave.

Damn males! Always trying to prove who's the strongest.

My new-found intuition told me that the four-legged predator was about to attack in order to protect me. *Damn the male!*

I jumped in the middle the moment he roared, and raised my hands on either side to discourage them from attacking each other. "Stop!" I yelled, and the sabertooth sat on his haunches—his stance still one ready to pounce the moment things went sideways. At least he was obedient, I thought, and I heard the animal chuff, which I was pretty sure was the sound of his laughter.

Distracted by that realization, it took me a minute to notice the silver line that went through and linked every one of us, forming a full circle. I raised my hand and touched it carefully. My fingers went through it. At the contact, though, I felt warmth and a deep connection to the other three forming. Their emotions were mine, just for a millisecond. For the first time in my existence, I truly belonged.

A LOSING BATTLE

KALI

All my life, it was just me and my father, whom I was never able to impress. He always wanted more of me. No matter what I did, I was never good enough. After telling him about that frightful evening—and having him accuse me of lying and being immature for trying to get his attention that way—we grew further apart.

Being the daughter of a highly decorated general, it was always assumed I'd gained my rank due to our family connection. That could not be further from the truth. I always had to work the hardest, always had to prove I was worthy. I had gone through three wars to get to where I was today, or more accurately, where I had been before I got abducted.

Lost in my musings, I didn't realize they were staring at me. I felt a soft breeze caress my back right before hands enveloped me from behind. I tensed. The only one there had been the animal, and it definitely hadn't had arms.

Foreign words tickled my ear—but in my head, I understood

their meaning—just before he kissed my neck where he had stung me with his tail. He told me he would protect me.

What's happening? Am I dreaming, or am I losing my mind?

His chuckle rang inside my head. I turned in his arms and was taken aback by how handsome he was. He took my breath away.

He had copper hair, a straight button nose, and high cheekbones. His skin was like the animal's fur was imprinted on it, silver-gray with black spots and stripes, and it was equally silky smooth. His eyes were the same intense electric-blue color.

Mine, on the other hand—I was certain—were wide with dilated pupils as I took in his nudity. I willed myself not to look below his waist…it was futile. My gaze took all of him in.

I scrunched up my brows as I realized that even though it looked like he was naked, he wasn't. The garment he was wearing had the same coloring as the rest of him, and as I stared, more of that material seemed to be coming out of his bare skin—covering the rest of him.

The sight was disturbing and mesmerizing at the same time, and I wondered if he could do it at will.

I shook my head, trying to knock some sense into me. The whole situation was crazy, which reminded me of the small, but important detail I'd momentarily forgotten.

"Where is the animal?" I asked while trying to twist out of his arms to check the room.

His lips didn't move, yet his words—*Beast and I are one. We are shifters*—were clear in my head.

I needed to get out of this crazy person's embrace; I needed room to breathe and think. Placing my palms on his pectorals, I pushed him away, but failed to budge him even an inch.

He smirked, but sobered when the doctor's aggravated voice

sounded loud in the room. The shifter dropped his hands, and I stepped away as they started conversing tersely.

Taking a moment to reevaluate my situation, I considered my options. What all three of them had in common were their out-of-this-world good looks. *Shit!* What I was thinking about was their size, not how masculine they were, and definitely not how much they made my lady bits tingle. They were at least a foot taller than me—and at five nine I wasn't short myself—with broad, muscular shoulders, and abs for days. There was no way I'd win in a fight against them. I had to bide my time.

'Monakrivimou, the Healer wants to implant a translator. It's what they tried to do earlier. I don't want you to accept. I can't shield you from the procedure's pain.' The shifter's words in my mind startled me, bringing me out of my reverie.

I rolled my eyes at him. Did I look like someone in need of protection? Looking at the other two, I nodded my head positively to show them I agreed. Communication was key. I wanted to know where things were going. Plus, if I could understand what they were saying, escape would be that much easier.

They led me back to the other room, and the silver-skinned alien sat next to me. The purple-skinned one growled, but refrained from saying anything.

I tried to mentally prepare—it was a thick needle, after all, and I wasn't a big fan.

The doc set it next to me, with a pointed look at the shifter, who seemed immovable. With a gentle touch, he turned my head and sprayed something behind my left ear. Immediately after, it started tingling.

Hm...it's some kind of anesthetic.

He was so light-handed, I didn't feel the needle pierce the skin.

But the moment whatever was in the syringe entered me, it felt like an electric current was frying the neurons in my brain. My eyes watered, and I bit my lip to keep from screaming. A coppery taste filled my mouth and a wave of nausea threatened to overpower me.

Unexpectedly, the alien next to me shifted. Before he got the chance to pounce on the doctor, the other one intercepted. The predator's snarls were grating on my ears, and the sounds of objects crashing onto the floor were overly loud.

They were locked in battle when the pain started receding and I could focus on them. The newbie's suit was torn and stained with blood. He was only defending himself and pushing the animal away.

I tried to connect with the predator—Beast, he'd said his name was—the same way he'd connected with me. Rage was driving him hard, and I couldn't find a way through the red haze. How could I call him back? My gut told me I could.

Please stop. I'm fine now, I reached out but it didn't work.

I jumped off the table and walked toward the shifter, only to realize I hadn't taken a step. The doc's hands were restricting me.

"He's not stable. Arana was tortured beyond endurance, it's dangerous for you to go near his sabertooth," he warned.

"Let go. I can bring him back," I ordered.

"No," he insisted.

Beast turned toward us. He'd heard, and he was mad. His infuriated roar spurred me into action.

I pried the red-skinned alien's hands away and stepped closer to the predator.

His lips were curled and his long teeth were gleaming white. He wasn't looking at me, so I knew I was safe.

What I couldn't understand was why I felt the need to gamble my life like that for three aliens, two of whom were my captors. Being certain that I was the only one who could prevent this from turning into a bloodbath didn't make matters any easier.

"Bad kitty," I admonished while inching closer, aware that the sheet tied around my body wasn't enough of a protector against this lethal predator's weapons. "Don't look at them. Eyes on me."

Goose bumps formed on my arms as a rush of excitement ran through me the instant he complied. Having power over such a terrifying being was exhilarating.

"I'm fine. It's over. I need you to change back so we can talk," I demanded.

The sabertooth approached me, his gaze level with mine. *'He hurt you.'*

The husky voice in my head belonged to the animal, not the male. "Not intentionally," I replied.

He just raised his head and started licking the tender spot behind my ear. The rough surface of his tongue tickled me. Laughing, I tried to push him away. He didn't budge—not until he was satisfied with his job. Then he stepped back, closed his eyes, and let out a few deep puffs. He was trying to shift, but fury was still riding him, blocking whatever he needed to do to shift. When he growled in frustration, I took his muzzle between my hands. His eyes snapped open. With slow movements, I petted him between his eyes then scratched him behind his ears.

"Come back to me." I didn't know that my voice could sound so tender.

The next instant, I found myself holding his face. His skin was as soft as his fur. Our eyes locked, and I couldn't avoid what was coming even if I wanted to. Which—at that moment, weirdly enough—I didn't want to avoid.

His hand found its way to the base of my neck and he fisted my hair. The slight pinch made me gasp, and he dropped his eyes to my lips. When his found mine again, the hunger I witnessed in the vibrant blue swirls surprised me. His other hand was wrapped around my waist, and he pulled me flush against his body. The sheet that covered mine did nothing to keep the contour of his muscles from imprinting on me. He slowly bent his head and locked his lips with mine.

My eyes fluttered closed, and everything else faded away. It was a gentle kiss in the beginning until he coaxed my mouth open. Then he poured all of his emotions into it, melting my defenses. He sucked my bottom lip, bit it lightly, and then soothed it with his tongue. The rough, raspy texture of its surface—in such contrast with his soft lips—surprised me, and I gasped.

A growl rattled in his chest—the vibrations found a target in my core, melting it and making me want things better left alone. Then his tongue entered my mouth and silenced my thoughts.

Vaguely, I heard the newbie speak and the doctor reply that the Saberian was my mate too, and had every right to kiss me.

His words were a bucket of ice-cold water thrown over me—stunning me, bringing me back to reality.

My body had gone into overdrive—I could almost hear the blood rushing through my veins, and I didn't have the mental capacity to even think about what it all meant. I pulled back, breaking the kiss. "Mate?" I stammered, but turned around to address the doctor. "What do you mean he is my mate too?"

The shifter's hand was still clutching my hair. He tugged to get me to turn.

"Let me go," I barked, and he dropped his hands.

I prowled toward the doctor.

"Explain," I ordered, without caring about how uncomfortable he was.

If I could annihilate them with a look, I would.

"You are my mate," the shifter said, and I spun around. "Otherwise, I wouldn't have marked you. Saberians have only one mate in our lifetime," he informed me—his demeanor calm when mine was about to explode.

"She isn't just your mate, warrior," the newbie interjected.

Then the doctor added, "She's ours too. Wravukians only get one mate as well in our lifetime."

The silver-skinned alien furrowed his brows, and seemed lost in thought for a moment before he squared his shoulders and looked at me.

"It appears this alien female evoked a Sacred Union. Even though I've never heard of a cross-species Sacred Bond, it seems we have one," he said.

Oh, hell no! As if one alien believing I'm his isn't enough, now all three think they have a claim on me?

"Hold your horses, cowboys—"

"We don't have such animals here," the newbie replied, perplexed.

"We aren't cowboys," the shifter added.

"It's an expression," I snapped. "What I tried to say, before I was interrupted, is I have a say in this too. I'm no one's mate. I don't want a man or a mate or whatever you are!" I tried to keep my voice steady, to convey I meant business, but it hitched at the end, betraying the fear that was taking root.

"You don't have a say. It is what it is, and we'll deal with this unusual situation," the newbie ordered, and I huffed at his declaration.

"Who do you think you are telling me what I have a say in?" I barked—mad at him and uncaring about our size difference. I'd stabbed him once already, I could do it again.

If he thought I was a pushover, he was sorely mistaken.

"My name is Rorc. I'm the Admiral of Wravuk's Second Fleet, and Captain of its lead ship, the Nur. You will obey me," he ordered.

"Guess again, genius" was my retort.

The nerve this guy has. Pfff.

"I think we all need to rest, have a bath, and then sit down and get to know one another over dinner. Aren't you hungry, Mate?" the doctor inquired.

"Don't call me that! My name is Kali, and I demand you take me back to Earth."

I knew I was being petulant, but I had started panicking again; they were convinced I was their mate, whatever that meant. This situation was ridiculous. How did I manage to get involved in all this?

"Your place is with us," Rorc growled.

I looked up to find all three of them watching me—expressions sober. They were serious.

'Monakrivimou, let us take care of you. You went through a lot, I can feel your panic. There is no need for it. We will provide for your every desire,' the Saberian told me telepathically, while out loud he said, "You have nothing to fear."

I stood still, when what I really wanted was to curl into the fetal position. They were not planning to let me go, a small part of me was thrilled, but I squashed it. I would have to find another way to return home. One thing the army had taught me was to pick my battles. So I would do as they said—for now. Making them believe

I'd stay was imperative. They would drop their defenses at some point, and then I'd escape.

"Fine. Can I get something to wear, or should I parade around half naked?" I asked. With everything going on, it'd completely slipped my mind that I was naked underneath the semitransparent sheet.

Well, I hope they enjoyed the show because that's not happening again.

My declaration was followed by three distinct growls, and I saw the doctor stomping to another room. I kept the smile to myself.

He returned holding an alien square piece that was cool and soft to the touch with its weaved texture; it almost felt like cloth, but it didn't look like it.

"How am I supposed to wear that?"

I tried to take it from him, but he pulled his hand away.

Jerk.

"Remove the sheet," he said.

I crossed my arms over my chest.

He mimicked me.

"You have got to be kidding me," I huffed.

"I need to show you how our uniform works. It is armored. Please, remove the sheet, I need to place this above your heart." His tone was gentler.

Why was it so hard to let my flimsy covering drop? Two of the three had already seen me naked. Of course we had been otherwise occupied, and they weren't focused on me as a woman, yet hunger was as present in their eyes then, as it was now. I mulled it over recognizing—with a heavy heart—that it was my scars I didn't want them to see.

They were perfect—exuding masculinity and strength effortlessly—whereas I was flawed, in more ways than one, and now they'd realize it too.

Well maybe they'd return me home once they really saw me.

Why that thought was upsetting, baffled me, but I dropped the sheet. My eyes followed the fabric's movement and locked on the bunched material on the floor.

Their swift intakes of breath were loud in the silence.

"Who hurt you?" Rorc asked.

I looked at him over my shoulder—his eyes had gone wide and he wasn't blinking. "When?"

The doctor trailed his finger over the healed wound above my chest. His touch felt electric when that area had lost sensation after the surgery.

"Why didn't the males of your species protect you?" he said.

I opened my mouth to reply, but Arana beat me to it. "She's a warrior." There was admiration in his voice.

"I'm a soldier, like you all are," I clarified, and tried not to fidget.

They were all staring at me. Two of them looked a cross between appalled and angry, whereas the third looked proud.

"Are you going to show me how to put the uniform on or not?" I snapped. Only once in my life had I felt this exposed, and I'd hated it.

He placed the little square over my heart, and I could feel it pulse in tandem with the vital organ. He took my hand and pressed my forefinger against its surface. He let it go and it stayed on me. It contracted, and then a liquid-like substance slowly spread all over my body. When I was covered from the neck down, it solidified yet remained weightless. I moved my arms and legs experimentally; the alien material retained its elasticity.

Rorc stepped in front of me, hooked his finger under my chin, and applied light pressure until I looked up.

"You will never have to fight again," he vowed—his tone solemn.

This guy was hot, but was also getting on my nerves. "Guess again, genius."

"You—" he started, but didn't get to finish.

"Actually she will," Arana interjected. "She is the Queen of Saber."

"You're going to let our female fight?" Rorc's body was quaking. "You're out of your fucking mind if you think I'll allow it," he growled, and stepped aggressively into the shifter's way.

The doctor got between them, successfully diffusing the situation. "Why don't we move to my quarters, to feed our mate and answer her questions?"

"Like I've said, I'm not your anything," I insisted. Even though it was starting to feel like a losing battle, I had to make them see reality.

They looked at me like I'd grown horns on top of my head. If they wanted to harm me, they could have easily done it here. Being alone with them in another room would not make a difference, and now that the doc had brought it up, I was hungry.

"Fine," I acquiesced. "Lead the way."

SACRED UNION

ARANA

To say my world had once again been upended would be an understatement.

I was blessed with a Sacred Union. My mate's taste still lingered on my lips. My joy would be indescribable if I had the slightest inkling how to get my people to accept the Wravukians. This was a complication I didn't need, and while I expected Beast to be throwing a fit at having to share his female with others, he was simply basking in her presence—mellow for the first time ever.

Or we could kill them now and be done with it. She won't care either way, Beast suggested.

Okay, maybe not so mellow after all. *Don't even think about it.*

Oh, but I'm thinking about it. One of us has to, and you're too much of a coward to do it.

A barely audible hiss of displeasure escaped my lips, and she glanced backward at me.

Despite our connection being so new, her soul was already picking up on my distress, and she had known how to placate my sabertooth earlier. I could feel her inner turmoil too. She was confused, scared and determined to escape. Little did she know that I would never allow such a thing. She was strong, but she'd never escape me.

The Healer ahead of us stopped outside of an entrance and placed his palm on the scanner.

What would I do about them? They were her mates too, but we hadn't completed the Union and it wasn't in my makeup to share. Not the most precious being to me. I had marked her first, and even though we hadn't completed the Mating Ritual yet, our bond was strong already. I had an open path to her mind as she had to mine.

A pang of sorrow zinged through me as I reminisced about the Saberian females, who'd been a force to be reckoned with. Beautiful, alluring and lethal. They had been more powerful than the males of my species, and when they had been with young even more so. Could we actually give her a sabertooth? Beast was certain, but Changing an alien female had never been done, as far as I knew. Maybe the Elders would have more information.

I had to get us out of here. I could sense that the Admiral didn't trust me. He was right, and I was certain he wouldn't give her up without a fight. I only needed them to slip once, but I didn't want her to witness it. She would become scared of me and that was the last thing I wanted.

She spun around—her body tense—and glared at me. "Whatever it is that's going through your mind, stop it," she ordered.

Wanting to test her limits, I curled my lip at her and released a soft growl.

Her hand went to her hip, but what she instinctively reached for wasn't there. Her eyes narrowed and her jaw set.

Feisty, Beast purred with approval.

On purpose, I projected an image of her on all fours and me reddening her sweet bottom with my hand, into her head. I saw the blush creep up on her face and neck, and I smirked. She humphed, turned around, and entered the Healer's private quarters.

The door clicked shut behind me, and I rested against the wall next to it. I didn't want her to try anything silly and possibly get hurt. The two males in the room with us were my Pair-bonds. They were unable to hurt her, as was I, but I didn't trust anyone else not to.

She perused the room and went to lean against the window to my left.

The two Wravukians stood in the middle of the sitting area across from me.

Our mate crossed her arms across her chest and lifted her chin when she noticed we were all taking her in.

The Healer was the first to break the silence. "I believe introductions are in order. My name is Meskiagkasher—though just Mes will do—and I'm the Wravukian King's Second Son, as well as the Nur's Arch-healer."

One would expect getting to know us would calm her down—instead, she tensed.

"Rorc, as he's already told you, is the Admiral of the Second Fleet of Wravuk and Captain of the Nur," he said, and looked expectantly at me.

"I'm Arana, King of Saber, and my sabertooth is Beast. Together we are the fiercest warrior alive." I let the Wravukians absorb what that meant for them—maybe I'd get lucky and they would withdraw their claim on our mate—before I continued, "And you, Kali, are our mate." Her name sounded exotic, but so right falling from my lips.

She pressed her arms closer to her torso and shook her head. "You're mistaken," she said to me, then turned to Rorc. "I just need you to take me back to Earth, and then you can move on." She started pacing the room, but continued, "I'm sure a Prince, an Admiral, and a King won't have trouble finding another mate."

Beast picked up on her agitation and unsheathed his claws.

I knew the other two could hear his low growls; they didn't comment, though—too focused on our female.

The Healer, who seemed to be the most level-headed out of all of us, tried to calm her. "Kali, what is going on between us is unusual for us too, but it's real."

"Nothing's going on," she barked, then continued at a lower volume, "fate must be playing a joke on me! First, I get kidnapped—by aliens nonetheless—and now, my captors inform me they're my mates. What a clusterfuck."

"We aren't your captors," Mes said as Rorc grunted and threw his arms up in the air.

"We rescued you from the Arkad, along with the other females. When I came down, it was to let all of you know we were returning you to your planets," the Admiral said.

He was struggling, trying to collect himself in order to answer her calmly when she'd just insulted the integrity of the two Wravukians.

My mouth fell open. I shouldn't have been able to sense his emotions, yet the pathway uniting us was open and unobstructed. Fuck. If our bond was this strong so soon, I wouldn't be able to sever it without repercussions. I composed myself and returned my attention to the conversation.

Hope blossomed on Kali's face. "Will you return me to my home too, then?"

The joy in her voice made us cringe.

We would give her the world, but we could not give her that.

We could not let her go.

"No." I uttered the single word she did not want to hear. But I couldn't lie to her, nor did I desire to do so.

She was strong—she would get over the fact that she would be calling Saber home from now on.

"The Sacred Line formed. You saw it with your own eyes. You.Are.Our.Mate. Your home is with us," I continued. Her emotions were leaking through our bond to me, and my sabertooth was getting angrier the more time passed that she didn't calm down.

She stopped in her tracks and speared me with her stare. "This line you speak of means nothing to me."

Beast was affronted by her disregard for us. *You need to mate her, Arana. She feels our connection but she's ignoring it. Bringing her sabertooth closer will tie her to us.*

Mes was rubbing his temples, his breathing elevated. Rorc had started pacing around the room, bound to wear a groove in the floor.

Was it like that for every Sacred Union, or was it just us? Everyone's inner turmoil seemed to compound from one to the other.

"To find one's true mate is rare for Wravukians. A Sacred Line hasn't formed in decades," Rorc told her.

"Let's all sit down. We'll answer all your questions, Kali." Mes's tender tone was cajoling.

When she didn't move, I pushed away from the wall and approached her. She didn't budge, instead raised her head—eyes flashing with defiance.

"Would you force a woman to accept you?"

"Of course not," I said as I furrowed my brows.

"Does it matter what a woman wants?"

I didn't know what she was getting at, but I replied nonetheless, "Yes."

Backing away, she said, "Then know that I can never be with a man...I don't want you...any of you."

My stomach clenched with the sudden onset of nausea. I pressed my lips tight and lowered my head. Her rejection cut deeply and the room spun.

Don't you feel it's something else holding her back? Beast, who'd been a quiet observer for the most part, said. *Reach out to her through our bond. She's scared.*

My sabertooth's words were a balm to my soul.

"I need to go to the bathroom," she said.

Mes got up. "Come, I'll take you."

She hesitated but approached him.

"I need to show you how to remove your uniform," he said, and extended his hand to her chest.

She stumbled back while her eyes flashed fire. "You're not seeing me naked again." Then she smirked and added, "Why don't you show me with your uniform?"

I snickered and told Beast, *A challenge if I ever heard one.*

His tongue lolled to the side, giving me his equivalent of a smile.

"If you want to see me naked"—Mes smiled as he raised his palm over his left shoulder—"you only have to ask, Mate." He pressed two fingers to his collarbone and his uniform dissolved, leaving him bare in front of us.

He might be a Healer, but his build was that of a warrior—no doubt due to his ancestral line. He'd successfully protect our mate if need be.

Wravukians, like us, weren't averse to nudity. Kali, on the other hand, gasped and slapped a palm over her eyes.

"Put your clothes on," her shrill tone demanded.

Rorc chuckled. "You asked him to show you."

Mes—still naked—approached her and brought his lips to her ear. "Is my appearance not to your satisfaction, Mate?"

She shuddered and stumbled back, then pursed her lips, squared her shoulders, and dropped her hand. Our mate had fire.

"I do not care one way or another about your appearance," she growled, and stepped into his personal space. "Stop calling me mate."

He bent so he could look her in the eye as he told her, "Little liar, I heard your heart fluttering as fast as the wings of an archilochus fowl when being chased by hawkr predators." Then he wrapped his arms around her delectable body and pulled her close, right before his lips claimed hers.

Instead of experiencing rage, disdain, or even envy at seeing her with one of them, I felt a flush of adrenaline tingling through me. The moment her body yielded, and softened in his arms, the feeling morphed into burning lust.

Rorc moved closer, put his hands on her waist, and leaned down to inhale the scent wafting from her hair. Then his lips found the side of her neck and a moan escaped her lips.

Witnessing her pleasure at the hands of my Pair-bonds sent all the blood straight to my groin.

How the fuck would I convince them to let her go? There was no way the Wravukians would give her up, not after her reaction to their affection. But most importantly, did I really want to take her away from them?

Beast, you're oddly calm about this.

It's a fool's errand trying to break a Sacred Union, he replied, and curled up with a humph.

The sexual tension in the room was almost tangible. We were all caught under its spell when Kali, who was still locked between them, tensed. Her hands, which had been clutching Mes's arms, were now pushing him away—but failing to budge him.

The others' lust-filled minds were slow in catching onto the shift in her mood. She took a swing at the Healer's side and head-butted the Admiral before escaping from them.

"Trust me when I say, Mate, this behavior will only earn you punishments," Rorc said, taking a step toward her.

She bent her knees and raised her fists in front of her face. Her defensive stance showed she didn't realize that we'd never hurt her, that any punishment we dolled out would end up in her pleasure.

"I don't trust you as far as I can throw you," she said.

What did trust have to do with throwing someone? I wondered.

Mes furrowed his brows, not really understanding the meaning of her words either.

"What are you talking about, female? I weigh at least twice as much as you," Rorc replied, just as perplexed.

Kali's mouth went slack. "Female? Female!" she shrieked, and then attacked him.

Rorc deflected most of her offensive moves, but she got in a couple of good hits. She was a warrior, so I gave her a few ticks to vent her emotions—it would also be good for my Pair-bonds to witness her strength—before I enveloped her in my arms, picked her up, and placed her away from the other two.

"We seem to have a problem," Mes, the calmer of the two said as I held my wildcat back from attacking Rorc again.

Beast's soft purr vibrated in my chest and our mate stopped struggling.

She pressed her palm to my skin. Fire from the contact seared my insides.

"A problem? We fucking have to share the same mate with a Saberian!" Rorc growled.

It was interesting that he didn't mind sharing, just that he had to do it with me too.

She tensed in my arms, and I wanted to punch him for interrupting our connection.

"The solution is easy. I marked her first. She is mine. You can find your own mate." I tried to keep my tone down. After her reaction to the Admiral's words, I needed to tread lightly. My gut was telling me that she wouldn't appreciate it if she heard me talking in such a proprietary manner about her.

Rorc stepped aggressively my way before Mes reached out to stop him. He shook the Healer's arm off and started toward me again.

Placing Kali behind me, I straightened to my full height. Did he think to intimidate me with such behavior? I'd faced way worse than Wravukians who, for the most part, were an honorable species.

He bumped his chest to mine—ruffling both my and Beast's feathers.

I bared my teeth and let a snarl escape while standing my ground.

Our battle of wills was broken by the female's exaggerated huff.

"I'm not yours. And I'm not his either," she said, and threw her arms in the air. "I belong to myself."

"Let's all sit down and have a civilized conversation. We all have questions that need answers," Mes suggested again, his tone demanding yet gentle.

It was interesting to see our mate react—without putting up a fight—to it. Her scent dispersed in the room behind her, and it was like a punch to the gut, almost bringing me to my knees. She was calling out to me and she didn't even know it.

Deep breaths through my mouth helped dispel the haze that was threatening to come over me. When she chose a seat opposite the Wravukians, Beast was appeased. I headed her way but the expression in her eyes stopped me in my tracks.

Then she dared to order, "Not here."

She'd soon learn who was in charge, so I'd give her a pass this time. Still, I prowled toward her because she'd riled up my sabertooth too, and he pushed at me to not allow her to think she'd be the dominant one.

"Have your fun now, my Queen." I leaned over, caging her between my arms. "While you can." My voice sounded more gravelly than usual, the animalistic rasp more prominent. "You can have it your way…for now."

Fear sparked in her eyes, and Beast roared at me for scaring our mate.

Back off, you cur.

It hadn't been my intention to frighten her. Although, being a little scared could work in our favor. I straightened, then sat on the unoccupied couch.

That moment the Healer's comms beeped, and a holographic screen flashed with a report.

"What did Barianh find?" Rorc asked.

"Sacred Unions were cataloged in the old archives," Mes replied absentmindedly—as he was still reading—then added, "but never a cross-species one."

His answer chilled me to the bone and all three of us turned to look at her. I had to trust that once the Sacred Line had formed, we were compatible. But we couldn't know what effects the bond would have on her.

Mes's thoughts were along the same lines as mine because he asked her, "Earth of the Solar System is categorized as a primitive planet in the Intergalactic Enosis database and contact is strictly prohibited; what species are you?"

"I'm human, and if contact was forbidden, I wouldn't be here now, would I?"

Anger mixed with something else rolled off Kali in waves, and she shifted into a defensive position. The changes were subtle, but we all noticed.

"You have nothing to fear. I can and will protect you," I declared, as much to her as to the other two.

Both males emitted a low growl—I easily picked up—in front of our mate. Beast wouldn't tolerate such behavior, and pushed for the shift as I jumped to my feet—ready to allow it and teach them a lesson—but then her voice broke through the anger.

"Arana."

Just my name coming from her lips, sounding so foreign but so right, was enough to calm me down. I wanted to hear her say it again—or better yet—scream it in the throes of ecstasy.

"Arana!"

She must have picked up my train of thought because this time it was a reprimand. Our Sacred Bond was getting stronger with each passing tick.

"Can someone explain what this Sacred Bond is that you all keep thinking about?" She looked at each of us expectantly.

Mes took the reins. "We'll answer all your questions," he promised, then said, "but before we tell you about that, let me explain a little bit about our species."

"Why do I have the feeling I'm not going to like what I hear?" she mumbled under her breath—but our senses were heightened, and we heard her.

"Kali, this is important. You need to understand," Rorc scolded her.

As if he pressed a switch, her body went rigid and fury swam in her eyes. "Why is that, Admiral?"

I felt his displeasure at the snark in her voice, yet he didn't chastise her.

"Because it is the reason why we cannot let you go," he said, sighing.

She froze, momentarily stunned by his answer. As the shocked silence stretched, she clenched her fists and ground her jaw.

"Wravukians, as well as Saberians, mate for life," Mes quickly interjected, to diffuse the situation. "I will only speak for us. Arana can fill in about their Mating Ritual afterward. In the past, either the males of my species would find their Fated Mates—which would lead to a powerful Union that would produce very strong offspring—or they would choose a female to mate with. When the former took place, neither party had an option. The attraction was instant, and it would escalate until the Mating Ritual was completed. At the moment of the Ritual's completion, a line the color of the male would unite the male with the female. That line would keep the couple united when they moved from this life to the next." He paused, giving her time to ask questions, and when none came, Mes continued, "When the latter took place, the Mating Ritual would be considered complete when both partners carried the mating mark. Many centuries ago, though, there were even more powerful Unions. In those, trios or more partners were Fated Mates. Those Fated Unions were extremely rare then, and we thought they were extinct now." Mes finished the part he wanted to divulge and looked expectantly at me.

It was rare for an outsider to be privy to a species' Mating Rituals, so it was an honor to learn about the Wravukians' ways. But it was also clear it wasn't the one that had manifested earlier between us.

I cleared my throat. There were many things they would need to learn about our Union, but Kali wasn't ready to find out about all of them just yet, so I chose my words carefully. "Sacred Mates form one Pneuma; they are halves of one soul. They complete each other and the physical attraction is instant. Similarly to the Wravukian customs, either our females would choose who they paired with, or they would wait to find their mates. But in my species, the females had the power to awaken the Sacred Bond. When in the presence of their mates, the females' voices would evoke the Sacred Line and it would unite the pair, forming a full circle."

"Which is what happened when I told you to stop," Kali said.

I nodded and continued, "We formed a Sacred Union. It's such a rare occurrence that only two have been registered in the Elders' Athenaeum, and they manifested centuries ago. Saberian warriors and their sabertooths are dominant and possessive. I don't know how those two Unions made it work."

I locked eyes with both males. They knew I had left a lot unsaid. Parts she wasn't prepared to hear, such as that the Saberian Queen would have to fight to be accepted by her people. Nor was she ready to hear that the second time we mated, I'd bite her, and bring forth the sabertooth Beast had given her.

WE CAN'T LET YOU GO

MES

Kali's eyes were two huge round saucers, and she was looking at us like we'd grown multiple heads.

The influx of emotions stopped abruptly. She'd raised her shields so fast that it worried me. The room was still and quiet, exactly like Wravuk before a cyclone.

"Let's assume for one second that the light is on but nobody's home. I need you to spell it out for me, as alien culture is not my forte. You both mentioned instant physical attraction and mating." She gulped and swiped her palms back and forth on her legs. "When you say mating you mean um…sex, right? That you want to get intimate…with me?" Her face flashed a rosy color as her voice trailed off.

Skipping the part I didn't understand—our female loved speaking in riddles, maybe it was a thing her species did—I tried the word, "Sex?" I liked it. "Yes," I said, answering her question.

"No freaking way," she snapped. "You expect me to have sex with the three of you?" She shot up and moved to the farthest spot from us. "As if one wasn't bad enough," she mumbled, then said decisively, "No. No way."

Another rejection.

I ran my hand through my hair, pulling at the roots. My essence had enveloped her; I hadn't imagined that. She was my mate…our mate. Why wasn't she attracted to us? Was I mistaken? No. The Sacred Line had formed, uniting us all. When I'd kissed her, her body had come alive in my arms.

There must be something else holding her back.

Then it hit me.

"Do you have a mate back on your planet waiting for you?" I asked, and the other two males went completely still, eyes focused on her.

"No."

"Thank the Creator," Rorc mumbled, and approached her.

I felt his need to envelope her in his arms as strongly as if it were my own.

As soon as he wrapped his fingers around her arm to pull her closer, it was like he threw her for a loop. One tick she was frozen, and the next she struggled like a cornered wild creature that knew it was about to meet the Creator. The Admiral's confusion permeated the air, but her terror gripped me and brought me to my knees. The images flashing so fast in my mind's eye that I couldn't grasp their content.

Her emotions had an immediate effect on Arana as well—whose sabertooth burst from his skin.

"Open the door and let her go. Now," I ordered before throwing myself in the predator's way. Through our newly formed bond I could feel him trying to control Beast—who'd responded to her distress—and failing.

Rorc picked up on the urgency in my voice and slapped his palm on the scanner next to the entrance.

The door opened and Kali, who had tears running down her face, ran.

I needed to comfort her, but I could only deal with one crisis at a time. No one would dare harm a female. She was safe on the ship. But if Arana did not get a handle on his sabertooth, we were all in grave danger. One Saberian was enough to cause serious damage.

“Beast, whatever happened is in her past. We are not a threat to her,” I explained knowing he was a predator, but also as sentient as the rest of us. “Arana, get a handle on your sabertooth,” I cajoled.

Beast curled his lips at me and growled, before focusing on Rorc. *He’s responsible for my female’s distress.* His gruff timbre filled my head.

“Fuck, Beast! I did not hurt her. I’m her mate. Same as you!” Rorc replied, trying to get through to him while watching for the tiniest change in the sabertooth’s posture. He knew he had a fight on his hands.

“It wasn’t your Pair-bond that caused this reaction. Something happened to her and his touch brought back memories,” I added, hoping to get through to him.

Instead, he took a feeble swipe at me with his poisonous tail and bypassed me, rushing full on into Rorc.

Arana seemed to be having trouble trying to control Beast, who didn’t even acknowledge what we’d told him.

The predator jumped at Rorc, who evaded to the left at the last tick. In doing so, though, he hit his hip hard on the corner of the table, lost his balance, and went down.

Beast, without losing a beat, pounced on him.

I jumped on top of the sabertooth, locking his tail between my legs.

He rolled sideways, trying to dislodge me. When Rorc punched him under the jaw, he howled and bit Rorc on the shoulder.

Fuck! He wouldn't stop. Taking my knife out, I thought about my options. I couldn't hurt him, but a distraction would be enough to free our Pair-bond. Before I had the chance to act, Kali appeared at the entrance.

"Stop," she pleaded.

The Second in Command was right behind her. He took in the scene, aimed his gun at Beast, and barked, "Let him go, Saberian."

Our mate jumped in front of the gun. "No," she ordered, but Cubjornh's loyalty lay with Rorc, not with an alien, so he didn't budge.

It caught the attention of Arana, who jumped off Rorc, shook me loose, and prowled toward the guard—deadly intent in his eyes.

Our foolish mate blocked his way.

"Kali, no! Get back." I put all the alpha command I could muster behind my words, but she continued, undeterred. "He is beyond reason now." Feeling helpless, I stepped toward her, practicing, in my mind, the move that'd get me between them, when Beast turned his head and roared at me—a loud warning to stay back.

"It's all right," she crooned, and stepped right into the predator's space.

Ice-blue eyes were laser-focused on her; he curled his lip.

She slowly raised her hands, unafraid—our mate was magnificent. Gentle fingers went through his whiskers and stayed at the sides of his muzzle.

"Did I cause this?" she inquired, but didn't wait for an answer before she continued, "I'm sorry. It was a long time ago, but I'm okay now. I didn't want anyone else to experience that."

Then she did something none of us anticipated. She brought her face closer to Beast's head and laid her forehead on his. The sabertooth purred, his tense body relaxed.

"Please, Arana, come back to us." Her soft-spoken words seemed to penetrate her protector's anger, and he shifted. The moment his paws turned to hands, he enveloped her in a hug and buried his face in her hair.

"Admiral, do I arrest him?" Cubjornh asked—gun still pointed at the Saberian.

"No, leave us," he ordered his Second in Command—who hesitated, causing Rorc to cross his arms with a grunt and narrow his eyes at the other Wravukian.

"Ror—"

"Are you disobeying a direct order, Vice Admiral?" His taut voice was a warning by itself; if one added that he'd just pulled rank, trouble was brewing for the poor soul.

I snickered. Cubjornh was his oldest friend, but if he wasn't careful, he'd find himself on my operating table soon enough.

"No, Admiral." He saluted, then my Pair-bond dismissed him, and he left the room.

Kali gasped and left Arana's arms to examine Rorc's wound. "You're hurt."

"Rorc, shield your emotions," I reprimanded at the same time a menacing snarl echoed in the room.

"It is nothing. I will heal soon enough."

She looked at me for confirmation, and I nodded my assent after checking it. Surprisingly, the bite wasn't deep. It wouldn't need sutures. Our advanced healing abilities coupled with the nanites in his blood would take care of it in just a couple of hours.

"I'm sorry, Rorc. We both lost it. Our bond is stronger than I expected," Arana said.

"Don't worry about it." He excused the action as inconsequential.

Her emotions swamped all of us the moment he'd touched her. It was a chain reaction of effects. We needed to know what had happened to her. I watched her from my peripheral vision. Strong and fearless, she had no trouble facing a sabertooth head-on, yet now that she was in the room with us, the skirmish feeling she'd had earlier returned with a vengeance.

"Kali, you have to tell us," I pleaded.

Her body jerked and she looked once at the door.

Arana, who was behind her, bent and whispered in her ear, "Don't. I need you…we need you."

Her expression turned pained, and light tremors racked her body, but she stood tall. Her shoulders rose and fell with her deep breath, and her steps were steady when she walked to the seat she had vacated. All the while, I felt her raise mental walls block by block. Considerate mate. Her words might say rejection, but her actions showed care.

Arana acknowledged her effort by kissing the top of her head before sitting down—missing her scowl. Or maybe he saw it because he felt pretty smug about himself, and based on the hostile vibe I was getting from Rorc, he sensed Arana's mood too.

It was as much interesting as it was unsettling the fact that around her, I couldn't shield myself. Being a wide open receiver to their emotions, unable to protect myself, was dangerous. Was it because of the Sacred Bond? Or was it her?

Her voice brought me out of my reverie.

"It happened fifteen years ago, and I haven't let anyone else touch me since then…."

"What. Happened?" Rorc barked. He was never one for subtlety.

She paused, and I was about to scold my brother for scaring her—she needed to get this out in the open—when she continued, "I had just graduated from Army Basic Training, and was to be transferred to another military base when my father's best friend called me into his office. He was the Lieutenant General, but I had grown up with him around," she explained, each word turning her voice tauter. "So I didn't think anything of it when he'd wanted to talk to me. I made a grave mistake by trusting him." Her hands trembled and she clenched her fists. "He assaulted me. I was inexperienced and weaker then. He was stronger and I failed at defending myself. Since then I worked my ass off to become stronger, faster, and better than the men on the base, so something like that never happened to me ever again. And it hasn't."

I was certain she wasn't aware of the tears that had escaped her eyes when she'd recited this abbreviated version of what had traumatized her. I was, though. And each one felt like poison dripping on my heart. My mate had been hurt, and I hadn't been there to comfort nor avenge her. I'd already failed the most important person in my life.

A screeching sound drew my attention.

Claws had extended from Arana's fingertips, tearing the metal armrests he was clutching.

Rorc, on the other hand, was awfully quiet. The quakes—I wasn't sure he was aware of—rocking his body was the only sign of his inner turmoil.

We've all failed her. My heart sank at the realization. How could she possibly love us after such betrayal?

"Assaulted?" Rorc's voice sounded dead, but I knew the havoc taking place in his head, remembering what had happened to his sister. "He beat you?"

Please, Creator, let the answer be yes. I silently prayed.

Kali lowered her eyes to the floor while shame and sadness swamped her.

"No. He raped me," she whispered.

The blow coming from those four words had me doubling over.

Rorc shot up and started pacing the room—the fury emanating from him taking shape, nearly becoming a tangible entity.

Growls full of pain rattled in Arana's chest. Completely still, he seemed like he was holding onto his sanity by a thread.

The different emotions battering at me made breathing hard. I had to find a way to dissipate the excess energy.

"Did your father avenge you?" Rorc asked through clenched teeth, "Did he kill him?"

Her sudden sob pierced our souls. "No," she gasped, and her tears began to flow unchecked, bringing all three of us to our knees.

I could no longer keep my distance, and the others couldn't stay away either.

Rorc knelt on her right side and clasped her hand in his.

I did the same on her left and cradled her hand in both of mine, hoping to absorb and ease some of her pain.

Arana wiped her tears with his thumbs and kissed each of her eyelids before lowering himself to the floor in front of her.

Our predicament forgotten, our gazes met and we silently vowed to avenge her. We didn't have to say the words, we communicated the unsaid promise through our bond.

"Monakrivimou, tell us," Arana coaxed.

We had to know the whole story, and it was better she told us now, so we'd never need to revisit this traumatizing memory again.

In a quiet voice she asked, "What does munnacrevmu mean? You've called me that before."

If she needed a bit more time to gather the courage to tell us the rest, we'd give it to her.

"It means you are the one and only of my heart." His thumb slid back and forth over her cheek while he seemed momentarily lost in thought. "You are the most precious being for us, Mate. We will never hurt you. Although I won't guarantee I'm not going to hurt them. They heal quickly."

The sides of her mouth tipped up, and he kissed the top of her head once again.

"Tell us," he coaxed.

She gave us a curt nod. "My father didn't believe me. He told me his best friend had divulged my promiscuous behavior and how he had gently turned me down. That such an upstanding member of the Army would never behave like a monster, and that my imagination was running wild. He even called him to our house that night, to clear the air between us." She shuddered and rushed the rest in one breath. "The General had humiliated me, accused me of being an ignorant little girl who had yet to learn how to be a woman able to attract a man. I never spoke about it again. If my own father didn't believe me, no one would."

She pulled her hands from ours and got up; Arana, though, pulled her in his arms, effectively blocking her escape.

"I believe you," he said.

"We do too." I spoke on behalf of both of myself and Rorc, who was having a hard time reigning in the fury that was seeping to me through our connection.

There, from his kneeling position, he opened his arms and said, "Please, let me hold you. I need you, Kali."

In all our years together, I'd never seen him plead for anything or act submissively. Yet now he did so purposefully, when I knew he did not have a submissive bone in his body.

Arana tightened his hold, but she gently unwrapped his arms and turned right into Rorc's embrace.

He pulled her close, placed his head in the crook of her neck, and inhaled her alluring aroma. The red haze swirling over him slowly dissipated.

The desire I'd been suppressing reared its head and demanded to be satisfied. Her scent—I'd been ignoring—invaded my senses, making my mouth water. Unable to stay away, I walked up to them. When her gaze landed on my face, her eyes widened. Was my deep-rooted need so obvious?

She let go of Rorc and came into my arms. Was she aware she nestled her body into mine? Did she realize she made me so hard, my body ached?

I kissed the top of her head and let my lips linger. She felt like an oasis in the middle of a desert, like the tastiest delicacy a starving male could have. The sweet scent of her arousal filled my nostrils.

I slid my forefinger under her chin, and tilted her head upwards. Her beautiful gray eyes drew me in. "We will never betray you," I vowed.

"But you won't let me go."

"We can't let you go," I corrected. "You are the one for us. Our souls are entwined already. Don't you feel it? Ask us for the moons and the stars, and we'll do everything in our power to deliver them to you. But don't ask us to sentence you to death. If we separate, it will affect you too. Sacred Mates don't do well apart," I told Kali, but I wanted my Pair-bonds to hear as well. I caught snippets from both of them thinking of taking her away from the others, but that wasn't how a Sacred Union worked. Cross-species or not didn't matter, and the sooner they realized it, the better it'd be for all of us.

Inwardly, our mate rebelled at my statement; outwardly, though, she remained calm. She took a step backward, and I let her go. I hadn't lied to her, but maybe she needed time to come to terms with our new reality. Moving closer to the windows, she was lost in thought once again. This time the walls she erected effectively blocked me out. At the same time giving me a reprieve from the other two males' feelings.

I hated it, and the feeling surprised me. But not knowing what was running through her head was worse than the battering I got from the influx of everyone's emotions and thoughts.

"Admiral, the transfer of the females over to Admiral Thora is complete," Barianh informed us before it added, "Arch-healer, the female's heartbeat just skyrocketed. I'd advise a tranquilizer to calm her. The Earthlings have a singular and fragile heart."

"Enough," I ordered the AI. Barianh's suggestion was extreme. "Kali, what has you worried?" I asked.

She ignored my question, but turned and spat at Rorc, "You said you would return them to their planets. You lied!" If she could shoot lasers with her gaze, Rorc would be dead by now.

He raised his hands, palms out. "I hadn't anticipated finding my mate. Thora is an honorable male, whom I trust. He will take them back. We are heading to Wravuk. We're taking you home."

"We're not staying on Wravuk," Arana growled.

This would be a problem.

"Home…right," Kali said—her voice barely above a whisper, her tone ice-cold.

It scared me.

She looked at the door and then at us, when Mavjerik requested entry.

"Access granted." The entrance opened under Rorc's command.

The troop was standing there next to the two Mardonian females. They searched the room, and the moment they detected Kali, they ran straight toward her, hugging her tight.

"I wasn't going to leave you alone," the adult female told Kali.

Our mate's mouth gaped open. "I can understand you," she exclaimed. Her face lit up with joy.

Did she have so little faith in me? Of course she understood. The translator I had injected in her would translate all known languages.

"Yes," the other two said between laughs. The young female, though, kept looking worriedly at us.

"We'll give you some space, Mate. Let Mavjerik know when you want us to return," the Admiral told her and, without waiting for a reply, walked out the door with us at his heels.

OUR DNA WILL ALTER KALI'S

RORC

Quakes were racking my body—and inside where no one could hear—I was screaming, disgusted at myself. What good was I? I had been too late to save my sister, and I hadn't been there for my mate either. I was barely holding it together. I needed to move. Despair was slowly choking me. "We'll give you some space, Mate. Let Mavjerik know if you have need of us," I told her, and walked out the door without waiting for a reply.

We needed to sort out the situation we found ourselves in before things got too out of hand.

"No one gets in the room, Mavjerik," I ordered as soon as I exited my quarters.

He stood to attention. "Yes, Admiral."

Walking over to the Training Bay, the other two males followed me. What better way was there to solve our issues, and maybe release some of the anger that was riding me hard, than a good sparring session? A few of my troops were practicing, but they'd pay us no mind. I stood inside one of the fighting arenas, but before I could say anything, Arana beat me to it.

"Once we land, I'll take her to Saber."

Fucking Saberian.

"No," I barked, and charged into his personal space.

"I'm the King and she's the Queen. How do you think this is going to work, Admiral?" Arana growled, standing his ground.

Mes, the level-headed one, tried to reason with him, "We'll all have to comprom—" the Saberian interrupted before he could finish his sentence.

"I am the King! There won't be a compromise. I have to rule. My warriors are slowly dying. Kali will bring back hope and the will to live," he said through clenched teeth and narrowed eyes—an angry rumbling sound deep in his throat.

"She'll be better off if you let her go." I bumped my chest to his, fucking angry with what he was suggesting. "Your kind has your Queens fight to prove their worth. Isn't that how you do things? How do you expect an Earthling to fight your best fighter, a sabertooth intent on killing her?"

The way Saberians elected their Queens was common knowledge. It was not safe for Kali to be there. She didn't have armor under her skin, or claws for that matter. She was a soft female, to be made love to, to be adored.

"She's not just an Earthling anymore." He cleared his throat. "She will soon have a sabertooth too," he added in a quiet voice.

Time stood still for a moment as his words registered and shock short-circuited my brain.

"Um, what do you mean?" I asked at the same time Mes said, "Has it been done before?"

Saberians weren't reputed to be a welcoming tribe. Had anyone ever been Changed? Was it even safe? How would it affect my mate? Questions swirled in my head until a sour smell pulled my attention to my surroundings. Feeling others' emotions was Mes's specialty, but since the Line united us, I could pick up the emotions of the stranger in front of me who was my Pair-bond. Shame had its own scent, and it'd suddenly filled my nostrils.

"We're Changing her. Beast initiated the process. And no, not that I know of, Healer."

I saw red. I grabbed him by the shoulders and threw him across the fighting arena. "You're Changing her without knowing if she will survive the fucking process! I. Will. Kill. You," I yelled, and attacked him.

The Saberian didn't shift this time, but stayed in his biped form. Shame was radiating from him, but it was too little too late.

I charged him, drew back my arm, and punched him in the face —my knuckles catching his jaw. It hurt, but it was fucking satisfying when his head snapped backward.

He straightened slowly. A thin red line trickled from his bottom lip. He wiped it with the back of his hand and snarled. "This is your one free pass, Wravukian."

I watched, somewhat mesmerized, as the torn edges of his skin knitted back together, when his words registered.

"Challenge accepted, animal," I spat before attacking him.

Panting, I lay on the floor next to Arana, who had one arm thrown over his eyes and the other wrapped around his torso.

It turned out that in his biped form we were equally matched, and the Saberian gave as good as he got. He could have shifted anytime, yet he hadn't, and my respect for him grew.

Every breath sent a sharp pain shooting from my ribs to my chest. My jaw was tender, and the cut on my eyebrow was still bleeding. My accelerated healing had kicked in and soon, with the help of the nanites in my blood, I'd be as good as new.

Mes's shadow reached us first. "Are you two done?"

"It's disconcerting how indifferent you've become to my injuries lately," I teased.

"Pffff," he snorted, but I caught the tips of his lips lifting before he schooled his features. "You'll live."

Arana snickered, then coughed to cover it up.

I expected anger to bubble up to the surface—I still hadn't forgiven him entirely—instead, quiet acceptance filled me with peace. This is not what I had pictured when it came to my mate, but it was what I was given. Being part of a Sacred Union meant sharing her, but it also meant more protection for her.

"Get your lazy asses up. While you've been playing, I've been thinking. We need to talk," Mes said, scowling, then walked away.

We both scrambled after him.

"Something worries you," Arana stated.

And now that he mentioned it, I sensed it wasn't our antics that had agitated my best friend.

He led us back to the Healers' Bay.

"Arana, lie in the pod. I need a blood sample, and I want to scan you for viruses and foreign substances."

The Saberian crossed his arms over his chest. "Why?"

Mes stopped disinfecting his hands to look at our Pair-bond. "I've never examined your species before, but when I worked to save your life, I took blood samples. I wanted to make sure the Arkad hadn't poisoned you. I noticed a retroviral sequence—a retrovirus attacking your nucleotides—but your DNA's immune system was fighting it. A microbe was what had caused Yenoctonia, right?"

Arana's shoulders fell and he clasped his head in his hands. "I might have transferred it to Kali," he said, not really answering the question.

"Yes," Mes confirmed.

A knot settled heavily in the pit of my stomach with this new revelation. "Can you kill it, or at least neutralize the virus?" I asked, dreading the answer.

"Maybe. If I have enough—"

"There's more," the Saberian cut him off mid-sentence.

"Tell us," I ordered, furrowing my brows when I didn't even get a snarl.

Hm, maybe he can be trained, I chuckled, but then sobered quickly. Our mate's fate was on the line.

His sharp inhale echoed in the room, and I could sense his inner battle through our pair-bond. "What I tell you must not leave this room, and it mustn't be recorded." His serious tone was foreboding.

"Barianh, lock the room and do not record this conversation," I ordered.

"Authorization code required, Admiral," the disembodied voice replied.

"SPS230221."

"Authorization granted. The Healers' Bay is on total lockdown in 3, 2, 1."

"It's safe. Tell us."

"It wasn't a local microbe that claimed the lives of the invincible Saberian females during Yenoctonia." Arana's eyes turned glassy, momentarily lost in whatever past memory haunted him, before he squeezed them shut and continued. "But a virus created to target them specifically." He ground his teeth. "The male warriors were unaffected."

I cracked my knuckles. I wanted to punch him again. "You knew this, yet you initiated the Change?"

"I didn't have a choice, Admiral."

My neck hurt from the tension. "There's always a choice," I shouted, and reached for the emergency blaster on the wall.

"Stop," Mes ordered.

I ignored him and was about to grab the weapon when he blocked my way.

"You aren't helping," he barked. "Do you really think you can kill your Pair-bond? Kill a part of yourself?" He shook his head from side to side. "What's done is done, Rorc. We need to work together." My eyebrows reached my hairline, but he persisted, "She has rejected us repeatedly. Unless we win her heart, we won't complete the Mating Ritual, and that way lies madness."

"The Healer is right," Arana said, and Mes—eyes narrowed—spun toward him.

"We are Pair-bonds whether we like it or not. Neither of you can break the bond, so you two better get used to the idea, and get acquainted now before we return to our mate. A male has already hurt her." If I were a lesser male, I would have fallen to my knees under the weight of his fury leaking through our bond before he contained his emotions and brought himself under control. "We need to help her heal, not cause her more pain." With that, he retrieved the tools he had prepared, walked to the Saberian, and started examining him.

I cleared my throat. Mes was right, but it was fucking hard to come to terms with our Union. I couldn't touch on the subject of her assailant without rage blinding me…he would pay, but first, for her sake, I needed to accept the situation we found ourselves in. "What else does the Changing process involve?"

He seemed reluctant to divulge information—his inner struggle evident in his electric-blue eyes—but he caved. "This has never happened before, so I'm not sure. My sabertooth, though, is certain that I need to mate her soon. My semen will flow into her and unite with her body, boosting the Change that started when Beast stung her. The third step, that will equip her with the power to shift, will be our bite."

"We need to abide by the Wravukian Mating Ritual as well, Arana." The Saberian opened his mouth to speak but Mes continued, "We don't have a choice either. It's a compulsion that will become stronger the longer we ignore it. Lie down," he ordered while he tapped a few commands on the med-pod's command center, then took the blood sample to another machine—and not a tick had passed by, and he was furiously taking notes.

He opened his mouth and closed it, as if wanting to say something and changing his mind. Finally, he asked,"Which is?"

Mes was too busy, so I answered, "Each family has their own ceremonial dagger. It is used to slice the palms of the males, who must immediately link their hands. The joined blood will flow in a cup, and then their female will drink from it. Attributes from the dominant line will be passed on to the Pair-bond and their female. But for the Union to be completed, the males must mate the female together."

"Similarly to yours, our DNA will alter Kali's," Mes said, and moved to release Arana from the med-pod.

I was aware of the fact—it was common among the Wravukian

mates for the less dominant one to gain traits from the stronger line—but hearing my Pair-bond confirm it filled me with trepidation. Would her small and fragile body, already undergoing a Change, withstand these additional traits? What if, instead of protecting her, we ended up killing her?

Unaware I had spoken out loud, I started when Arana spoke.

"We need to trust our Creator. He blessed us with a Sacred Union. We were made for her—she is our true match. Our DNA will make her stronger, not kill her."

Mes drew himself to his full height—chin lifted in defiance—daring us to challenge him. "I'll examine her blood and inoculate a sample with the virus to test her reaction to infection. We also need to consider the influence our blood will have on her genetic material following the Mating Ritual, especially since Arana's sabertooth has begun mutating her DNA already, so I'll do a preliminary investigation to learn the possible extent of the changes. Once we know she's safe, I'll need to examine Saber's soil, water, and air to determine whether the planet is habitable for our mate."

"Of course," I agreed readily, then stared at Arana, waiting for his decision.

If he denied, I would find a way to end him and keep our mate alive. Losing one of her three mates would hurt her, but it wouldn't cost her life.

"All right," he acquiesced. "I'll have one of my warriors bring you samples."

Well, I guess I won't have to kill my Pair-bond after all.

I humphed a breath and both males looked at me.

Mes, knowing where my thoughts had been, shook his head. "You're so bloodthirsty."

"Only when the circumstances demand it," I chuckled.

A high-pitched alarm rang through the speakers, startling all of us. "Meskiagkasher, the Imperial's Arch-healer requests your presence immediately," the ship's AI reported.

"What is the issue, Barianh?" Mes asked.

"Unknowns breached the lead ship of the First Fleet, the Imperial. The threat was dealt with, but Prince Callibohr was severely injured."

I felt the darkness he always kept under control swirling, unraveling, and threatening to swallow him whole—and potentially all of us in the process. Mes was a powerful Healer—he could bring beings back from their journey to the Vaults of No Return—but that was only one side of his gifts. Like everything in the universe, it needed to balance, so the other equally powerful side could end life just as easily.

He shut his eyes, pinched the bridge of his nose, and stood still for a few moments, trying to rein in his emotions. Through our bond, I shared my strength with him until I felt him relax his shoulders.

He opened his eyes and nodded his thanks before he said, "Let him know I'm on my way." Then he raced to the Teleportation Bay.

I sprinted to the Bridge with Arana behind me. He wasn't allowed in there, but I didn't have the time to argue, not when Mes's brother was in danger.

"Admiral, our long range sensors are picking up five ships—origin unknown—heading to the Imperial. Do we engage?" Cubjornh asked as we stepped in.

Noticing the Saberian, his eyes widened, but he kept his thoughts to himself.

I perused the wide viewscreen that was now zooming in on the hostile spaceships. Arana froze, and I felt his tension through our bond. Did he know who they belonged to? Their sleek triangular shape was unusual. I hadn't seen them before, but then again we hadn't entered the Pyxis System yet, and I wasn't familiar with all the crafts the species inhabiting the Aquar System possessed.

Ignoring his low growls, and knowing my Vice Admiral would have used proper procedure, I asked, "Did they respond to our warnings?"

"Negative."

"Try again," I requested, and waited.

Static was my answer.

'These are the same ships that attacked our people.'

I startled hearing both my Pair-bond's and his sabertooth's gravelly voice in my mind. *'No time like the present, then, to kill two birds with one stone,'* I replied before I focused on the task at hand.

"Cubjornh, send ten armored warships to intercept and take down the hostiles," I ordered. "Cairbre, activate shields and bring the Nur within range. Neutralize any threats within five astronomical units of the Imperial."

MISSED MY OPPORTUNITY TO RETURN HOME

KALI

Wow. They believe me. They don't know me but they were genuinely enraged on my behalf.... Just, wow.

My emotions were a jumbled mess. I couldn't believe I had shared the most humiliating moment of my life with them.

They hugged me—something not even my own father had done when I'd told him.

I hadn't been able to think straight with them in the room. My body had gone into overdrive, uncaring of what they were asking of me. For fifteen years, I'd never lusted after a man, and now these three aliens—with their ripped physiques and smoky voices—were causing my hormones to run amok. Realizing I was a hussy in hiding was disconcerting, and on top of that, the nearly constant purring in my head was giving me a headache.

What the heck have they implanted in me?

Their voices slowly faded the farther they went, but their emotions didn't. I could feel Rorc's disgust with himself, Mes's fear and Arana's determination, as if their emotions were my own. I pictured walls—so high and thick they were impenetrable—and the foreign feelings lessened. I would not worry about them. They were obviously grown-ups. If they fought, maybe they'd end each other and I wouldn't have to deal with three frustratingly gorgeous males.

My chest ached and I rubbed it to ease the pain.

Why did the thought of them being no more hurt so much?

Matesssss, whispered a husky voice in my head.

Heart racing I spun, looking around wildly.

My new friends sounded very different, so neither was the one who had just spoken.

I must be losing it! Maybe I will wake up soon and find myself lying on my bed, in my cozy apartment...but mates? Plural! This is stuff I wouldn't even conjure in my wildest dreams.

Yet deep down they felt right.

Croco's worried voice pulled me back to the present when she said, "Did they harm you?"

"No, they didn't. Getting the translator—on the other hand—was painful, but they only wanted to help" was my sheepish reply. I didn't want her to think ill of them. After all, they had saved us. "Although, it might be malfunctioning since I've started hearing voices and purrs," I mumbled under my breath.

"Momma, is the female all right?" asked the little girl in a lilting voice.

"Scckrkassh, what have I told you? She is right here. Be polite. You can ask her," Croco gently reprimanded.

Even though she was alien, the little girl was adorable in the way only children are, and I didn't want to put her on the spot. So I knelt to reach her height and answered the question before she needed to repeat it.

"I'm very well. Thank you for asking." I smiled and got up.

"Um…we haven't met properly. I'm Kali." I offered my hand for a shake, but Croco just stared at it. "Oops! That's a custom where I'm from. No need, I guess." But before I could lower it, she startled me by grasping it, sniffing it, and then rubbing the back of my palm on her cheek before letting it go.

I was surprised by how soft her light-green skin was, when the dorsal part of her body was covered in some type of osteoderm.

"Kalissh," she tried my name before introducing herself. "My name is Trrskeiirrssh, and this is Scckrkassh, my youngling."

Her daughter followed her mother's example, grabbing my hand. I tried not to flinch when she sniffed my skin—her teeth seemed quite sharp, but she was careful not to hurt me.

I tried to repeat their names, and my attempt had them laughing out loud.

"I'm so glad I amuse you." I couldn't help but laugh too. "I don't mean to offend you, but do you mind if I call you Tris and Kas? I doubt I'll ever get it right, otherwise."

They both shook their heads and tested the names I'd given them. Big smiles split their lips and put their pointy teeth on display. They were my only friends. The only two who had stayed back.

Frowning at the realization, I said, "Wait a minute! You missed your chance to return to your planet."

"We cannot go home." Tris enveloped her daughter in her arms when she started emitting a hissing sound.

Confused, I watched as her mother's slight pats on the back and whispered words slowly calmed the agitated child.

"I'm sorry, I didn't mean to upset you." The remorse rang clear in my voice.

Kas left her mom's embrace and hugged me fiercely, causing my joints to crack. "Wow! You are strong."

Tris reprimanded her gently, and the little one loosened her hold but did not let go. That was all right with me, so I hugged her back.

"Our planet is a harsh one, where only the strongest survive. My mate died defending us. If I'd stayed, Scckrkassh would be next—a new mate would not want another's youngling—so I took her and we fled." Her voice caught on the last word, and I realized she was putting up a strong front for her daughter. I reached out and enveloped her in a one-arm hug as well.

Even if they couldn't return to wherever they were from, they could have chosen to go to another planet. Staying here with me meant a lot.

"Thank you," I whispered, emotion choking me.

My own mother had abandoned me and my father when I was four. I didn't really remember her face anymore, but knowing I wasn't enough for her to stay had left a wound that never truly healed.

And here I was somewhere in the vast universe, with three males wanting to make me theirs and a new friend sticking by my side. The faces of my teammates—Stallion, Atlas, Cobra, and Bishop—popped into my head, amplifying the ache in my chest. I didn't know if I'd ever see them again, and they would search for me. They wouldn't stop until they found me alive or discovered my remains.

I have to go back.

Tris squeezed me and let go, breaking the embrace.

"Where are the Wravukians taking us?" she asked.

As if mentioning them, conjured their presence, the wall I had erected tumbled down, and the males' emotions swamped me. Fury made my blood boil, and pain exploded in my jaw. *What the heck are they doing?* I groaned and focused on bringing my shield back up. "I'm not sure," I said, and blinked rapidly to clear the black spots from my vision. I rubbed the sore spot and added, "They're disagreeing."

"Why?"

I sighed. "Arana wants to take me to his planet, the other two want to take me to theirs."

"Well, only your mate can make that decision," she clarified.

"That's the problem…they claim they all are my mates."

The audible crack of her jaw dropping didn't bode well for me. "When two true mates find each other, there is always a sign," she said.

Oh hell!

"A silver line united all of us—"

She clapped her hands and shrieked in delight, startling me.

"That means you'll have more protection. You and your younglings will be safe."

I got where she was coming from, but come on, there were three of them.

"Where I come from, this is not normal. Each woman has one man—" or woman, I was about to add, but she had cocked her head sideways, her eyes slightly widened. "One female, one male," I explained, and left it at that when she nodded.

"I don't understand your species. The more mates, the more blessed the female." She shook her head—lost in thought while I contemplated her words.

Did these aliens have it right, and we humans have it wrong? I briefly wondered when an overly loud alarm had us doubling over and covering our ears. I ran to the entrance and pounded at the door.

It whooshed open, but the hallway was blocked by the bulky body of the guard my mate left in charge of keeping everyone out, and us in.

"What happened?"

Eyes brooding, he looked us over. "Nothing for you to worry about, female," he said, dismissing me.

Before he could react, I punched his throat—putting all my weight behind the move. His eyes widened in surprise and he fell on his knees, gasping for air.

"Stay here where you're safe, Tris," I said, and sprinted out of the room.

This was my chance. They wouldn't ring the alarm for no reason. Either they were under attack, or someone else was. I was certain they'd take their spaceships to fight the threat. I couldn't miss this opportunity. "I'm sorry, Tris. I have to get back to my people," I mumbled as I ran to their Docking Bay.

No. Mates, the unknown voice whispered in my head, but I ignored her, and the fact that the thought they'd find another woman hurt more than I was ready to admit.

This time I managed to evade all the Wravukians, who now wore somber expressions accompanied by murderous intent as a result of the attack. It was unsettling how easy it was to read them. I always had a knack for sensing certain emotions and intentions, but what was going on now took things to a whole different level.

Luck seemed to be on my side, for once, since many spaceships had their ramps lowered, and the aliens were too busy with what was going on to notice me. I sprinted as stealthily as possible up the ramp of one of the spaceships and quickly found a small space to wedge myself in that'd protect me from turbulence until I hijacked the craft.

Soon the whirring sound of the hatch closing filled the space, and the floor trembled under my feet as the pilot powered up the engines. Suddenly, my body felt super heavy and my back was pushed into the side of the nook I was hiding in. It felt like someone was sitting on my chest and I started to feel dizzy, but as suddenly as the change happened, it returned to normal, and I could draw oxygen into my lungs again.

I stood still, trying to avoid puking all over the place. When I finally had a handle on my bodily functions, I looked around. Luck was still on my side. The wall opposite from me was mounted with all kinds of alien weapons. Guns weren't a great idea inside a vehicle in outer space, so I went for a knife. I eyed the selection until one caught my eye. It was too short to be a sword and too long to be a dagger—it was perfect for me. For a moment I was distracted by the beauty of the flame-shaped blade, until I heard the alien's voice.

Without wasting another second, I sprinted to the cockpit. Its entrance opened automatically. The pilot's head jolted to where the sound had come from and froze when he saw me. Taking advantage of his surprised reaction, I jumped behind him and held the knife to his throat.

"Change of plans," I said, and applied slight pressure. The protruding ridges nicked his skin and multiple beads of blood marred the dark-bronze surface. "Turn this craft around. You're taking me back to my planet."

"Where is your planet?" Unperturbed by the cut, his voice was cool and collected. As if his life being threatened was of no importance.

That meant one of two things. Either he was afraid and didn't want to agitate me further, or he was that good of a fighter and knew he could thwart me at any moment.

I doubted it was the former. "Earth," I said, glad that my voice was steady and composed.

He turned back to the craft's controls and typed. He was definitely not afraid of me.

"Why are you changing course, Joren? Head to the Imperial right now!" the Admiral yelled.

"Ignore him," I ordered.

"We can't hide. They have access to our viewscreen, they see us," the soldier said, but obeyed my command.

Was he humoring me to give me a false sense of security before he took over?

"Your people need all the help they can get. I'm going to beat you to a pulp for insubordin—" Rorc sounded again but stopped abruptly.

'Keep our mate away from the intruders.' Arana's voice was as clear as if he'd been sitting next to me.

I might not understand aliens who thought they could dictate what I could and couldn't do, but I understood war. And I was taking one of their fighter jets away. I wouldn't be able to stand myself if they lost the battle because of me.

"Turn around," I barked. "You heard your Admiral. They need all the help they can get."

The alien lost some of his color.

What the fuck? Did he just turn paler?

When he didn't move, I jammed the tip of the knife into his leg. "I'm sure you won't need your leg to pilot, so turn the fuck around, and don't make me say it again."

He grunted and I startled—the weapon remaining steady in my hand.

I hadn't meant to stab him, but apparently I'd misjudged my strength.

"But…you're a female, to be protected—"

Something in my expression made him stop mid-sentence. If I didn't need him to pilot the damn ship, I'd have annihilated him with the look I was giving him. What was wrong with the men of this species?

He moved his fingers over the different commands, and soon the Imperial was in front of our viewscreen.

I'd been expecting Rorc's anger, but the wrath coloring the undercurrent of his voice surprised me. "Mate, you're playing games you cannot win. Your disobedience has earned you your first punishment."

My breath hitched as a shiver raced down my spine. Had my nipples just gotten hard because the infuriating man mentioned punishment? No way was I sticking around for such a thing, no matter what my body wanted. Or so I'd thought. But the moment the thought crossed my mind, the spaceship stopped, and all the controls turned off.

"The Nur is now in command of the fighter," someone reported, and then Rorc said, "You'll remain there until we retrieve you."

Fuck! I hadn't anticipated them controlling their crafts remotely. Pulling the knife out of Joren's leg, I stepped back—my attention still on him. When he didn't move aggressively toward me, I allowed myself to wallow for a moment because I had missed my opportunity to return home.

Weirdly enough, the sadness I'd been expecting to settle over me and smother me like a heavy blanket during a warm night never came. The heaviness due to knowing I was stranded with aliens was absent. Instead, elation swept through me, and excited butterflies took flight in my stomach in anticipation of what this new adventure would bring.

Lost in retrospection, I reacted a moment too late to the shrieking alarm—failing to grab something to hold onto. I flew across the cockpit. The soldier stretched his long arm, snatched me out of the air, and pulled me flush against him, engulfing my body with his.

In his attempt to secure me, though, he squeezed too much, cutting off my air supply.

"Can't…breath." The words were barely audible, but he relaxed his hold immediately while still keeping me securely pinned.

All of a sudden, the screeching sound of metal tearing blasted through the spaceship—making Joren hunch in on himself, forcing me to bend. I covered my ears, but my hands offered little protections against the hackle-raising noise.

The soldier cursed under his breath, released me, and rushed to grab weapons. "Can you use a blaster?"

I was trained to use a wide variety of weapons. How different could an alien one be? "Yes," I said, and sprinted toward his arsenal. "I want that one." I pointed to a blaster on the smaller side, but perfect for me.

He pressed his thumb to the base of the grip; it lit for a moment, then the light went out. "The trigger is here on the left side. Use your thumb. The kick back is intense. Brace yourself. And for Creator's sake, don't blast me."

The crash course was interrupted by loud sniffing.

What the heck? Was a freaking bear in the room with us?

Joren's bulk obstructed my view. I leaned sideways to take a look and instantly regretted it as the heinous creature made eye contact with me.

He lifted his horned head in the air—his nostrils flaring—and opened his snout to reveal double rows of pointed teeth as he shrilled, “Maaaattttte.”

THE RIGHT TO REFUSE A UNION

KALI

Joren pushed me back and jumped to block the hideous creature who was advancing toward me.

This alien's voice was the stuff of nightmares, and had he just said mate? I gulped down the sudden lump in my throat. He was shorter than me, but seven times my size in breadth, his huge belly flopping grotesquely over legs with three-toed feet. Vertical lines of short spikes protruded from his chest, and from his thick tail resting on the floor, while longer ones protruded from his elbows and upper arms.

An uncontrollable shudder swept through my entire body as I turned to the side—presenting as small a target as possible—and slowly retreated, putting distance between myself and the revolting alien that claimed to be my mate.

The thought alone caused bile to rise and burn the back of my throat. I dry heaved, then swallowed hard and pinched my lips shut. It'd be funny to see their reaction to my throwing up, but I didn't want to risk it. The bitter tang in my mouth suddenly made me desperate for a toothbrush.

Maybe my mates used them. Their teeth were blindingly white. The thought stopped me short. It was like a light bulb was switched on, illuminating the room and bringing everything into sharp focus, making my heart sink.

Thinking about the three aliens I ran away from didn't cause the same violent reactions I was experiencing by hearing this creature's claim. Thinking about them made me feel warm and tingly inside, despite trying my best to ignore the unsolicited sensations. Even now in the unfortunate situation I found myself in, my heart fluttered, and I shivered from desire. My body was on board with whatever they planned for us, even if it was taking my mind a little longer to catch up. I was attracted to them, but I hadn't allowed myself to acknowledge it. *Darn it, fleeing from them was the wrong choice.*

Heavy steps drew my attention. Behind the bear of an alien, beings with multiple sets of arms—the top two of which ended in serrated spears—and antennas on their heads, crowded the space.

"Pawns, Wravukian, kill. Grims's mate, mine," he ordered, and as one the beings that spookily resembled humanoid cockroaches rushed to Joren, tackling him, and burying him under their bulky bodies.

Luck, you had to run out on me now, didn't you?

Being kidnapped once by extraterrestrial beings was bad enough, but three darn times—even if the second was in order to be rescued—must have been some kind of record!

I started blasting the ones at the top, praying that the soldier remained alive and wouldn't raise his head without warning.

Loud thuds echoed, and I looked up to find the bear-like alien laser-focused on me and coming closer—undeterred by the gun in my hands that was now pointing at him.

You asked for it, fucker.

I pressed the trigger, but nothing happened. Had I just run out of whatever the equivalent of bullets were for this gun? I pressed it again, but it was useless. I aimed for the being's head and threw it with all my might, hoping it'd explode on impact. It clashed with his horns and bounced on the floor. I went for maximum damage, but instead got his ire and a show of teeth.

Damn it, I'm not going to escape unscathed this time, and I didn't even get to tell my true mates how I feel.

Then an idea came to mind. Keeping my eyes on the alien advancing on me, I let my mental walls crumble brick by brick, seeking to connect with them.

The sea of pain Mes was swimming in stole my strength, and I stumbled. I wasn't experiencing the pain the same way he was; I wasn't hurting really, my reaction was more because it's enormity had taken me by surprise. He sensed my presence almost immediately and cursed while managing to block me out. My heart bled for him, for through our connection, I knew it was his brother's pain he was absorbing in his attempt to save him.

Then words invaded my mind. *'Her sabertooth will protect her.'* Hearing Arana's voice was a balm to my soul, but his words were confusing.

Suddenly the spaceship lurched sharply to the side. Grabbing the first thing in sight, I managed to hold on while the pile of bodies in front of me tumbled across the floor, revealing an injured —but still alive—Wravukian. Unfortunately, the horned alien reacted fast as well. His claws raked the bottom of the cockpit, denting it and successfully stopping his slide.

A deafening boom had all of us diving for cover. The whistle of splinters that followed pierced my eardrums. Metal shards flew everywhere, and a loud hiss of pain reverberated in my mind the moment one found its new home in the arm I had used as a shield to cover my head. I reached up to pull it out when the piece fell out by itself. *What the fuck?* As I stared at the wound that had barely bled, the seams of my skin edged closer together and sealed—making the new wound appear a few days old.

Unable to wrap my mind around what had just happened, I filed it away for later. We needed to find a way to escape the hostile aliens, and through the smoke, I could make out a gaping hole in place of where the nook I stayed hidden not too long ago used to be. As it cleared, two figures became visible. One on two feet, the other on four paws.

I sagged from the instantaneous relief. They were able to fight these creatures. No doubt in my mind they'd be victorious.

Heat radiated through my chest. *They'd come for me.* The tips of my lips curled up, but as their eyes swiftly perused and dismissed me, their emotions and thoughts registered through our bond, erasing all traces of my smile.

Arana and Beast felt ice-cold inside. My escape had cut them deep. They'd heard my refusals but they'd planned to prove how worthy they were and hoped I'd accept them eventually. Sacred Mates could never abandon their other halves, so they were stunned when I'd been able to walk away. This rejection, they acknowledged—knowing its acceptance would cost their lives but unable to act against my wishes.

Rorc felt like an inferno, yet his mind was filled with an unnatural silence. The veins straining against his skin were the only sign of his inner turmoil. He was angry because I had left him. He was furious I had placed myself in danger. The more I focused on him, the more I realized the rage was just a mask hiding the pain my departure had caused.

My cheeks burned with shame.

I hurt them.

The truth was a hard pill to swallow, but I wouldn't lie to myself. I made the mistake, I'd be the one to make it right as soon as we took out the enemy.

My mates didn't hesitate to jump into the fray.

'Sever the head to kill them,' Arana sent through our bond.

Rorc repeated the warning and moved to cover Joren's injured side—who'd used the distraction to get up and grab another weapon—and together they fought the cockroach-like aliens.

Beast, intent on protecting me, positioned his enormous bulk between me and the creature who claimed to be another mate of mine.

The monster alien fell on all fours, opened his snout to reveal his pointy teeth, and snarled his challenge.

They stood still for a moment, measuring each other, before they exploded into action—a feat I had assumed impossible for the morbidly obese creature. Rearing up on their hind legs at the last second, their bodies clashed—a sound like a wrecking ball hitting the side of a building echoed within the metal walls. Locked in a lethal dance, I watched them with bated breath, unsure of how I could help. The bear-like creature bit, clawed, and tried to overpower the sabertooth without any success—he let out a high-pitched scream of frustration and redoubled his efforts. Beast—somehow remaining unscathed, and having had enough apparently—clamped his jaw around the alien's jugular and took a bite. His knifelike canines pierced his opponent's skin effortlessly, taking out a huge chunk. Next, he raked his paws diagonally from his opponent's left shoulder to right abdomen, making him stagger and step back. The sabertooth pounced on him, managing to throw him off-balance. Beast, having landed on top of him, went for the killing bite.

I was used to sounds of bullets hitting flesh. I was even used to how a knife tearing skin, muscle, and grinding against bone sounded. But I'd never thought I'd hear the sickening sound of a body part being detached. I averted my gaze to Rorc, who was cradling an unconscious Joren in his arms, but my eyes strayed and took in the rest of the scene. I lost whatever was left in my stomach right there. Breathing heavily through my mouth, I pinched my eyes shut.

An arm wrapped around my shoulder, and another curled behind my knees right before I was lifted in Arana's fully-clothed embrace.

How did his uniform appear then disappear? Was it a shifter thing?

I turned to nuzzle against his neck, hoping his scent would distract me from the carnage around me, only to have something warm and wet smeared on my cheek. The metallic smell indicated it was blood, and since Beast hadn't been injured, it meant it belonged to the dead one.

I spun the other way—not wanting to throw up all over Arana and myself—and dry heaved, thankfully without vomiting.

Soon we were moving into the other spaceship and the air cleared, offering me a reprieve.

"Not long to go, monakrivimou," Arana whispered before he kissed the top of my head.

I didn't know where he was taking me, and I didn't care. I felt safe in his arms. I opened my eyes to see Rorc's stiff back. I doubted it was because he was carrying Joren's weight.

"Thank you for saving me…again."

He didn't acknowledge me, confirming my suspicions, and fear of having messed up irreparably shook me.

"I hurt him, didn't I?"

"Yes, but he'll get over it." Arana dismissed my concern.

I doubted Rorc would get over it—but instead of contradicting him, I said, without meeting his eyes, "I hurt you too."

He didn't answer, and I didn't insist on getting one. He turned a couple corners and entered a room. With me still in his arms, he walked straight into the enclosed shower, and then lowered me to the ground.

Water started raining down on us from three different directions, washing the gore off us and bathing the floor red.

I stood there looking down—hiding.

Not knowing whether I had ruined everything was killing me, and I was about to ask Arana when he spoke.

"My feelings are irrelevant." His dejected tone made my chest constrict painfully. "A mate has the right to refuse a Union, even if it is a Sacred one."

"And would her mates let her go so…easily?"

"Her mates would love her so much already that they'd be unable to see to anything else besides her happiness…even if it killed them."

Love?

Snapping my head up to meet his eyes, I managed to lose my balance; my foot slid forward, and I would have fallen backward if it weren't for the Saberian's lightning-fast reflexes. As it was, I found myself safe in his embrace once again. I lay my forehead on his chest, his heavy breathing making my head bob up and down rhythmically—a motion I found surprisingly soothing.

He let me stay like that, without demanding more. But I wanted to give him more. As unpleasant as the experience with the bear-like alien had been, it'd opened my eyes to what I had been so close to throwing away. And for what? Was it because back on Earth having three men was considered unconventional, and my father would be disappointed if he ever found out his daughter was so… promiscuous? Or because staying with them meant I'd never see my team again? As valid as these reasons might have been, they weren't enough of a deterrent anymore.

Matesss mine. The foreign voice and I were in agreement.

I turned and lay my cheek between his firm pectorals. The ba-bump…ba-bump under my ear was strong and steady. *Ha! He has two hearts.* It was just another difference that didn't matter. I wrapped my arms around his waist, closing the few inches that separated us. "I don't want you to let me go," I whispered.

He stilled. "Are you accepting us, Kali? Our Union?" he asked, and held his breath.

I nodded, sure he'd feel it.

He wasn't satisfied. Keeping one arm around me, he lifted the other. Hooking his finger under my chin, he applied gentle pressure until I lifted my head and met his expectant eyes.

Anticipation, lust, hunger and warmth were shining in his ice-blue orbs.

Suddenly breathless, as if I had been running a marathon, I whispered, "I was afraid. I'm not anymore. So yes, I choose you, Rorc, and Mes. I accept our Union."

MY RIGHT TO CHOOSE

KALI

His eyes flashed fire and his mouth popped open in surprise. A giggle escaped from mine. He closed it, snarled, then bent and fused his lips with mine. A million butterflies took flight in my middle. His kiss was rough, demanding, all-consuming, but soon turned into something gentler, something reverent. His tongue's raspy texture, foreign and fascinating, made me wonder how it'd feel on my body, made me want things I'd never thought I wanted. The growls vibrating in his chest gave way to purring. Knowing it was Beast speaking to me this way made the moment extra special.

I placed my palms—fingers splayed—there. Feeling scars on his bare skin startled me, and I pulled back, breaking our kiss. "How did you—" I lost my train of thought as I took in how naked he was now that his uniform had disappeared again.

Oh my God! His muscles have muscles.

For the first time in my life, I felt ultra feminine. Compared to him, I was soft—even though I didn't have an ounce of fat on my body. I had trained long and hard to turn my body into a weapon, but he made it seem like I was just a pocket pistol to his machine gun. I might have drooled a little bit, too, until my eyes traveled further down and saw the evidence of his lust for me. My audible gulp was too loud in the close quarters.

Can a cock this big fit in me? In any woman?

Jealousy—green and ugly—filled me, and I got mad at the woman who could take his cock, imaginary as she was. I shook my head, trying to erase the unsettling thought. I didn't want to think about Arana with another woman. He was mine. I hovered my hand near him, and looked up at him for permission.

A smirk was playing at his lips, and I wondered if he knew where my head was at. '*Yes, I'm yours,*' he said in my mind, right before he took my hand and wrapped it around his shaft.

It was the first time I was touching a man's penis, and it was fascinating. Masturbating was never something to write home about as I'd never managed to climax; at some point I had tried to watch porn, to educate myself and maybe get back to the game, but the only thing I had succeeded in doing was bringing back unwanted memories. Memories I was thankful weren't surfacing at the moment.

He pulsed in my palm. He was so thick, my fingers didn't touch. The dark-gray skin was hot to the touch and as smooth as the surface of a full metal jacket bullet. I gave it an experimental squeeze. Arana sucked in a breath but didn't stop my exploration. I tightened my fist and pulled downward until I reached the base. Pre-cum beaded on the tip and I used my thumb to spread it all over the head.

I wonder what he tastes like...

No sooner than I had that thought, my patient alien seemed to have had enough. He pressed a spot between my breasts and my uniform changed consistency, almost liquefying as it returned to its case. He then removed it and set it aside before dropping to his knees in front of me.

"What are you doing?" Why was my voice this breathless?

"Your scent has been driving me crazy, monakrivimou."

A big palm on my belly pushed me backward until my back rested on the shower wall. Then his hands caressed my waist and rested on my buttocks as he bent forward, bringing his nose near my private area and sniffing. "I need to taste you, Mate."

Embarrassment colored my cheeks, but he wasn't paying attention. His fingers flexed on my bottom, my only warning before he lifted my center right into his face. A sound I'd never heard come from my lips escaped me. *Had I just squeaked? Oh my God.* I was about to demand he put me down when his tongue licked my opening. The rough texture—as if there were countless tiny spines on its surface—was a direct contrast to his smooth lips, the opposite sensations making my skin erupt in goose bumps. I moaned, and that was all the encouragement he needed.

I never knew that having someone go down on me would feel so heavenly. My body was on fire, and I could feel the tension building in my core. Every flick of his talented tongue made my body shiver and tremble. His mouth sucking and nibbling, as if he was savoring my taste, drove me even higher.

"Arana," I moaned—trepidation coloring my voice.

I didn't know where this was leading and it felt like it was too much—all my erotic synapses firing up, making the room spin and stars dance behind my eyes. I needed something but had no idea what. I ran my fingers through his soft hair, before fisting it—whether to pull or push him away, I wasn't entirely sure.

'You taste like Wandalh nectar. Strolling through the Serenity Gardens

will never be the same again, Kali, because whenever I scent the alluring aroma, I'll be craving you.' His sexy deep timbre sent a bolt of lightning straight to my core, making me shudder.

Then I felt his tongue enter me. *'Come for me, Mate,' he ordered.*

My whole body was feeling all kinds of tingles and I started freaking out. "I can't," I said, and pushed his head away.

He snarled at me, and when his eyes lifted to catch mine, the hunger in them made me gasp. "You can, and you will," he declared, and oh so slowly he brought his lips to my clit and sucked hard, then used his tongue to flick the magic button I never knew I had.

"Oh my God."

A sudden surge of pressure threatened to overtake me; my muscles clenched and my core pulsed. Waves of pleasure rolled over me—intensifying the foreign sensations tenfold—and I grunted in frustration. I wanted to come, but I just couldn't make myself.

'Silly Mate. It's not your job to make yourself come, but mine.' His self-assured drawl brought me right to the edge. Then, with his icy-blue eyes holding my gaze, he thrust two fingers inside of me—the suddenness of being stretched tipping me over and making me fly. I might have screamed his name but I was lost, soaring in the sky—my mind no longer my own. I was experiencing something I never had before, something scary yet simultaneously exhilarating.

He got up; the heavy weight of his cock resting against my ribs brought my fear of the unknown to the forefront of my consciousness, marring the bubble of happiness I was in. Would he fit in me, or would sex with him be too painful? Would I be able to offer him the same ecstasy he'd given me? Would it be so perfect I'd break into a thousand pieces? Would I be able to put myself back together again, or would I lose myself? My eyes flew open when his palm gently caressed my cheek—temporarily stilling my insecurities.

"Adorable, Mate. The Creator made me for you. Stop worrying about whether I'll fit or not. I was made to be exactly what you need…all three of us were." He laid soft kisses on top of my eyelids before touching his forehead to mine. His deep breath tickled me, his deft fingers working me slowly—keeping me on edge and muddying my thoughts. He waited for my answer, but for the life of me I couldn't remember the damn question.

He saved me from my suffering. "I need to be inside you more than I need air to breathe. Will you let me in, sweet Kali?" The plea in his voice and the earnestness in his eyes swept the last of my doubts away.

"Yes," I breathed, and the smile on his lips lit his whole face. But it only lasted for a second before it turned predatory, making me freeze like a deer in headlights.

A shiver raced down my spine, and a needy moan echoed in the shower as Arana withdrew his fingers. He smirked devilishly right before he guided my legs around his waist.

Restricting my movements with his hands on my hips, I found his control maddening. His shallow thrusts lit up nerves that I wasn't aware existed, making me wish for things I never had before.

He was preparing my body to accept his gradually, and I could tell it would be glorious, but God, I wanted more.

I was ready to make my demands known when he impaled my throbbing pussy with his cock, wrenching a scream out of me. I was soaking wet, yet it was a tight fit, and the pleasure bordering on pain sent me over the edge again.

Raking my nails across his back, I made him groan, and suddenly all his gentleness evaporated like the soft mist around us.

Thrusting in and out of me easily, now that I had gushed all over his rock-hard shaft, he didn't hold back. His hands clenching my waist and controlling my movements were bruising, but I didn't care. Between his kisses, his name—interspersed with the moans from my lips—became my mantra. Place, time, and reason became irrelevant as the pleasure coursing through my body slowly escalated, searing me, making me anew.

"Please," I begged shamelessly. I could see the edge; I was so close to it; I knew it would be magnificent with him inside me, and I wanted to feel it, but Arana wasn't letting me tip over.

"Fuck," Rorc grunted, and I jerked my head his way.

Seeing him there, with his hand adjusting his cock over his uniform, barreled me over the glorious edge. And I was right—this time I broke into a thousand pieces. The previous two times he made me climax paled in comparison. I was so overcome I opened my mouth to scream, but no sound escaped.

Arana, bending and biting the sensitive spot between my shoulder and neck, tumbled over the edge with me. His sharp teeth threatening to pierce my skin, along with the feeling of his seed spurting deep inside me, elicited another mini orgasm from me.

My cloudy mind slowly cleared, and my rapid breathing eased when I remembered we had an audience. I turned in Arana's arms, but Rorc wasn't there anymore.

"He's gone…is he mad?" I held my breath.

Arana chuckled, the deep and throaty sound shooting straight to my core, making me slick with want even though I just had him.

Geez, he's still hard in me.

I was amazed it hadn't hurt. I was amazed I could function when I felt like pieces of me were still lying scattered around us.

Then, like someone had thrown a bucket of freezing water over me, realization hit and I stiffened. "Um, Arana, we didn't use protection. What if I get…" My voice trailed off. I couldn't finish the sentence, the thought of becoming a mother terrifying.

"You're not going to get pregnant," he said, and I sighed heavily.

Stupid disappointment! Why would I even feel you? It must be the postcoital hormones coursing through my body.

I was in disbelief that I had enjoyed, no that was not accurate enough. I was in disbelief that I craved sex with Arana again so soon, and it was messing with my head.

"We didn't have sex, Kali. We mated," he growled, proving he was still entrenched in my mind.

"Stop that!"

"Why? Your way of thinking is fascinating."

Dumbfounded, I gawked at him. How could I possibly respond to that?

"Kali, you have the same access to my mind as I have to yours. This is the way between Sacred Mates," he said as he peppered my face with kisses.

"Is Rorc mad?" I persisted, not touching on what he had just told me.

"He's not mad, monakrivimou. He's horny. Open yourself to our bond. Feel him. Let him feel you." His voice dropped an octave, making him sound even sexier. "Let him feel your desire…" Arana trailed off while the back of his nails blazed a trail from my waist to my chest raising goosebumps in their wake. He circled my nipple with his fingertips, widening the circles until he cupped my left breast. I always thought they were too big for my frame, but watching it fit perfectly in his palm, I entertained the thought that maybe I was made for my mates too. He squeezed my mound lightly—making me lose my train of thought—and, without preamble, pinched my nipple between his thumb and forefinger, drawing a loud moan from me. "Do you sense him, Mate?" he demanded, the barely there growl under his words and his involuntary, shallow thrusts making my heartbeat kick up and our combined juices flow out of me and onto his legs.

Fuck, what had he just asked me? Something about sensing Rorc.... I closed my eyes to concentrate—to find the mental link to our bond, but Arana picking up the tempo made sure I didn't forget who I was with. It was difficult, but I managed to do as he requested. Rorc was standing in the middle of the cockpit, fists clenched, body tense, and panting heavily. *'Mate,'* I called out to him, not expecting to be heard. So when he jerked his head backward, I gasped.

Arana, feeling neglected, increased his tempo. If I'd thought the pace he'd set earlier was intense, it was now frenzied. I felt his powerful thrusts all the way to my breasts, and I would have fallen off him if it weren't for his firm grip around my waist, pulling me back toward him every time he pistoned his cock inside me.

"Open up, Kali," he growled, biting my earlobe, and I obeyed. "Share with him how your mate's cock in your pussy feels," he ordered, and I—putty in his hands— obeyed again. "Imagine when you'll have his cock in you...imagine when we'll fill your pussy and your ass—"

The forbidden image he placed in my mind's eye blinded me, pushed me violently over the edge, and I was lost. I thrashed wildly until black spots filled my vision and darkness threatened to pull me under. Shudders of pleasure racked my sweat-drenched body, and my pounding heart—I swear—was about to burst out of my chest.

I felt broken, but Arana's soft kisses over every inch of skin his lips could reach, and the soft caresses of his hands on all the other places glued me back together, slowly lowering me back to him from the high I was in.

It took me a while to calm down enough to gather my wits about me, and I was shocked to realize his cock still felt like steel inside me. "How can you still be hard? Is it an alien thing, or a you thing?"

He laughed, and it caused all kinds of warm tingles to erupt. But I was too sensitive, and they were too much after the however many orgasms I'd had, so I wiggled to be let down.

"It's a you thing," he chuckled. "I've been waiting for you for a long time," he said as he withdrew and lowered me to the floor.

My knees buckled, but I remained standing. "You mean you've never been with another wo—female?"

He shook his head.

Wow! He's gorgeous and he's a vir—

Remembering he was firmly entrenched in my mind, I stopped my thought mid-sentence, and I felt my cheeks burning.

"What has you flushed, Mate?"

Eyes on his chest, I traced his scars with a fingertip. "Why do you have these scars? When Beast fought earlier, it seemed like he was indestructible."

"The skin our sabertooth form has is a type of organic armor unique to our species, and the only one who could hurt us while shifted is another of our kind. Our biped forms are more vulnerable and show the scars." A fingertip had become ten, and now both of my hands were flush on his chest. The soft purring vibrations felt ticklish, and I nearly jumped out of my skin when an answering purr rumbled in my chest. "Worry not, Mate," he said, the moment he placed his palm between my breasts. His happiness bleeding through our bond to me. "We haven't fought a species, yet, that can injure our sabertooths. And soon you'll be as indestructible as me."

My hands fell limply to my sides. The sudden ringing in my ears drowned all other sounds. *I don't understand.*

"Kali?"

I heard the worry in his voice but my mind felt numb, and answering was as impossible as walking through quicksand. Then my brain kick-started, and thoughts started swirling so quickly it was hard to follow them. How could I possibly become as indestructible as him? I must have misunderstood. Had I contracted some kind of alien disease? I remembered hearing that other voice, now the purring. I was human maybe he meant something else, and the translator was malfunctioning like before. Yes, that must have been it, but I'd better ask. This was too important.

I looked up until our eyes met. "What do you mean? What am I becoming?"

His Adam's apple bobbed, and trepidation flashed in his eyes.

Oh my God, this is going to be bad.

He took a deep breath and said, "We're Changing you. We gave you a sabertooth and soon she'll be ready to come out." The words ran together as he rushed them out in one exhale.

"Changing me?" I parroted. This wasn't just bad, it was unimaginable. "How?"

I expected Arana to answer, but it was Beast who spoke through our bond. *'When I stung you, I started the process of altering your DNA, your organs, and your body. Arana's seed will speed the process and prepare your body for your first shift, and when you're both ready, our bite will imprint our scent on you and release her.'*

The euphoria that had filled me the moment my Saberian's cock throbbed and his warmth spread inside me—making me feel even fuller than before—disappeared in an instant, and the sticky evidence still trickling out of me made me curse under my breath. He gave me a precious gift moments ago, only to reveal it came with a terrible cost. My choice. Inwardly, I screamed to the universe the injustice of having something I vowed to protect with my life, or die trying, stolen from me. Again. Outwardly, my body shook with fury.

He clenched his hands, squeezing my arms, and bent to my level. "Kali, you've shut me out. Talk to me," he implored.

I shook my head, too stubborn to give him what he wanted.

"Kali," he growled, and the dominance in his voice reverberated through me, demanding I obey.

"You want to know what I'm thinking—the hard truth?" He nodded, relaxing his hold. "Fine! You're just like General Spencer," I said, and I regretted the words the moment they slipped from my lips. He was nothing like that poor excuse for a human. The alien shifter was caring, honorable, and a protector, but I was too angry to back down.

Arana sucked in a breath and dropped his hands, as if I was hot coals he couldn't bear to touch. His expression was stricken. "I'm nothing like him," he vehemently denied.

"How are you any different, Mate?" I spat the last word, and he flinched as if I had physically struck him. "You took away my choice."

"I didn't know what Beast was planning, Kali. Not until it was too late."

I heard the truth in his words, but it didn't negate the fact that they were one, and I was too far gone to see reason. "You two are a team, Arana. You're just as responsible."

Another flinch. "You're right, but we didn't have a choice. The compulsion was—"

My cold eyes must have given him pause because he stopped and hung his head.

"And if we act on our compulsions, how does that make us any different from all those who do what they want and hurt others?"

He didn't answer, not that I expected one anyway.

"Can you stop the process, or reverse it?" I asked, even though deep down I knew. He…no, not just him but all of them demanded so much of me. It was one thing choosing to stay here, create a future with them, but losing my humanity? Becoming something else? I couldn't wrap my mind around it.

Is it so bad to be taken care of by our mates, by me? That somewhat familiar voice in my head purred.

Yes, I answered her, wondering how the males would feel if I informed them they'd be the ones who needed to change in order to be with me. *And I don't need anyone taking care of me,* I said stubbornly.

She huffed, she knew I was lying to myself. Then she whispered hesitantly, D*on't you want me, Kali?*

I don't know you. I was alone all my life. Having you here with me is not natural for me. I tried to explain, to alleviate some of the pain my answer would cause.

What I didn't expect was to feel this visceral pain within that wasn't mine. Realization stopped me in my tracks. She was a part of me already. And how could I not accept a part of myself, no matter how unfamiliar it was?

I'm sorry, I want to meet you...this is just...weird, me talking to myself! I kept bubbling because I wanted her to stop hurting. But I also told her the truth. Once I made up my mind, I never went back on my word.

I'm Dawn, she said, her voice husky, still laced with fear of rejection.

"No," Arana said, breaking up our inner dialog, and the blow wasn't as hard as I thought it'd be. But I still needed to get away, to come to terms with my new reality. It took me a couple of tries to activate the uniform Mes had given me, but the moment my body was covered, I walked out the door with no aim in mind, and wept silently for what had—once again—been taken from me. My right to choose.

'We need you more than we need air to breathe. There is no reason to continue existing if we can't be with you, Mate,' Arana pleaded through our bond while Beast roared his pain. My reaction hurt them, but I was not ready to forgive them just yet.

DIE TO PROTECT HER

ARANA

"Fine! You're just like General Spencer." The seven words delivered a blow, stronger than any I had ever received, stealing the air from my lungs. She scrunched her face, and I let her go. Her aversion to my touch after we'd mated was worse than if she had thrust a knife into my gut.

"I'm nothing like him," I vehemently denied, and Beast—remembering how helpless we'd felt when we'd been unable to protect her from this vile male she was comparing us to—roared his frustration in my mind.

"How are you any different, Mate?"

Every muscle in my body cramped. It was the first time she'd acknowledged me as her mate, only to speak of the title as if it were a curse. My hearts skipped a beat, and then kicked up into a frenzied rhythm.

"You took away my choice," she added through clenched teeth.

Through our bond, her pain was seeping in, searing me with its enormity. "I didn't know what Beast was planning, Kali. Not until it was too late." It was the truth, but it was only a small part of it. I wasn't sure she wanted to hear the rest.

"You two are a team, Arana. You're just as responsible."

Yes, I was, but she needed to know all the facts to understand because even if I had known, I wouldn't have stopped him. "You're right, but we didn't have a choice. The compulsion was—" Her anger washed over me, stealing the rest of my words. I hung my head, squeezing my eyes shut. Fear of being unable to fix this overwhelmed me. I had found the one person who I was destined for and I was losing her. I was unworthy.

"And if we act on our compulsions, how does that make us any different from all those who do what they want and hurt others?" she asked, and I jerked open my eyes to find her cold stare, chilling me to the bone. I hesitated, trying to find the right words to explain that this was the only way to make her understand that if I could take her place, if I had to be the one to change, I'd do it in a heartbeat. But before I could put my jumbled thoughts in order, she asked, "Can you stop the process, or reverse it?"

I pressed my fist over my aching chest. Beast, hurt and upset she didn't want a sabertooth, curled in on himself. She would reject us, reject our Union. "No."

Fumbling with her uniform, she stood with her back turned to me. Memorizing her shape, every dip and valley, I saw some faint black spots across her sides. *Damn it! I'd been too rough with her.*

Beast surfaced in my mind. *You weren't careful with our mate,* he accused, ready to shred my insides to pieces, to take his pain out on me.

His closeness, though, enhanced my eyesight further, and I noticed the faint silvery stripes intercepting the black semicircles.

Understanding dawned on us, and we stared—dumbfounded—as she stormed out of the room.

Her sabertooth will be powerful.

True, Beast replied, *I already sense her.* Awe lightened his voice at the same time desperation to stop her from storming out of our life filled us.

'We need you more than we need air to breathe. There is no reason to continue existing if we can't be with you, Mate,' I cried, at the same time Beast roared his pain at having hurt the most important being in our lives.

Feeling her slipping from us—like water through our fingers—brought back pain I thought we had long since buried. I looked downward and saw my mother's broken body in my arms. I heard her voice saying that I'd find my Queen, that I should be strong. "Mother, I failed," I whispered. "I don't deserve her…but I won't stop until she's ours."

We'll win her back, Beast agreed, and I let determination, and the calm that followed, bleed through our bond to my mates.

She was right in that we took away her choice, and although it was inevitable, our way of doing it had been a mistake. We should have waited, explained first. We couldn't take our actions back, but it was time I made sure she understood we were sorry. We'd been prepared to let her go, if that was what she wanted. But then she chose us, and I tasted her and got lost in the haven of her body. How could I ever go back to a barren existence again? I would never let her go. We would treasure her, for she had sacrificed her life on Earth for us. We would die to protect her, but most importantly, we would live for her.

It was time I let my people know. With a plan in place, I marched to the cockpit and straight to the comms.

"Where's Kali?" Rorc asked.

"I was hoping she'd be here."

He stomped to me, fists clenched. "Did you hurt her?" he growled.

He assumed I'd hurt her physically, but I was incapable of doing so, all of us were. Still, I answered him. "No. I upset her when I told her I'm Changing her."

Rorc deflated at that and returned to his post. He understood because he would do the same.

"I need to contact my palace."

He nodded and opened a communication channel for me. It wasn't long before Urien's hologram appeared in front of me.

His eyes widened the moment he saw me, and he immediately tilted his head—revealing his neck—as he uttered, "Arana." His relief was palpable.

I smiled so wide my cheeks hurt. "We found her, brother."

"Well met, brother," he said, then his eyebrows furrowed. "Why are you on a Wravukian ship?"

Rorc snickered and Urien growled. His protectiveness rose, even though we were AUs apart, and there was nothing he could do.

"Long story, but—"

The Wravukian clapped my shoulder—interrupting me—and got in Urien's visual field. "Your King here got captured, and if it weren't for us, he'd be stretching his legs in the valleys of the Vaults of No Return."

My childhood friend bristled at Rorc's casual way of addressing his King, and stepped aggressively toward us as if he'd launch himself through the hologram and pounce on Rorc.

I intervened before things got worse. "Urien, meet my Pair-bond, Rorc—Admiral of the Second Fleet of Wravuk."

Slack-jawed, he froze. The sight would be comical if our situation wasn't so serious. I knew what was running through his mind, and they were the same worries I had. "And my other Pair-bond, Mes—Second Prince of Wravuk—isn't here at the moment."

"You formed a Sacred Union with…with Wravukians?"

"And a Human," Rorc chirped, overly amused by my warrior's stunned expression.

"What is a Human?"

"You'll meet her soon. She's magnificent," I said at the same time my Pair-bond added, laughing, "She's the one who wants to murder your King for Changing her."

That little tidbit snapped Urien out of his stupor. "Fuck," he exclaimed. "Arana, the Southern and Western Territories are rebelling because they believe you won't return, and the Elders will not accept—"

My roar caused the warrior to drop his gaze and reveal his neck, and Rorc to back away from me—his hand reaching for the blaster on his hip. The alloys in the cockpit vibrated, creaking and clashing.

Protect our mates and kill the traitors, Beast—as mad as me—suggested.

"It's not up to them. It is done. They either accept it or face the consequences," I threatened. Scenarios of how our arrival would be welcomed flashed through my mind's eye, each one making me angrier than the last, but also reminding me of Mes's request.

"Gather soil, water, and air samples and have them brought to me on the Nur immediately."

Without disputing my unusual request, he nodded, but like a

sabertooth on a hunt, didn't let the previous subject go. "What if they request the Queen's Fight?" he asked the moment I sensed her at the entrance.

"Then she'll fight. Announce the news, arrange the preparations, and get the Royal Guards ready. I will deal with the territories the moment I return," I ordered, right before I terminated the broadcast and turned to look at her.

"Is it safe to assume you were talking about me?" she asked, arms crossed across her chest. She was still mad at me.

Rorc closed the distance between us. "Our mate will not fight a fucking warrior." He shoved the blaster's nozzle at my chest.

"Saberian Queens fight. She's no exception," I snarled back, grabbing his neck and letting Beast's claws burst from my fingertips. I grazed his neck, warning him that we'd both go down—not just me, like he thought.

"Hey," she yelled, snapping her fingers at us while we were locked on each other. "Neither one of you will be deciding what I will or won't do."

She was wrong...so very wrong. At least about that, we were in agreement with the Admiral. As one, we turned and prowled toward her. Our brave mate stood her ground, lifting her chin in an act of defiance.

"We have every right to decide what you will or won't do. We're your mates." My Pair-bond's gravelly voice was laced with anger. He thought he wanted a meek female, one that would be at his beck and call. He was lying to himself.

I sensed that by questioning her honor, I'd be pushing one of her buttons. But I'd play dirty if need be. I wasn't losing her. "You chose us. Are you going back on your word, Kali?" She shook her head. "I still have your taste in my mouth." She gasped, and the vein on her slender neck started throbbing. "You still have my seed smeared on your thighs." She stepped backward; the sweet aroma of her arousal filled our nostrils, and it was more than Rorc could stand.

He pulled her flush to his body and his lips descended on hers.

At first she pushed him away, but then her hands wrapped around his neck and she was kissing him back.

I chuckled. If I hadn't just made her mine, I wouldn't be able to hold back either. Watching them was invoking all kinds of images in which we were playing with her body—building her desire with our hands and our mouths on her—and I didn't hesitate to share them through our bond.

Rorc groaned and deepened the kiss, devouring her; Kali moaned—the sound music to my ears. She didn't recoil from seeing us share her, so I stepped behind her and ground my aching cock on her delectable ass just as Mes's dilapidating pain, followed by savage and impenetrable darkness, bled through our bond, stealing our warmth and energy.

We hadn't completed the Mating Ritual yet, but I could already feel our Sacred Union's bonds, and the two Wravukians already shared a bond similar to the ones I had with my people. Rorc fell to his knee, and he would have taken a shivering Kali with him if I hadn't been holding her. The only reason I was standing was because Beast had instantly reacted to the looming threat, and was lending me his strength.

"Something's happened to Mes," Kali cried. "We need to help him."

"He's losing control," Rorc said as he got up, shudders racking his body. "I don't know if we'll make it to the Imperial on time." He turned to the controls and set course for the ship.

Already, I was imagining ways I'd hurt the one responsible for torturing my Pair-bond, before I showed him mercy and killed him. "Is someone hurting him?"

"Yes and no," Rorc grunted, when another wave of Mes's emotions rolled over us.

Kali fell on a chair and closed her eyes, intense concentration on her face.

Our bond was already strong enough that I could have tapped into their connection. I refrained from doing so, though, because I or Beast losing control in the confines of the small craft was even scarier. "Explain," I ordered instead.

"Mes's gifts are rare. He is an empath and a powerful Healer unlike any other. He doesn't only feel another's pain, he is able to heal the worst wounds, as if the patient's body is singing to him. He can absorb the other's pain and heal any wound by taking it into his own body. He has the ability to bring someone back before they enter the Vaults of No Return…or send them there. He isn't a Shield, so containing his gifts under certain circumstances is nearly impossible. Maybe that is the reason why the light that allows him to heal life shines so bright, it's blinding; but it's also the reason why the darkness inside him that balances it is equally powerful and destructive when his control over it slips."

Such powerful Healers belonged to the legends. Everyone had heard of them but no one had met one.

"Rorc, hurry," Kali murmured. Her body was here, but she felt far away. Her mental walls were up, keeping me out.

I didn't like it at all because if she needed my help, I'd be unable to reach her. We had to complete the Mating Ritual, then she'd no longer be able to shut me out of her mind.

YOU'RE SAFE WITH US

MES

"We need more plasma and blood. Brarn, the anticoagulant poison is working fast. But he shouldn't still be losing so much blood." I'd lost track of how long we'd been working with the Imperial's Arch-healer to save my brother's life, and we were failing. I was losing Callibohr.

One of his aides brought the vials, and Brarn connected the new lines.

"The Order of the Prime are proving to be more daring than we'd anticipated and are quickly becoming a formidable enemy."

I had no idea who they were, but the theme was always the same. Power-hungry species trying to rule over the rest of the universe. And of course my idiot of a brother had to be on the front line to protect those weaker than us.

"I swear next time I'll be the one to fulfill Cal's death wish and be done with it," the Arch-healer threatened, but the ache in his voice betrayed his true feelings. The older Wravukian cared about my brother as if he were his own son.

Heat was searing my insides, and fire was burning my limbs. The gift I was born with was warning me I was missing something important. I hovered my palms over the deep diagonal cut across Callibohr's back, on the spot where the spinal cord was exposed. There was something there…just out of reach. What was it? I had to open myself, but with so many people in the Healers' Bay, I'd be bombarded and incapacitated.

"Everyone out!" I ordered, and at that moment one of my brother's hearts stuttered and stopped.

Brarn had been the one to summon me, after trying for half a circle to save my brother and failing, so he didn't question my decision. "Out," he barked when the Healers weren't moving fast enough, and ushered them out.

Time had run out. I dropped the mental shields that were crippling my abilities. A barrage of fear and despair assaulted me, nearly bringing me to my knees. I clenched my jaw, inhaled and exhaled rhythmically, trying to align my center, before I placed my hands gently on Cal's back and rested my fingers directly on the cut. Closing my eyes, I let my senses flare. I concentrated on his failing heart first and jump-started it. The tik I sensed it would keep working by itself, I turned my focus back to the deep wound and the rest of his body.

They had put Callibohr under for the operation, yet he was experiencing the pain. His body was unmoving, but the receptors in his mind were on overload. I absorbed it, took it in me to lighten his burden. Black spots distorted my vision and I closed my eyes.

The dark monster residing in me, the one that craved the taking of life, and the other half of my healing light, opened its jaws—hungry, ravenous. I needed to save my brother. I had to contain the darkness long enough to do so.

Shaking myself, I tried to shut out everything else but Cal's biorhythm. There were two jarring notes disrupting the balance of his energy's flow. One was coming from the heart that had stopped, and the other from a fracture on one of the spinal cords. I opened my eyes and leaned over the exposed bones. There, right between an intervertebral disc and the unprotected vertebrae, was a tiny parasite—unlike anything I'd ever seen—wiggling its way into my brother's spinal cord. Grabbing the dressing forceps, I gently extracted it and placed it in a resealable vial. It wiggled and slithered, leaving a thin red line in its wake.

Suddenly, the med-pod's alarm started flashing. I looked up at the hologram—my brother's heart had stopped beating again, and the other was trying to compensate for the loss of blood flow until, in an utterly horrifying moment, it stopped too.

"No, no, no. Callibohr!" I yelled. I could feel his soul departing, and I couldn't tether it to his body unless I killed the other parasite attacking his hearts, first.

My mother's voice saying it was time to let go rang in my head. She had forbade me from releasing my darkness until I had harnessed its power. She was a Shield; she knew what it could do, and she was teaching me how to control it. But she died before I had the chance to master control.

I couldn't lose another person I loved. I couldn't let my brother die. I'd gladly pay the cost to bring him back, even if it meant losing my mates in this span of my existence.

I let all of my healing light tether to his soul—the only way to bring him back from the brink of the Vaults—thus allowing the darkness in me free rein.

The monster unfurled and stretched, slowly covering every

nook and cranny of the Healers' Bay, sucking the energy out of all living things in its wake, yet remaining insatiable, searching for more. I sensed the moment the two parasites died.

There was a small window to return my brother's soul to his body, and maybe I'd be able to rein in the monster now that I was older, stronger. Otherwise, I'd have to run as far away as possible before the darkness killed the one person I'd been trying so hard to save.

Centering myself, I regulated my breathing and focused on calling back the part of me that was the healing light. As it returned —with my brother's soul protected in its center—its rays touched the shadows, and the darkness recoiled, gathering its feelers closer to my body.

Hope blossomed that I'd be able to control the situation as it obeyed my order and hesitantly slithered back into my body. I watched as the hologram reporting Callibohr's biorhythm showed everything functioning as it should. He was safe.

The room spun around me and I staggered, terror momentarily paralyzing me. A rolling avalanche of emotions and thoughts crashed into me, suffocating me, and freeing the death of us all. The leash on my darkness stretched taut and broke.

I kept fighting to take control back as I raced out of the Bay, but hearing the soldiers I passed by coughing and struggling to breathe in my wake, meant I was failing.

Cal's wing was isolated from the rest of the ship, so I chose to lock myself in there, hoping distance would give me the time needed for what I had to do.

Safe inside his quarters, I banged my head backward on the wall and screamed as if my limbs were being ripped from my body—

because even though they remained intact, my soul was being torn apart, and the pain was so much worse.

Lying on the bed, I allowed myself the luxury of talking to her one last time. *'Kali, my sweet mate, I'm sorry. I'll be waiting for you in the next life span,'* I said, and hoped our bond was strong enough for her to hear me.

'Don't you fucking dare give up on me, Mes. I'm coming,' she replied, and her being here terrified me even more. I wouldn't be able to protect her.

'Don't let her near me,' I ordered my Pair-bonds, uncaring if the dominance—I usually held in check, but were unable to this time—would rub them the wrong way.

Her voice echoed outside the door. "Let me in. I'm not afraid of his darkness. He's incapable of hurting me, the same way Beast is."

I was too late. They were here already, and what she'd told Arana must have convinced him because she just burst into the room. But he was mistaken and it would cost our mate her life.

Damn if just the sight of her wasn't a balm to my burning eyes. And suddenly I wanted her to be the memory I'd take with me to the Vaults of No Return. Inwardly, my want fought with what I needed to do; I needed to tell her to run far away, before I destroyed the most important being in my life. Her.

I wrenched my eyes from Kali, to Rorc. "Please," I croaked, unable to move or say more. His stare hardened—I was certain he was mad at me for making him fulfill the oath we had taken when we were little and I had just lost my mother, the one in which we had promised if one of us was nearing the end, the other would end his suffering. His steps were heavy as he approached me. He placed the blade on top of my heart—one hand on the hilt, the other on top of it—and I couldn't hold his stare anymore. The pain from shards piercing my scalp all over slowly messed with my vision, but I needed to see her.

"Stop!" she screamed, and my Pair-bond froze.

No, no, no! I couldn't hold my darkness at bay anymore.

Then she was there, her palms gently cupping the sides of my face, and her tears sizzling on my burning skin. I tried to move my head, to break her hold, but I was too weak.

'Please leave. You must survive,' I tried to communicate through our bond.

"No. I can help you," she said as she closed her eyes. She took a deep breath and rested her forehead on mine. Her exhale was like a breeze of cool air, lightening my burden, shedding light on my bleak world, taking away my pain and all the battering emotions bombarding me, offering me a sweet reprieve. One that wouldn't be enough, but at least I'd be able to say goodbye.

Her shining light brought relief. My muscles relaxed, and I could function again. Then I noticed my darkness recoiling, right before shadowy feelers connected with her and slithered all over her body.

I thought losing my mother was the worst fear I'd ever feel. Coming close to losing my brother tumbled over that. But now terror, unlike anything I'd ever felt, gripped me. She was absorbing my pain, my darkness. I wrenched my face away from her hands. I wanted to be gentle with her, but I was angry at her. It was my burden to carry. I would not allow my female to pay my price.

I could not keep the growl from my pissed voice when I ordered, "Stop what you are doing right now," with every ounce of dominance I carried.

"No," she said calmly, without opening her eyes to look at me.

I shook her. My darkness kept invading her body. It would kill her. I would kill her.

"Beloved Mate, please, stop it!" I implored her, desperate. It seemed I could not get through to her. I was losing my mind, knowing I couldn't do anything to shield her. I started panicking—looking at my Pair-bonds, I pleaded for help, for they didn't know what she was going through right now. They didn't know the pain that she now knew.

"What's happening, Mes?" Rorc asked, hovering next to her, ready to grab her and run.

Shame radiated through me as I, the Healer, couldn't keep my mate from experiencing my pain. "She's absorbing my darkness, carrying my pain," I whispered.

She opened her eyes, and I momentarily got lost amid the calmness of her gray clouds. "Look at me, Mes," she ordered, and I obeyed. "Do I look like I'm in pain?" she asked, her voice gentle.

I tried to focus on her, but like a lost offspring, I was too agitated to focus and think clearly.

"Do I look like I am in pain?" she asked again, her voice firmer than before.

"No," Arana replied, since it seemed I'd lost my ability to speak.

But he couldn't know, could he?

"Yes, he knows," she interjected.

Was she reading my mind?

We all gawked at her.

A laugh escaped her luscious lips, and she covered her mouth with her hand. "And here I thought my mates were such big, bad predators." She laughed again, and this time she managed to pull a smirk out of us too.

"How is this possible?"' I asked her.

She suddenly trembled, and I was there, enveloping her in my arms and pulling her on top of me.

"Kali." I needed to know what was happening, that she wasn't in pain, that she wasn't lying.

"I'd never lie to you," she vowed, and I calmed. "I could always influence people. I always thought it was all in my head, but maybe not," she explained.

We were speechless. She was special. The rarest gem. But I needed to make sure.

"You're shielding me, but not feeling my pain?"

"Something like that," she told me.

I growled again. "Are you feeling my pain?" I demanded to know, so I'd find a way to shield her.

"No, not now. But I did earlier. And I needed to help, Mes," she explained, and I saw vulnerability shining through her eyes—as if she was expecting me to scold her for caring, or push her away for overstepping.

Besides my mother, no other female had cared to risk her own life for me. If I wasn't in love with her before, I sure was now. She had firmly embedded herself in my hearts. There was only one thing left to do to ease her worry. Lifting my head slowly, I gave her plenty of time to stop me. Instead, she closed the gap between us and pressed her lips on mine, giving me the permission I needed to take over. Fisting the silky strands at the base of her neck with one hand, and pulling her close with the other, I kissed her savagely—like a man in despair who had just been given a second chance. I kissed her reverently—like she hung the moon and the stars. And I kissed her devotedly—like she was a Goddess and I, a peasant.

The moment her taste exploded on my tongue, I was a goner.

Everything disappeared but her. Her slight weight on me offered comfort. Her intoxicating scent was welcoming me home. Her soft skin under my fingertips aroused my senses.

The bed at my feet dipped under someone's weight, and soon her low moans turned louder, making me crave so much more.

"Little one, tell me this is okay." Rorc sounded as breathless as I felt.

I broke our kiss because I needed to hear her answer.

The moment we laid our eyes on her, we'd fallen.

We'd become hers when the Sacred Line had formed.

Our attraction to her was irresistible, yet she was resisting. Her reaction was nothing like a Wravukian female's.

"Yes," she whispered—trepidation coloring her voice and excitement lighting her eyes.

I guided her leg over my waist so she lay astride me. Her cheeks turned a rosy color and were warm under my palms as I cupped them and pulled her downward.

Closing her eyes, her lips met mine, the earlier hesitation gone. When Rorc tasted the spot under her earlobe, her entire body shivered. Slowly, he lowered himself on top of her. The added weight pressed her center firmly on top of my aching cock. She squirmed, rubbing my length—the friction making me see stars. The sensation, along with the heated desire I felt emanating from my Pairbonds, awakened my inner darkness. Only this time it didn't want to drain the energy of everything living; its hunger was for her alone—demanding I take her hard and fast.

In an attempt to rein in the monster inside me, I tried to calm my breathing, slow my erratic hearts, and regain control of my senses. It was next to impossible, though, when my feelings were mutual. And as my anxiety that I'd hurt my mates spiked, I heard her moans of pleasure turning to moans of fear. The sound doused my dark side like nothing else could, and the lust-filled haze shrouding my mind cleared, allowing me control.

Kali gasped and started thrashing. Her body was here, but her mind was trapped in one of her memories, and she was broadcasting the images through our bond.

Rorc immediately lifted off her, but used his strength to restrain her arms. Arana placed his palms on her back, and I felt him immerse himself in her in an attempt to break her free from the nightmarish shackles holding her captive. I held her head still, and used my voice to bring her back to the present.

"Kali, we're not going to hurt you. Come back to us." Her panicked flailing stopped, and was replaced with wails. "My love, your nightmares can't have you anymore. Come back to us." I swept away the tears slipping free from her unseeing eyes. "Precious Mate, we'll protect you with our lives. Come back to us." I pressed a kiss on her forehead and looked at her haunted gray eyes. "We'll keep you safe. Always." I swore.

The other two aligned their bodies with ours, and we all wrapped our arms tight around her until her silent sobs eased, then stopped completely.

"I'm sorry," she sniffed, and hugged us back.

"You have nothing to be sorry about," I told her, and my Pairbonds agreed. "We cannot change your past, but we'll help you heal. Whenever your nightmares dare ensnare you, we'll be there to protect you," I vowed, because I knew Rorc and Arana felt the same way. "It's okay to fall apart, my love. We'll be there to find every shattered piece of you and put them back together until you're whole again. You're safe with us," I promised and hoped she knew truer words had never been uttered.

It seemed, though, that Arana had access to the thoughts crossing her mind that we hadn't because he tensed, and his growl drowned out the ship's constant background noise. It made sense, since his DNA was Changing her, for them to have formed a connection we did not yet possess.

"You are not leaving us," he decreed the same moment his fury washed over me, along with the echo of her words. *'The nightmares won't stop, only death will stop them.'*

"That's not happening." The razor-edge in Rorc's voice cut the silence that had fallen after Arana's revelation.

Arana, though, addressed a comment of hers that he alone had heard. "Our path is set, Mate! You can no more escape it than we can. If you need time to accept our circumstances, I'll give you some. We all will. But don't tempt me, because you'll find out what catching a predator by the tail does." His words were laced with warning.

Her next thought was clearly transmitted to all of us—*'I'm not afraid to die, what makes you think your threats scare me? It's my life to take. My decision.'*—and it chilled us to the bone.

I felt something rising underneath her skin, and we all witnessed her sabertooth trying to break free, futile as it was.

Arana jumped from the bed and roared his anger as his sabertooth burst free. He lowered his face to her level and pulled his lips back, snarling until Kali's animal retreated.

Rorc growled menacingly and encircled her throat with his huge palm, tightening it just enough, needing her submission. "When you didn't know, and thought of us as your captors, you considered taking your own life. I gave you a pass, then, because it was a valid reaction, but now..." His voice trailed off, too shaken to continue.

I felt ice-cold rage flooding my veins. I gripped her chin between my thumb and forefinger and guided her eyes to mine. My tone was gruff, but I had no desire to soften it. "We promised to be your silent sentries so no one will hurt you. That includes you." I inhaled to steady my inner turbulence. "I brought you to life once. I will do it again. And then we will punish your delectable ass for thinking you could take our mate from us." I didn't gentle my stern tone, nor hide the threat underneath pretty words.

Her demeanor changed in an instant. "You were in the helicopter with me…I remember now," she whispered, then turned to Rorc, who was now pacing around the room, too agitated to remain on the bed. "You were there when they operated on me." She drew a shaky breath, then said to the sabertooth, "And you, Beast, protected me in the desert…all of you were there with me, protecting me, saving me."

I was glad she was coming to her senses, but I was too scared to just let it go without a final warning. "Don't ever let that thought cross your mind again, Kali. We will not be as accommodating next time." My icy voice seemed to be her undoing.

A few tears trailed down her cheeks and she hiccuped. But we needed her to admit it. We already knew that if she gave her word, she'd keep it.

"We're waiting for an answer, Kali. You won't like the consequences if you make us wait much longer." I warned her.

"Fine," she yelled.

Rorc approached us, finally standing still. "Fine, what?" he demanded.

"I will not end my life," she acquiesced, and a great weight lifted off my shoulders, taking the terror that had gripped us all earlier with it. Her body slumped on top of mine, the confrontation having momentarily depleted her strength.

The energy from Arana's shift felt like a breeze caressing us. Kali's eyes widened at the sight of her naked mate, and the intoxicating scent of her arousal wafted through the air.

THE QUIET BEFORE THE STORM

RORC

Seeing that unsightly being threatening her earlier had taken fifty rotations off my life. With a fragile body like hers, he would have crushed her with a swipe of his spiked arm. Listening to her now considering ending her life was unsettling in and of itself, but it also brought back memories I wanted to forget. It was the last straw. Completing the Mating Ritual would give us access to each other's minds and would release Kali's sabertooth. We had to do it sooner rather than later. Would she still be herself, though? Would she still want us even if we didn't have animals ourselves, or would she keep Arana and discard us? Fear of losing her clutched my hearts in a vise. But if Kali resembled even half of the formidable female warriors, having a sabertooth would make her nearly indestructible. If losing her was the price to pay for her safety, the cost was worth it. Even if it killed me.

"I will not end my life," she promised, but I couldn't get the images of my sister flashing behind my eyes to stop. Her body bloodied. Torn. Dead.

Kali buried her face in Mes's chest. "I'm not usually a coward, I'll blame my lapse in judgment on outer space messing with my sanity."

She tried to laugh it off, but I couldn't let her. I was still too ruffled, and she needed to get it into her pretty head that she shouldn't be afraid to show us her true emotions. We loved all sides of her equally.

"We all have our weak moments, little one," I pushed through my teeth, wanting to reassure her, and failing.

Her eyes jerked to mine, then—having picked up on my mood—her brows furrowed. She got up, turned, and knelt on the edge of the bed in front of me. "What do you need?" Her seductive whisper caressed me, tantalizing my senses even though I was certain it hadn't been her intention.

I gripped her hips—my fingers flexing of their own accord—and pulled her closer. "You." My voice was raw, vulnerable.

Her pink tongue darted out to wet her lower lip, rocking my composure. "I'm yours." Her words stopped time, destroying my control.

My body reacted instinctively. My hands slid fast over her back —the uniform an unwelcome obstacle depriving me of the tactile sensation I craved—to the hair at the nape of her neck. She pressed her body a little harder against mine, her eyes jumping from my eyes to my lips, then fluttering closed. I grabbed a fistful, tugging lightly. A gasp parted her lips and I claimed them, my tongue plunging into the depths of her mouth, her unique flavor addictive. I groaned. I couldn't hold back anymore. Breaking the kiss, I guided her hand on top of my uniform's activation nanites.

"Press it," I ordered, but really left the choice up to her. If she didn't want us to go further than this kiss, I'd stop. Even though it'd kill me or—I snickered—cause my balls to fall off.

She raised an eyebrow at me and applied pressure. Her warm skin on mine sent the blood left circulating in the rest of my body straight to my groin, leaving me lightheaded for a moment. When her gaze dropped to my torso, her breath hitched; when it dropped even lower, her lips parted and she gasped.

"Are all aliens this well-endowed?" she asked as her fingers trailed lightly across the length of my straining cock.

A low, feral sound slid from Arana's throat while Mes's darkness unfurled, seeking to destroy any other male she might be interested in.

I pulled the strands still fisted in my palm harder, making her yelp. I eased my grip when she bent her head backward and looked me in the eyes. "You're playing dangerous games, Mate." My gravelly tone warned her to tread carefully.

"Geesh! As if having three males is not enough." After an unsuccessful attempt to push me away, she awkwardly crossed her arms over her chest. "I was just curious, is all."

I leaned in, not allowing her space. "If you are curious about others, it means we're not doing a good job of being your mates."

Mes traced his lips over the exposed skin of her long neck before he bit her earlobe, making her shudder. "I think it's time we corrected that, don't you?" He said, and pressed her uniform's activation nanoparticles, then took the armor plate off her body—leaving her bare for my eyes to feast on.

Magnificent, breathtaking, a sight to behold, and ours. The Change was evident on her body, as spots and stripes similar to Arana's decorated her skin—when before there were only faded silver lines. Would my markings adorn her skin, as well, after we completed the Mating Ritual? I couldn't wait to find out, and suddenly just looking at her divine body wasn't enough.

I gently cupped her face. "You're so beautiful. More than I deserve, but I'm keeping you." I let go, but not entirely. Keeping the pads of my fingers on her skin, I slid them across her neck, making her shiver; I swirled the dips of her collarbone, then continued the downward path between her perfect breasts, goose-bumps breaking out on her skin; I traced her new markings, making her laugh. Then I followed the exact same path with my tongue, biting and kissing her along the way, her breathing slowly becoming ragged.

I pulled back to admire my work, the pink love bites sprinkled over her lithe body. "Beautiful," I whispered.

Mes wasn't idle either. He had been playing with her nipples the whole time, and now his right hand was spreading her pussy lips wide, revealing a little pink nub. When he ran his finger over it, she trembled and cried out. *Fuck.*

"Are you wet for us?" I teased. "Should Mes check?"

Mes inserted a finger in her, and she groaned, "Oh my God."

The hard pebbles on her breasts were beckoning me, so I captured one with my lips and the other with my thumb and fore-finger. I stroked it gently at first, flattened my tongue and licked, then pulled as much of her round mound as I could fit into my mouth before releasing it with a pop. Her moans and groans formed the sweetest symphony. Her body did not lie, and I wanted to discover every little thing that would make her sing and her breath hitch. I changed the rhythm from gentle to rough, sealing my lips around her nipple, sucking it in my mouth, and using my tongue to duel with it. I let go of the nipple I was holding because I wanted to play with the little nub Mes had revealed earlier. The moment my thumb slid over it, she cried out—her body convulsed and her knees buckled.

"Damn it, Kali, your pussy is strangling my fingers," Mes groaned, and I wanted to feel it.

Releasing her nipple, I pulled back to watch her as I added my own finger to the two Mes had thrust into her. Her walls contracted around me; she was tighter than a vise—how were we both going to fit in her? Worry started creeping in and I squashed it. She was our mate. We were made for her and she for us. I pumped slowly, exploring her, feeling a raised ridge—so different compared to the smooth area surrounding it—I played with that spot. The moment I synchronized my movement with my Pair-bond's, she screamed and exploded around our fingers, gushing all over our hands.

I had been teetering on the edge of my control the whole time, but this...seeing her come apart was my undoing. I fell back on the bed and took her with me.

"Watch your weight," I warned Mes, as that was what had triggered her panic attack earlier, while I placed her over my aching cock without preamble and pulled her down on top of my shaft.

Staying still to let her adjust to my size, and let Mes prepare her back entrance, was the hardest thing I had ever done.

Suddenly, she tensed and snapped her head backward to look at her other mate. "I've never..."

"I know, my love. Trust us to know how to pleasure you. We would never willingly do anything to hurt you. We'll always make sure you enjoy everything we do. And if there is something you don't like, we'll stop and listen," he said, and his words had an immediate calming effect on her.

The pressure on my cock eased for a moment, and then became

even stronger than before. I cursed under my breath. "Hurry, Mes, I cannot stand it much longer. Her pussy is strangling me."

"She's so tight, I can't—" he grunted.

"More," she demanded, and Arana—who'd been distant so far—stepped closer.

He put his hand on Kali's neck and applied pressure until she lowered her body and her breasts smashed into my chest. He then knelt next to my shoulders and wrapped his fingers around the base of his cock while gently guiding her mouth toward his shaft.

Mes inserted another digit in her ass, making her moan loudly. The thin barrier between her two entrances did nothing to block the feeling of his fingers in her other opening. When he used a scissoring motion to stretch her, she gasped, and the Saberian—who had been sliding his tip back and forth over her lips, smearing them with pre-cum—took the opportunity to push past her lips and into the warmth of her mouth.

"Mes, get in her now!" I barked—I was about to blow my load like an untried offspring.

And thank fuck for small favors because he withdrew his fingers and replaced them with his cock. Kali started tensing again, and both I and Arana squeezed her nipples making her gasp around Arana's shaft and relax enough for Mes to slip in until he bottomed out.

Heavy breathing and frantic heartbeats were loud in the space as we all spared a moment to take our mate in. She was impossibly tight with both of us in her, and her mouth was full with her third mate. Realizing I was still pinching her nipple, I released it. So did Arana, and the blood rushing back to the sensitive area had her screaming. As if the muffled sound awoke us from a trance, we started moving. Scissoring in and out of her, we allowed her to get used to the fuller sensation. Soon, though, we were pumping in tandem—the friction so pleasantly unbearable, threatening to send us over the edge. I wrapped my fingers around her neck and felt her throat working to take Arana.

My groan added to the melody we were creating. She was our haven and we didn't want to ever leave. But her pussy had other ideas. The tremors started in her core and spread outward, rocking me, rocking all of us. She gasped and we held our breaths too, anticipating…the quiet before the storm. Then she screamed. The force of her explosion shattered us, blasting our gentleness to smithereens, reducing us to our baser instincts, violently drawing the seed from our balls. But I was happy to oblige her. Pistoning into her without holding back, I released my seed into her sheath. Through the thin barrier, I could feel Mes filling her with jet after jet of his cum, and under my palm I could feel her throat working furiously to swallow Arana's essence.

Arana pulled out first, and when her body slumped on top of mine, we gently withdrew as well. She shuddered, goosebumps rising on her skin, but her eyes remained closed. The other two males lay on our sides, each draping an arm over her—finding the thought of breaking contact completely unbearable.

"I understand why Beast did what he did, Arana, and what he needs to do. It's okay…I'd probably do the same thing if I were in his position," she mumbled before her breathing evened out and sleep claimed her.

Relief—that she had not rejected us, had not rejected our Union—filled us, and a smile broke across my face when I realized I could sense her and my Pair-bonds more clearly now. I let my eyes close as peace, unlike any I had ever felt, settled over us at last.

SECOND KING OF SABER

MES

I groggily opened my eyes and frowned at my uniform—currently a discarded vibrating armor plate on the floor. It had disrupted the first peaceful sleep I'd had in a long time. I had falsely thought these past years of meditation would have taught me how to contain my inner darkness, how to cultivate inner peace. What a fool I'd been! What I had painstakingly achieved was nothing compared to what my mate freely offered. Discovering she was a Shield was a pleasant surprise, and now I was in awe of this delicate yet so powerful being. Hesitant to leave my mates' warmth and cocoon of serenity, I waited for the alert to stop. Its incessant vibration, though, meant my brother had awoken.

When I slowly pulled my arm off her, Kali opened her eyes.

"Go back to sleep, love," I said as I caressed her cheek. "My brother needs me."

"Do you need me to come along?" Her voice, husky from sleep, sounded even sexier. Her thinking about my needs over her own melted my hearts.

The partially formed bond intensified my desire to complete the Mating Ritual ten-fold, and I doubted any one of us could wait for an official ceremony. Getting up and walking away from my naked mates proved to be harder than I'd expected, but the buzzing insisted I should. Knowing that the moment we returned to the ship, we'd have access to Rorc's ceremonial knife and cup—the two instruments needed for the completion of the Ritual—helped. "No. I'll be back soon," I told her.

She closed her eyes and was fast asleep before I'd finished my sentence.

I chuckled. We had exhausted her.

In a few ticks I was dressed and out of Cal's room. In my hurry, I almost ran into Remux.

"I'm sorry, Prince Meskiagkasher...Arch-healer," he stuttered and bowed. "Arch-healer Brarn sent me to get you."

I clapped the apprentice Healer on the back, subtly easing his worry. "Take me to him."

He led me to the infirmary but didn't follow me in. I thanked him and entered to find a furious Brarn looming over my brother. In my mind's eye I could see the steam coming out of the Arch-healer's ears, and the fire flashing in of his eyes. I chuckled, my brother had the tendency to elicit extreme reactions from those close to him.

Brarn jerked his head my way and threw his arms in the air. "At last, Mes! Maybe you can get your thick-headed brother to see reason."

Cal growled at him, "I'm still your Prince." Even lying on his chest, his head sideways, he was an imposing figure.

"And I'm your Arch-healer! And guess who has all the power to make decisions when it comes to wounded royalty? Me," he yelled.

If I didn't diffuse the situation soon, these two would go at it for hours. "And I'm Mes, now that we've gotten the introductions out of the way, shall we have a calm discussion like adults?"

A red-faced Brarn spun. "I need a break," he said, and stomped toward the Healers' office.

A victorious smirk curled the tips of Cal's lips until he coughed and groaned aloud, mirth gone, as well as some of his color.

"You do know that he has at least three ways he could kill you without leaving a trace, right?" I taunted my big brother.

He chuckled and groaned again. I rushed to his side. My fingertips heated—the Healer in me taking over. The clear, gel-like protective layer over his injury didn't hide the extent of the wound.

Hovering my palms across the slash's length, checking it was healing properly, I felt anger rising in me. "Why do you always have to dive headfirst into battle, Cal? Your fleet is there for a reason," I chastised.

"For the same reason you wouldn't let your Healers fumble for a cure for an unknown contagious disease, but you'd lead the research."

He had a point. "You're the future King of Wravuk," I deadpanned.

"And you're Second to the Throne," he replied without missing a beat.

I hunched my shoulders, the weight almost unbearable for a moment. "But I never gave up, Cal. I found her…she lights my darkness and dims my light, giving me a reprieve. Gifting me with peace," I whispered.

It was hard to get things through my brother's head when he was in such a mood, but it seemed this got his attention because he, above all, knew the price I had to pay daily for the gift I was born with. He knew what the darkness cost my soul, and the toll the healing light took on my physical form.

"I never expected to live long enough to see it, but I always knew you'd find your mate." The words left him in a rush—as if he were relieved that he would no longer have to worry about me, and could finally move on with his plan to die honorably.

"Don't give up," I said, unable to mask my authoritative tone under the plea.

"Brother, you were lucky. You found one who quiets your demons. I've met many females, bedded most, but none of them were able to quiet mine." His tone was dejected. "Besides, you're forgetting one small detail—the Throne can't be passed on to an unmated Prince. You being newly mated changes things." I narrowed my eyes at him, my temperature rising in proportion to my anger. If he thought he was off the hook, he was sorely mistaken.

"That can't happen," I declared, "and you will find her too…or them, like I did."

He chuckled. "Ordering won't make it re—" he stopped. Blinked. "Them?" he asked, surprised.

I couldn't hold back my smile. "Yes. I was blessed with a Sacred Union."

"Who are your mates?"

Better to start with the familiar.

"Rorc—"

"Well, no surprise there," he interrupted. "You two have been inseparable since you were little. Although, I can't imagine him allowing females under his command. Unless it was a female you saved?" He stopped muttering and looked at me expectantly.

"No, you're right, he doesn't. She was one of the females we saved from the Arkad." I stalled, suddenly not sure how he'd receive the news. "Her name is Kali."

"Kali?" Lost in thought, he smacked his lips repeatedly, making popping sounds. "That's an unusual one for a Wravukian. Where is she from?"

I clenched my suddenly clammy hands into tight fists, and Cal's eyes followed the gesture. Delaying the inevitable was pointless. "She's from Earth. Human. And my other Pair-bond is Arana. The King of Saber."

I wasn't sure what I was expecting, but it was definitely not Cal's barking laughter interspersed with grunts of pain and the slapping of his hands against the bedding.

"Ha. Ha. Funny. We'll see who will be laughing when you find your mates," I said, but soon found myself doing the same alongside him.

Brarn burst into the room to see what the noise was about. "What's going on?"

"My little brother…found his Sacred Mates…Brarn, meet Mes… Second…King…of Saber," Cal wheezed, between laughter and grunts of pain.

The Arch-healer's eyes widened comically and his mouth popped open. My brother laughed harder.

"Callibohr! You're going to undo all the work we've done," I admonished, and he slowly calmed down.

Brarn finally found his words and asked, "Is it true?"

"Yes," I answered before pinning Cal with my stare. "And that means the Throne of Wravuk can't be passed on to me."

I was always honest with myself and there was no point in lying now. The Arch-healer's reaction hurt. It wasn't hostile, but it wasn't welcoming either. And it had me worried. How would the rest of the Wravukians receive the news? How would my father react? If he rejected my mates, I'd lose the only parent I had left.

Hearing my brother curse under his breath as I walked out of the room filled me with satisfaction, and helped set my worries aside. Soon we'd be on Wravuk, and whatever lay in our future, my mates and I would deal with it together.

LOVE ETERNAL, LOVE TRUE

KALI

I pressed my hand on top of my heart. I could have sworn the darn organ was trying to fly out of my chest since my mates told me of their plans.

The moment we returned to the Nur, I was ushered to Rorc's quarters with instructions to freshen up, and relax, for we would hold the Wravukian Mating Ceremony as soon as they returned to me.

Stunned that it was happening so fast, I stumbled into the bathroom with the intention of washing my face. But that did nothing to calm my nerves. Thinking that water all over my body would help, I took my uniform off and climbed into the shower. When that did nothing, I filled the tub and immersed myself in the hot liquid.

Oh my God. Oh my God. Am I doing this? Yes, yes I am. I'm doing this. What would my father say? Well, he wasn't here, so there was that. I'd miss my team, but they had their own lives to live. They'd be happy for me if they knew. I had to find a way to send them a message. But staying with my mates meant I'd be alone. The sex was out of this world with them, and totally worth it, but outside our little bubble they had their jobs, their lives before I came into the picture. How would I fit in their world? I would always be the alien one. What if their families didn't like me?

Shit! Trying to distract myself wasn't working. The water wasn't doing anything to loosen my tense muscles, and my freaking heart either wanted to escape my chest or was about to have a heart attack.

I'm here, Kali. Dawn's lilting voice filled my mind. *I'll always be with you, and I'll protect you against anyone who tries to hurt you,* she said shyly, as if expecting a backlash from me.

After the initial shock, I'd had time to come to terms with sharing my body with another. And while my initial reaction of horror—filled with images of alien monsters bursting from my skin and eating me alive, admittedly watching all those sci-fi thrillers in my free time had skewed my opinion—had passed, I realized I actually liked the idea of having a badass sabertooth of my own.

I owe you an apology. I'm sorry for how I acted, I told her, and felt her coming closer to the surface of my consciousness. *I can't wait to meet you,* I said, and it was the truth.

Her elation at my declaration filled me as if it were my own. My arms tickled, and I looked down to see fur sprout from my arms and recede in a wave. It was awesome and weird at the same time.

Our mates are here, she purred, and I could both hear and sense them in the adjoining room.

They were calm and eager, and their emotions were what settled the roiling in my stomach, and slowed my rapid heartbeat.

Let's do this. I got out of the tub, dried myself, and reached for the silky dark-purple garment Rorc had given me. As I draped it over me, it caressed my skin and lowered my temperature. It was some kind of dress. A beautiful golden brooch clasped the fabric together over my right shoulder while leaving the left one bare. I chuckled. It made me feel like a Greek deity of old about to meet her followers. The high slit revealed my thigh and my female bits every time I put my left foot forward. The attire was scandalous. It made me feel divine.

They were waiting for me, bare-chested, in the middle of the room around a small round table that hadn't been there before. The objects on it caught my attention. There was a cup, not overly big, that I could easily hold in my hand. The perimeter of the rim was decorated with the same gold alloy. The bowl consisted of two parts. Clear glass was nestled in some kind of golden metal depiction of Wravukians engaged in celebration. Beneath it, the stem was maybe half an inch long, and the base solid gold.

The dagger next to it drew my eyes; rose gold and silver metals covered the bottom of the hilt, and it seemed as if fire, or maybe water, was flowing toward the guard. The same design seemed to cascade from the guard toward the pommel, but the two never touched. The two triangular quillons each held a small clear gemstone, and at the base of the blade the same wavy pattern as on the handle glided along, with another small clear gem near the base. And there, in the middle of the guard, sat a triangular clear jewel three times bigger than the rest. The two-toned metal alloys twisted and entwined, forming the short sharp blade.

It was the most beautiful weapon I had ever seen. I felt it calling to me. As if it were pulsing to the beat of my heart, beckoning me closer. So absorbed was I by the two objects that I hadn't noticed the absolute silence in the room. But when I did, embarrassment colored my cheeks. I shifted from one foot to the other, accidentally exposing my left leg and—based on the groans coming from my mates—my center as well.

"Is everything all right?" I asked, more to break the awkwardness than anything else.

"Yes, little one. Come here," Rorc said.

I gulped a big mouthful of air, and Dawn purred to remind me she was right there with me. I went to them, and Mes placed me in such a way that I was facing all of them, yet the table remained between us.

Arana caressed my cheek before he let his arm drop. "Do you trust us, monakrivimou?"

"Yes."

Answering without hesitation filled them with elation, and I could feel it through our bond. Nervousness started creeping in, but before it could take root, Mes placed his left hand over the cup.

Rorc lifted the gorgeous dagger. "Souls aligned, with blood we bind. From now, for always. Love eternal, love true," he recited, and sliced diagonally across Mes's palm. My Healer didn't even flinch, but let his blood flow into the cup until the edges of the wound seamed together—forming raised ridges—and his life force stopped running.

Then he took the ceremonial knife and repeated, "Souls aligned, with blood we bind. From now, for always. Love eternal, love true." And cut Arana's offered palm. My warrior kept his left hand over the cup too until his blood stopped running and another scar was created.

Would he cut my palm too? I vaguely wondered as I watched, enthralled.

Arana repeated the process on Rorc. His low timbre as he uttered the Wravukian vow resonated deep within my soul.

Before I could ask them, three sets of eyes locked on me. Rorc retrieved the dagger and stepped closer.

"Mate long lost…" His gravelly tone was too sexy for his own good and distracted me from his action.

I didn't feel the knife slicing me, only the burn spreading from the tender spot all over my chest. I stared at the thin trail of blood that had leaked from the cut under my left collarbone.

Rorc leaned down, kissed the already healed scar before licking the red liquid, and stepped backward to allow Mes to take his place.

My beautiful red alien, with the captivating yellow-gold eyes, bent a hairbreadth from my lips and whispered, "But now found," right before he claimed them. Too soon his lips traveled to my chin before moving lower along my neck to where the second slice had now left a permanent mark on my skin. I exhaled in a rush when his warm tongue tasted my blood.

Arana took Mes's spot in front of me. I already felt tipsy from desire, but when our eyes connected, and I witnessed the hunger etched in them, I went from tipsy to drunk in an instant. He lifted the dagger between us and arched an eyebrow. My other two mates had shielded me from the action, thinking I was too fragile to withstand the pain. My Saberian King, though, was challenging me. And I wouldn't be myself if I didn't rise to the challenge.

Eyes locked on the dagger that no longer had clear gemstones, but crimson ones, I watched, enthralled, barely feeling the sting as the tip sliced my skin in two and each ruby-red drop beaded across the cut before sliding down my chest.

Without taking his eyes off me, he placed the weapon on the table and watched, enraptured as my skin mended itself. A soft snarl rattled his chest as he lifted his nose and scented the air, before he lowered his head. My eyes closed of their own accord, and I moaned aloud when his rasping tongue gathered the life-giving essence. He kept licking me like I was his favorite treat, and I might have orgasmed if he'd kept it up, but he stepped back, breaking the spell he had weaved over me.

I was panting harder than if I'd just crossed the finish line of a marathon. The smooth fabric rubbing against my rock hard nipples and arousing my body, had me ready to beg my males for relief. The heat in my core demanded relief, making me want to lay on the table, open my legs, and let my mates feast on the juices smeared on my inner thighs. I had never been as aware of my body as I was in that moment.

The restraint my mates were showing awakened my wicked side. I wanted them unable to resist the temptation I was offering, I wanted to make them lose control. But before I could enact any of the images running through my head, Rorc picked up the cup, repeated the vow, and drank before passing it on to Mes, who did the same. When Arana had taken a long sip, all the while staring at me over the rim of the cup, he offered it to me.

I didn't hesitate to wrap my fingers around it. Maybe I should have been disgusted by the notion alone of drinking their blood, but Dawn's zeal added to my eagerness, and I needed to taste them...like they had tasted me. The aroma wafting from the cup—nothing like the coppery scent of human blood—indicated a delicacy awaited. Cradling the cup near my chest, I recited the vow, "Mate long lost, but now found." The Sacred Lined that had formed not too long ago, uniting us, shimmered to life. "Solitary lives forever renounced." A solid bridge replaced the rickety one linking our minds, providing an unobstructed path to their minds and mine. "Souls aligned with blood we bind." The silver thread flickered crimson for a moment as happiness, lust, love—my males' emotions—filled me to the brim. "From now, for always...love eternal, love true." Bringing the rim to my lips, I could taste my mates. Lifting it, their combined essence trickled in my mouth and I swallowed every single drop, irreversibly solidifying our bond.

The hunger I felt was reflected in my males' eyes, and as they surrounded me I became giddy with delight, for they would soon quench my thirst. Only to be disappointed when they kissed me passionately—stoking the embers of my desire to an inferno—and then retreated, allowing me space I did not want.

A prickling sensation covered my body. Dawn, as equally annoyed as me, wanted out. As she crawled under my skin, a low, feral sound slid from Arana's throat, and when it did, she retreated behind me. I snarled at him, mad that he'd scared her—I already felt protective of her—but even more aroused by his show of dominance.

Funny how I'd thought I wasn't attracted to men or women before, when all along I had a specific type that just didn't exist on Earth. The alien dominant type.

My Saberian—rejoicing in my discovery—stepped in front of me, dragged a finger over the visible part of my leg, then slipped it under my dress and between my folds before plunging it in me, wrenching a loud moan from my lips. "Monakrivimou, both of you have to wait. We can't release her here," he said, bringing the finger that was dripping with my juices into his mouth. He groaned and I felt a smidgen of satisfaction at not being the only one suffering. "If we give in now"—he dragged a breath through lips I wanted to bite—"we won't be able to stop."

"Fine," I grudgingly acquiesced.

All of their comms beeped at the same time and within minutes they had left, as if relieved they wouldn't have to fight to resist me anymore because they'd be otherwise occupied.

Blue balls. That would have been the color of my balls if I were a man.

I can't believe they left me hanging like that, I huffed to myself, and almost jumped out of my bones when Dawn replied, *we'll get them soon enough.*

A little bloodthirsty, are we? I teased, and she gave me the figurative lift of the shoulder before she retreated to wherever she went inside my head.

"Now what do I do?" I said to no one, but then had an idea. I wasn't completely alone on this ship, I had a new friend, who was probably mad at me for escaping without her. It was time to visit Tris and Kas and make amends.

THE ROYAL QUARTERS

KALI

When the door opened and in walked Mes, he found me, Tris, and Kas hugging each other tightly.

"I am sorry to interrupt, but I don't think you will want to miss this, Kali," he said.

They didn't know this about me yet, but I hated surprises. "Miss what?"

He just laughed at my sulky tone. "We have arrived at Wravuk. Come see our planet." With that, he turned around and left, expecting me to follow.

Tris just looked at me, and if she had eyebrows, I bet they'd be reaching for the sky with the incredulous look she was giving me.

"Oh no, you two are not getting out of it! You are coming too," I told them, and pulled them along as I trailed after my mate.

Mate. The word was so unusual, so new, and I wasn't sure I'd fully come to terms with the consequences of my decision. The ceremony we'd held in Rorc's room was equivalent to a human wedding. I had three alien husbands. Tris, who'd noticed my new scars and inquired about them, had danced on the spot when I'd explained what they meant. I was excited too, but I couldn't shake the feeling of waiting for the other shoe to drop.

My Healer led us to the Bridge. Rorc, standing in the middle with his back to us, was the most imposing figure there. The Wravukian crew around him was busy piloting the spaceship, yet they occasionally stole curious glances at us, most of which seemed open and friendly. The moment my eyes fell on the viewscreen, though, my jaw hit the floor. The view was magnificent!

The planet in front of us was oval-shaped, and the color of the atmosphere around it was emerald green in some places and amethyst purple in others.

I must have stopped in my tracks because Mes took my hand and led me to a chair. He indicated two other spots for my friends.

Mes looked at me sideways. "Do you like it?" he asked the moment Rorc placed his hand on my neck, startling me.

'Someone's feeling possessive,' I giggled.

'I don't like the way they're looking at you, stripping you with their eyes.'

I was in serious trouble, finding his guttural timbre sexy. If a man had talked to me like that, I would have clocked him on the head and swept the floor with his body.

'I'm not in the market for a new mate, so by all means they can look as much as they like,' I told him through our bond, then added out loud, "Yes." Was that my voice that sounded so breathless?

He seemed pleased with my answer, so I focused on the breath-taking view in front of me. As we neared, I realized the green spots were probably covering liquid surfaces, whereas the purple ones, the land. When I managed to take my eyes off the beautiful planet, I saw quite a few other planets, smaller in size, around Wravuk. And behind it were…two suns. The bigger one was similar to our sun, bathing everything in a golden-yellow light, but the smaller one bathed everything in a pale-turquoise hue. The weird thing, though, was that it seemed like the suns revolved, and not the planets around them.

A million questions were racing through my mind. All around me a chaotic order prevailed while Rorc barked orders and his crew relayed the needed information. Sooner than I'd thought possible, we had entered the planet's atmosphere and were descending toward its surface.

The landing was smoother than an airplane's and everything worked like a well-oiled machine. I guess they had done this quite a few times in the past, but—nonetheless—new found respect for my mate developed, embedding him a little deeper in my human heart.

I could almost taste the excitement in the air. The Wravukians hadn't been home for a while. Momentarily, I wondered how I knew that, but then Rorc dismissed everyone but the skeleton crew, and the happy ruckus that followed distracted me. As the soldiers slowly scattered away, awkwardness replaced the novelty of the experience. Usually, I was the one giving orders, but not this time, and it wasn't often that I didn't know what to do with myself.

Next to me, Tris looked expectantly at Rorc. I felt like hissing at her for looking at him like that, but I wasn't the jealous type, and that was a very bizarre reaction, so I ignored it.

It must be nerves. I need a gun.

Yes, I would feel so much better if I had a gun.

The whole time, Mes kept looking at me—eyebrow raised, and a smirk playing on his lips.

I ignored him too.

He chuckled.

Infuriating male.

"Let's go," Rorc ordered, and I bristled at the command.

Tris nudged me softly and I got moving, but I couldn't understand the heat rising in me, nor the jumbled emotions that followed.

Arana met us outside the Bridge. His hair was wet, and a few drops of water were sliding down his neck and onto his armor. The urge to lick every last drop—before it reached the garment he was wearing—arose, fast and sharp. The image was so vivid that for a second I wasn't sure whether I had actually taken the two steps that separated us, and dropped on my knees, or if it was all in my head.

Arana groaned while Rorc growled.

"Kali, you are killing us!" Mes complained.

My face flushed. During the Mating Ceremony, and while the Sacred Line had been uniting us, there was a moment when their emotions had swamped me. But then desire had coursed through my body and overpowered every other sensation, making me forget about everything but having my mates. Was it possible, now that we'd completed the Ritual, they had access to my mind? To my thoughts?

"Let's go. The King is waiting for us," Rorc gruffly ordered, and walked ahead of us.

I would press the matter later. I was about to see another King! The notion was a bit intimidating, but after so many years living under my father's thumb, I figured no one could be worse.

Mes slid next to me and bent to my ear. "Yes, we shouldn't leave Father waiting," he said before sucking my earlobe into his mouth.

I froze, but Arana placed his palm on my waist and applied pressure. I followed them, lost in thought. I'm sure Mes meant to lighten my mood, but crap. I was about to meet my father-in-law. Or at least one of them.

As we exited the ship, the three men surrounded me, boxing me in. Mes took my left side, Arana my right, and Rorc walked in front of us. Tris and Kas behind me completed the squad. They formed a solid wall and I had a difficult time seeing what was around us.

The palace looming in front of us was huge, awe-inspiring, and difficult to miss, due to its enormous size. It reminded me of a cathedral with the different domes in the corners and colorful roofs. All around the perimeter of the building, fight scenes were depicted. Who were they fighting? Enemies or previous Kings?

I could barely see the one-story houses we were passing by. We were surrounded by aliens. Not just Wravukians but also various other species. I wanted to see, but they weren't budging. I tried to catch their eyes—wanting to wither them on the spot—but unfortunately, no one paid attention to me. They kept alertly looking around, scouting the area. Scowls were permanently etched on their faces, along with something else that I could not identify.

Was I in danger? It didn't feel like it. My gut would have given me a warning. I managed to duck between Rorc and Mes and peak at our surroundings. A mass of aliens, all of whom appeared to be male, stopped what they were doing and stared at us. Then it hit me.

My mates were staking their claim.

Cavemen! I thought, but Dawn just purred happily. *What the fuck?* I almost lost my footing, and I would have fallen if Arana hadn't caught me.

"Easy," he coaxed, but I could not settle.

Do you enjoy this shit? I'm not a trophy to be paraded around, I told my sabertooth, but she couldn't care less. She loved their possessiveness. It meant they'd be great mates who'd take good care of our offspring.

Whoa there! Don't even start thinking about children yet, I ordered, and was ignored completely.

Lost in my musings, I didn't notice we'd entered the palace and been ushered to the King until I heard his booming voice.

"Son," he exclaimed, and rushed toward us. Right before he barreled into Mes, he stopped and hugged him tight. He held his son for a few minutes and I even saw a tear escape him.

I didn't know what kind of reception I'd been expecting, but it was definitely not this. Did Kings cry?

Mes gently disengaged from his father's embrace, and then the King turned to Rorc and enveloped him in a bear hug as well.

"I hope my son is not giving you too much trouble, Admiral?"

While they were occupied I had the opportunity to study him. I knew he was older, but his age didn't show on his face. He didn't look any different from the others, except for the color of his skin and eyes. I could not discern any other differences. His muted-gold skin appeared to be smooth and spotless, and his eyes were an intense yellow. The combination was quite an unnerving sight; he exuded power from his every pore. He wore the same uniform as Rorc, but had a different insignia on his chest. He did not wear a crown, and he was bald.

Despite everything, I could see the slight resemblance between him and Mes, and now I knew where Mes had gotten his eyes from.

"Where are my manners," he admonished, and turned toward me and Arana.

We had been standing a bit farther back, but the moment the King noticed us, Arana straightened and stepped in front of me.

That ruffled my feathers, but when I tried to sidestep him, he growled and stopped me with his hand.

"King Nathraichean, well met." Even though Arana's voice was respectful, he didn't bow his head like Rorc and Mes had when we'd first entered.

They clasped each other's arms. "King Arana, welcome to my humble abode."

A few seconds later they let go. My Saberian mate stepped to my right and introduced me. "This is my mate."

I was about to rip Arana a new one when the King distracted me by bowing to me, before turning to him and wishing, "May you live a long, healthy, and prosperous life with your mate, and may the Creator bless you with many offspring."

This time the Saberian returned the bow. Then one of my other mates cleared his throat, and Arana regarded me for a second before amending, "Our mate."

They must be fucking kidding me. I had a name, and it wasn't mate.

"What?" The King spun on his heels to look at his son.

"She is our mate. Arana's, Rorc's, and mine."

"A Sacred Union?" Nathraichean mused, then did the most bizarre thing. He inched closer, sniffed the air, and then his eyes locked on the spot where my mating marks were as if he had x-ray vision and could see underneath my uniform.

But I had just about enough with the weirdness, King or no King. "Your mate has a name, and if you don't address her properly, you won't have one for long," I interrupted, my voice bordering on rudeness.

All four males looked at me incredulously. I guess the local females did not speak when the males conversed. Pity!

And then the King laughed. Out loud. A rolling on the floor kind of laugh. When he sobered, his eyes flashed with something I didn't recognize, and it occurred to me that maybe my behavior in front of a King was bordering on improper. I told myself to lower my attitude a notch lest I wanted to find myself in a dungeon instead of a bed, but then I noticed my friend and her daughter were missing, and my good intentions flew right out the window.

"Where is Tris?" I demanded.

No one answered my question, so I snarled at my mates and turned around to go look for her. But before I could take a step farther, Arana's arm sneaked out and caught mine.

"She is outside. My Father will have a hearing with her after us," Mes informed me.

Then the King's demeanor changed, and he started laughing again. "Oh, she is a handful I see. Maybe it's for the best then," he said between laughs. "You two need the challenge," he told Rorc and Mes before calling out to a guard.

Said guard seemed to appear out of thin air, making me jump. Seriously where had he come from? No one else seemed startled by his arrival.

"King," he bowed. "The Imperial has landed."

"Thank you. Please take my son and his mates to the royal quarters," he ordered. "I have something to attend to. In the meantime, enjoy your stay," he said to my mates, then walked up to me and hugged me. "Kali, Sacred Mate, welcome to the family." Flabbergasted, I stood frozen in his arms. He chuckled, released me, and exited the chamber.

Okay, I'll pretend that was not weird, not weird at all.

The guard asked us to follow him.

"Mes, did you grow up here?" I asked, curious as to how royalty was treated in his culture.

His cheeks darkened a shade and I was ninety-nine percent sure he was blushing. "Yes, I did," he said, without elaborating further.

I pouted, and he just shook his head in exasperation. His eyes, though, betrayed his true emotion when they lit with his smile.

The Royal Guard stopped outside two huge doors and left us to get settled.

Arana entered first, perused the space, and when he deemed it safe, he stepped aside to let us pass. I bounced into the room, excited to see where my Healer had grown up, but I stopped in my tracks and had to do a double take. The place was ginormous. My whole apartment back on Earth could fit in here, along with my neighbor's too.

In front of me, floor-to-ceiling arch windows let the suns' lights bathe the room. Behind me there was an enormous bed that could easily fit all of us. Images of the three of them naked over me filled my head. *Get your mind out of the gutter, Kali!* I chastised myself, there was more to discover. What could pass for sofas and futons were scattered in the room—tastefully placed. All the walls were adorned with the same type of art as the outside perimeter of the palace. But as I walked toward the huge fluffy pillows on the floor near the bed, I saw that the aliens it depicted were in various positions during intercourse.

Geesh, King Nat! Subtle much? I rolled my eyes, and it was then that I noticed the mirrored ceiling. *It's like Mes's father wants a grandkid today!* No. *Nope. I'm not touching on that.* I averted my eyes quickly and my gaze fell to a small sunken pool next to the inviting pillows. *Tempting, oh so tempting,* but my stomach chose to make its demands known, and parallel to the wall on the right side of the room, there was a huge dining table with a feast fit for a King set on it. *Ha! How fitting*. I had two of them with me in the room—well, a Prince and a King, who was awfully preoccupied with his comms.

Suddenly, a little detail I had overlooked became too glaring to ignore. "Um...Arana, you are a King. What does that make us?" I asked, and it was eerie how three sets of eyes focused solely on me.

I COULD ONLY CHANGE SO MUCH

KALI

"You're hungry. We'll eat first, then talk."

I didn't like Arana's answer at all. I thought my question would have an easy answer, but apparently that was not the case. My stomach grumbled again, and Rorc took my arm and led me to the table.

The food they had given me on the ship was nutritious, but plain and drab looking compared to the banquet laid out in front of us. The exotic scents floating from colorful and unusually shaped fruit and vegetables, and a variety of fish and meat, reached my nostrils, making my mouth salivate and my stomach complain again.

Rorc pulled out a chair, sat, and pulled me down on his lap. I sprang right back up, but his arm across my legs kept me from going anywhere. "Settle, little one," he said, and placed a lingering kiss on my neck.

I had no idea how he could make everything sound like a

command—but it rubbed me the wrong way—and then he'd go and do something sweet and confuse the heck out of me.

Mes and Arana prepared four plates with various delicacies and placed them in front of us before they took their seats on our sides.

I eyed the mouthwatering food warily.

Mes noticed. "What is it, Kali?" he asked.

"Are these foods compatible with a human?" Getting food poisoning would be the way to make an impression on my mate's father.

He leaned in and placed a chaste kiss on my lips. "You made quite an impression already, Kali. He wouldn't think ill of you for getting sick," Mes replied, and I hadn't realized I'd spoken out loud.

Arana, not wanting to be left out, picked up my hand and brought it to his mouth. He started with a kiss, and ended with a nip of the soft skin between my thumb and forefinger that caused my core to clench. "Trust your sabertooth, Kali. She will only let you eat things that are good for you. She will protect you, as we will."

Rorc chose a fuschia-colored vegetable and lifted it near my mouth.

I reached out to take it and he tsked me, then brought the food closer to my lips.

Was he expecting me to eat out of his hand? What was I? A pet? I pinched my mouth shut.

"Open," he ordered with his gravelly voice.

No matter how compelling he sounded, I was a grown-ass woman. I could feed myself, thank you very much. I stubbornly shook my head.

"Open," he repeated, using the same commanding tone he'd used on his crew, and my traitorous body obeyed.

I opened my mouth without meaning to do so.

His fingers lingered a moment too long between my lips, but all three of my mates seemed enthralled by the sight of me eating that bite. I felt awkward, the attention I was receiving unfamiliar and uncomfortable.

"Get used to it." Arana's low drawl was an answer to my intimate thoughts once again.

I found it disconcerting, having someone tap into my thoughts unexpectedly. But they didn't give me much time to ponder before Arana and Mes followed Rorc's example and fed me more bites.

"I can eat by myself, you know," I insisted.

"We know," Rorc replied, smirking.

Bastard.

Okay, so they would not let me eat by myself. With my anxiety levels rising, I ate as fast as I could to end this torture.

Suddenly all three of them froze.

"Why would you feel this is a torture, monakrivimou?" Arana inquired, hurt turning his voice deeper.

"You're our mate, and it is an honor to provide for you," Mes added.

"It is our responsibility to keep you fed and satisfied. Is this not the custom on your planet?" Rorc asked, brows furrowed in confusion.

Once again, I had their full attention while they waited patiently for an answer.

Was it like this on Earth? I didn't think so, but then again I didn't have any experience in relationships. I didn't know what couples did in their homes. Was it so bad to let them feed me? It clearly made them happy.

When the fuck had their happiness become my priority?

Lost in my musings, it took me a minute to notice their smirks. Apparently, they found my confusion amusing.

"Enjoy your food, Mate. It doesn't matter what Earth males do because this is what we're doing. Get used to it," Rorc decreed, and a flash of fury ignited a fire in me, but it was put out, just as fast, the moment I felt Arana's hand on my thigh, trailing upward. I might have been wearing their uniform, but I felt his fingers on my skin blaze a trail toward my pussy.

Mes brought another piece of food to my mouth and I opened with a gasp when my other mate's wicked fingers applied pressure to my clit. Mes's thumb lingered on my lips, and I wrapped my tongue around the digit before he withdrew it, making him groan.

I grinned-two could play their game. Then I bit the fruit, and its taste exploded in my mouth. I moaned. It was delicious.

My Healer's answering smirk was devious. He slid his palm down my neck—his fingers clenching around my throat just long enough for him to feel my pulse racing, answering to the power he wielded—and down my chest. Then he pressed lightly, deactivating my uniform.

Rorc cupped my breasts and used his legs to spread mine—offering my other mates full access to my center.

Arana caressed my nether lips with the tips of his fingers softly, gently. "You're soaking wet, monakrivimou. Is it all for us?"

I was about to come back with a snarky reply, when Mes picked up a turquoise fruit and smeared its juices over my lips.

Sensuously slow, his tongue licked every single drop—making me forget what I was about to say. Then he thrust his tongue in my mouth and, like a ruthless pirate, stole a kiss.

At the same time, Arana plunged two fingers in my pussy, filling me to the brim, stretching me, nearly tipping me over to paradise.

Too soon, he removed them, and I whimpered at the loss. But he wasn't done. He picked up something that looked like watermelon, put it in my mouth, and waited until I closed my lips around his fingers, too. I'd never tasted myself, and the decadent act put me right on the edge.

Arana withdrew his fingers from my mouth, and placed them where I was aching for relief the most. I lifted my pelvis, silently begging him to allow me release, when he spread my juices between my cheeks. Feeling overtly vulnerable and exposed, I tensed, but Rorc—who'd been gently squeezing and massaging my breasts—pinched my nipples hard; the abrupt change effectively distracting me from the actions of my Saberian mate, who took advantage of the diversion and worked a finger in me. "This is mine next time we mate. I will take you from behind while you have another cock filling your pussy, and a third stuffed in your mouth. We will pound into you, make you beg, make you scream, and when we allow you release, I will bite you here"—he leaned in and grazed that sensitive spot between my neck and my shoulder with his sharp teeth—"and make you ours."

And damn, but I wasn't prepared for the explosion that followed. I cried out, or I might have screamed; I wasn't sure which. But it wasn't because I found the idea of my mates controlling me in bed and me obeying their commands sexy, and it most definitely wasn't because I found the idea of welcoming two of my mates into my body at the same time scorching hot.

Arana withdrew his finger gently, making me shiver and whimper, as nerve endings I never knew I had were still too sensitive from my orgasm. He chortled, and I focused on him. "I know what goes on in that pretty head of yours. You can lie all you like—your body will betray you every time," he said.

I really hated lying to myself, but what did the truth reveal about me? I wasn't a submissive woman, and I could never live with controlling partners. Growing up under my father's thumb, I had fought hard for my independence. I wasn't about to change now, and I needed to make that clear to these dominant aliens before it was too late.

Wanting to be taken seriously, I tried to close my legs, but Rorc had them trapped, and he wouldn't budge. Instead, he brought his hand over my private parts and played with the juices slowly flowing out of me. He was further proving my point.

"Giving me an orgasm or two doesn't give you the right to control me. I might have enjoyed it"—my aliens bristled at the word might, but I paid them no mind—"I won't lie about that, but if you believe you'll be giving orders and I'll be blindly following, think again." I said my piece and waited. For what, I wasn't sure. Would they yell? Would they try to intimidate me?

Rorc's fingers stilled. "Why wouldn't you?" Honesty and curiosity rang true in voice, right before he continued what he was doing.

I felt my face heat up. They would actually make me spell it out for them. I dropped my eyes, the situation more embarrassing than I'd expected.

Mes placed a finger under my chin and applied pressure, making me lift my eyes to his. "Why, my love? Tell us."

How was it possible to condense women's rights into a few sentences so they'd understand, when it took human men decades to come to terms with what was our birthright? "In my society, women don't follow men's orders all the time…we have a mind of our own…we're free to do as we please." I struggled to explain, knowing that even though what I'd said was true, it didn't apply to all women.

Mes tilted his head to the side, pursing his lips, deep in thought.

I looked over my shoulder at Rorc, whose gaze had gone distant, and then at Arana as he wandered a short distance, shaking his head and then returning to us.

Well it was safe to say, based on their reactions, that I had failed to convey the right meaning. Sighing, I let my shoulders slump.

"Why wouldn't females in your society do what the males told them? They're responsible for your pleasure, for your well-being. Don't you trust them?" Mes asked, genuinely puzzled.

Did I? That was the million-dollar question. When it came to my team, I'd say yes, with my life, but if I was being real with myself, outside our missions, my trust came with conditions. And as far as other men went…my scars were too deep to allow for faith in them.

This time I sensed Arana as he poured himself to our bond, accessing my mind, finally understanding exactly what I was failing to say.

"We only ask you to obey us without question within our chambers. Trust us to know how to please you. To know exactly what you desire, what you need, monakrivimou."

"So you don't expect me to do as you say, always?" I held my breath.

"No, not always. Only when it comes to your pleasure and your protection, little one. Those are our privilege and our responsibility." Rorc's answer still ruffled my feathers. They knew nothing about me and they already thought I needed their protection.

I heard Arana snicker, but that did not keep me from giving the male behind me a piece of my mind.

"I am a Brigadier General, Rorc. I have fought in wars. I've led Black-ops—my team and I have eliminated targets others couldn't. I've earned my rank. I don't need to be protected."

"She did incapacitate three of your soldiers, Admiral…and she stabbed you…while naked," Mes interjected, trying to lighten the mood, but Rorc lifted me off him, got up, and started pacing—his agitation palpable.

The aversion I felt at having hurt him took me by surprise. It also made me see things from a different perspective. Was them protecting me such a bad thing? Wasn't it the same thing my team did when it was us against the world? The aliens in front of me weren't just my team, they were the mates I had committed myself to. I could certainly water my wine a little bit if that would calm him.

I walked up to him, stopping him in his tracks. Placing my palm on top of where I assumed one of his hearts might be, I waited until his eyes locked on mine.

"I am not familiar with aliens, so I will listen to you when it comes to my protection," I said, and felt his muscles relax. "Until I learn," I warned. I could only change so much. "Then you will have to share the reins, Rorc. I'm not a damsel in distress."

We're a warrior, Dawn added, and he must have heard her through our bond because his eyes widened in surprise.

"You have to meet me halfway because I need to stay true to myself, too." I pleaded my case and hoped it would be enough. I could not be smothered. I was raised to be independent and all my attempts at impressing my father had strengthened that trait.

Instead of answering, he grabbed my hips and crushed me to his chest before claiming my lips in an all-consuming kiss. His hands found their way to my bottom, cupping my ass. He lifted me and I wrapped my legs around his waist, grinding on his clothed cock.

Trepidation warred with excitement, for I knew what was coming, and I didn't wish to stop it.

DID THEY REGRET THEIR DECISION?

KALI

We were about to complete the Mating Ritual. Anticipation was thick in the air, and excitement filled my mates. They'd teased my body to a fever pitch and any trepidation I might have felt earlier was replaced by immense need.

Rorc discarded his uniform and sat on the edge of the bed. His erect cock bobbed, smearing pre-cum on his abs.

I was a soaking mess, and if I could smell my arousal, I bet my mates could too. Still, a fleeting thought about whether he would fit passed through my mind, but soon he was lowering me on his thick cock, and any coherent thoughts disappeared. He was splitting my folds in two, but it felt so good as I fully sat astride his lap.

The firm grip he had on my waist, though, kept me from moving like I wanted to.

I clenched my core muscles, making him groan, and hoped he'd move. But to my dismay, he remained still.

"Rorc, please."

"Not yet, little one," he said, and lay back, pulling me down on him. The vein on his shaft pulsed frantically—matching the beat of my heart—betraying his hunger.

"Fuck…" I exclaimed as the action had his pubic bone pressing on my clit—making stars dance behind my eyes. In this new position my butt was lifted, granting Arana, who had positioned himself behind me between Rorc's legs, access.

Mes—who'd gotten on the bed too, next to Rorc's shoulder—delved his fingers into my hair. "So impatient, love," he said, and fisted the strands, using them to maneuver my head sideways to exactly where he wanted. With his other hand, he squeezed the base of his cock. I licked my lips at seeing the excitement gathering on the tip of his shaft. "Open," he ordered—his voice lower than usual, smokier—and I did, needing to taste him, needing him inside me. His slow pace was torture. He didn't allow me control, and I did everything in my power to make him lose it. My tongue traced every single ridge and bump along his length; I flattened it and licked him, then circled the head, making sure to taste every single drop he'd give me.

"Hurry," Rorc growled, and I wondered what he was talking about. He was the one keeping me from moving, but then cool liquid was massaged between my cheeks.

I couldn't keep my body from tensing, but I somehow managed to keep my jaw slack. Two chuckles were accompanied by a tortured grunt. *Oh my God!* I could just picture what I'd look like if someone walked in.

Arana feathered kisses along my spine, taking my focus off what his wicked fingers were doing to my ass. And as Mes tightened his grip in my hair, pulling my head backward, he further derailed my train of thought.

The new position allowed him to go deeper; he moaned as he

hit the back of my throat, and stayed there until I swallowed. Just before I started panicking, he pulled out, and as soon as I took a breath, he pushed back in, repeating the whole process over and over again, increasing my body's temperature to dangerous levels.

Rorc's body was so rigid beneath mine, that if he so much as moved an inch, he'd break into a thousand pieces. He lifted his right hand off my hip and rested it on my throat, feeling what his Pair-bond was doing to me; showing me he was in control; needing my trust. Although he could crush my trachea with little effort, I wasn't afraid. I knew he would never hurt me, so I didn't fight him; Instead, I pressed my neck into his palm, eliciting a loud moan from his lips.

Lust blinded me. *'Arana, hurry,'* I pleaded—the need to feel them inside me overwhelming. But even more intense than that was the desire for what they had dangled in front of me when they'd explained what the Sacred Union meant. I craved the bond that would unite us forever. I'd never feel lonely again. We'd form a family unit, and no one would be able to take that away from us.

My mate obeyed and I felt the crown of his cock pressing against my entrance until the ring of muscle gave in. He slid in his huge length unhurriedly, but I didn't want slow, and in my effort to entice them to start moving, I squirmed; Rorc lost his grip, and I was about to get what I wanted—sweet friction—when Arana's hand between my shoulder blades pushed me down, and threw me for a loop.

Reality changed, and I was held against a hard surface, the scent of polished wood filling my nostrils. All I could see through the dense fog was General Spencer's chair and the yellow wall behind it. Oh God, he had trapped me again. Struggling got me nowhere, and I knew what would come next. The pain, the humiliation.

I heard the pained roars of a big feline, but I couldn't see any near me. I desperately wanted to help the wounded animal, but I couldn't even help myself.

Someone called my name and I felt more than a pair of hands on me. The sinking realization that there were more people in the room with us this time stole my breath. I wouldn't survive this.

My name was called out again, the voice familiar, safe. I fought tooth and nail to hold on to it.

Two warm hands cupped my face, wiped my tears. Thumbs pressed on my temples, and slowly the mist clouding my vision cleared. The memory became more distant with each passing second—as if someone had shoved it behind a closed door—and the space between us allowed me to return to the present.

I blinked and was met with worried stares—the distress emanating from my mates leaving a bitter taste in my mouth. Still panting, I mumbled, "I'm sorry," and buried my face in Mes's chest.

We were still connected. My Healer was holding my head, while Rorc and Arana were still semi-hard inside me. They were thick enough that if they had pulled out while I was struggling, caught in the throes of the nightmare, they'd have hurt me. Their silence, though, scared me. Were they mad at me?

'Never at you, monakrivimou,' Arana told me through our connection. I lifted my head, unchecked tears running down my cheeks.

"We'll be more gentle." The remorse in Rorc's voice broke my heart. He felt it was his fault, when it was all mine.

"No, you're not to blame. That male is responsible, and he will pay." His tone chilled me to the bone. I loved the sentiment, but it would get us nowhere. The General was back on Earth, and we were in space. No one would punish him for his actions. But I didn't want to talk about that.

"Can you read my mind too?" I joked, trying to change the subject.

My Admiral laughed at that, and the vibration went straight to my core. "No, but I can read your face, little one."

"What did we do that triggered that memory?" Mes asked. His clinical tone, oddly enough, helped me to further calm down.

Arana answered before I could. "The trigger was my hand on her back pushing her down. I'm sorry, monakrivimou. It won't happen again. I'll be more careful."

At that, I broke down—the floodgates opened, and I started sobbing like my soul was being torn from my body. I was damaged. What was I doing with these alpha males that they'd have to watch how they touched me, alas they triggered a panic attack? I was so selfish, thinking I could keep them. They would get tired of me not being able to satisfy their dominant natures. The ones I knew they were already suppressing because they thought I was breakable. And maybe they were right. How long before they dumped me, and how would I survive it when I was already so attached?

"Stop!" Mes's authoritative voice felt like a whip.

I cringed, but my body obeyed, and soon my sobs quieted.

"My love, it kills us to feel the pain that poor excuse for a male has caused you," he said as he used a cloth to dry my face. "Let us extract the seed of doubt he planted in your mind." He kissed my eyelids. "Let us take the pain away." He kissed the tip of my nose. "Let us replace the bad memories with beautiful ones," he finished, and claimed my lips, blowing air on the dying embers, reigniting the flames within me.

"You are what we need, monakrivimou. No other female exists for us, but you. Never fear us leaving you. There is no chance of that happening…ever," Arana seductively whispered in my ear the words I longed to hear before his lips softly bit the crook of my neck—a promise of what was to come—throwing fuel onto the fire that was burning me from the inside out.

Rorc pulled me from Mes, breaking our kiss. "All the riches of the universe cannot compare to how precious you are to us, little one," he said, and pressed his lips to mine. "You hold parts of our souls." He nibbled my chin. "You brighten our darkness, and bring us peace. You are our safe haven." He grazed his teeth over my throat and along my collarbone. "Even if the only liberty we were afforded was to hold you, we would do it forever," he whispered, and pulled my nipple into the cavern of his mouth, turning the blaze consuming me into a roaring inferno.

My mates had stopped my tears. They had given me the words that were a healing balm to my damaged soul. They surrounded me with love in my most vulnerable moment. They wound their way into my heart, and they awakened a hunger in my body nobody could sate but them.

"I need you," I said, and this time I wasn't ashamed to admit it, nor afraid to surrender to them.

They maneuvered closer to the side of the bed, and Mes remained standing so that I could take him in my mouth without having to lay flat on top of Rorc, but while leaning on Arana's chest. Their wandering fingers—over my breasts, over my clit—played my body like a fine-tuned instrument.

This was it; we would complete the Mating Ritual. I was ready, moaning loudly and panting heavily. God! They had me on the edge, about to orgasm, and they hadn't even started moving yet.

"You won't come yet, Mate." Mes's order went straight to my clit, making my insides clench and his two Pair-bonds groan.

It had the opposite effect of the one he'd wanted. He noticed, and he grabbed my chin between his thumb and pointer. He was not as gentle, but I didn't mind at all. I wanted to get over my PTSD; I wanted my mates to freely enjoy my body without the threat of a panic attack hanging over our heads. But I also knew it would take time.

"Open your mouth."

I really loved Mes's dominant side. I did as he asked, and he slowly fed me his cock. His taste exploded in my mouth—it was delicious and reminded me of dark chocolate, rich, decadent. I was sure the men on Earth did not taste like that, from what I had heard.

Without warning, they started moving in unison and I screamed around Mes's shaft. The sensation was so intense—the feeling of being painfully full had me teetering on the cliff's edge.

Their every thrust was laced with reverence; their every touch was laced with love. Happy tears pooled in my eyes. This was what I thought I'd never have, what I'd almost given up on.

Grunts, moans, growls, and rugged breathing intertwined, composing a unique symphony, all our own. They increased the tempo. Their movements became unsynchronized, matched the turmoil in my core, and fed the power of the tsunami waiting to be unleashed.

They pistoned into me a few more times before Arana suddenly withdrew completely.

Before I had time to protest he plunged into my pussy, squeezing in next to Rorc, and stretching me to limits I didn't know I had. The wave that had been building in strength crashed ashore, propelling me into the ether as I exploded into a thousand pieces. I had never felt anything like it. I was flying high when Arana bent and latched onto the spot where my neck met my shoulder. His sharper than usual fangs broke my skin, the momentary pain adding to my pleasure, intensifying my orgasm to a whole different level. I felt them all freeze—the quiet before the storm—before their cocks constricted, then thickened even more, and spurted their seed inside me. The burn of being stretched to the max, along with Mes's addictive taste, prolonged my climax. Yet he only gave me a little bit, before he pulled out of my mouth.

I was lost in a haze of continuous pleasure, when I registered the fact that he had not come like my other two mates. I was about to tell him I wanted more, when he took Arana's place. The newest invasion threw me screaming into another orgasm.

After what seemed like forever, my spasms subsided, and Rorc—along with Mes—withdrew from me. Somewhere along the way, I had closed my eyes, and as I opened them again, I saw the silver line—now even more pronounced than before—uniting us in a circle. Simultaneously, I heard their awed voices in my head, and a stream of emotions flooded into me.

As one, my mates turned and looked at me, their expressions full of awe.

'I can hear you, I can feel you,' Rorc said through our bond.

'Our treasure,' Mes added adoringly.

'Mate.' Such a small word packed such a deep meaning. Arana suddenly tensed, and I felt the other two stand at attention, equally alert.

"What is it?" I asked.

Did they regret their decision?

Arana stepped back and within the blink of an eye, Beast stood in his place.

Then I felt it—a burning sensation starting in my toes and my fingers, it kept flowing upward, the heat intensifying to unbearable levels, making me cry out. I stretched my arms, trying to ease the ache, and saw the fur erupting from my skin. I felt terrified that I would lose myself.

'Don't fight the Change, monakrivimou,' Arana begged me.

He was scared, so were Rorc and Mes. This had never happened before. Their fear almost made me panic when I heard her, Dawn.

I will protect you. Don't be afraid. We are one.

I had chosen my mates, this life, my sabertooth. I was not a reneger.

I exhaled slowly and let go. I found myself on the floor. Shiny silver fur covering my limbs. Breathing hard, I tried to stand on my four paws. The sensation was disorienting. I was there, but I didn't have control of this body, not exactly. Dawn was there, next to me. I tried to take charge, to make us stand, but we collapsed in a heap on the floor.

'Let her take the reins, Mate,' Arana guided me.

It wasn't easy to let go completely, but it worked because we were now standing. My sabertooth was so elated she roared and turned aggressively toward our mates.

Sting...sting...sting... she trilled to herself, preparing herself for something I didn't understand.

What are you doing! I berated her.

They can't handle us, Dawn hissed.

What? Haven't you seen their massive bodies? Of course they do! I yelled at her, suddenly afraid of all the power coursing through this form. Stupid cat!

No, not yet, she said, and attacked Mes, who was closest to us. She pounced on him, our weight pushing him to the floor, our tail connecting to his neck, before Beast threw us off him and jumped on our back. She tried to dislodge him from on top of us, but she was inexperienced, this body too new and uncoordinated. He maneuvered us beneath him and stood above us with his wicked claws on our belly. When Dawn snarled, he clamped his teeth on our neck. The burning sensation indicating his thirteen-inch long, knifelike canines had grazed our skin.

My crazed sabertooth didn't like it, and she used her back paw to tear into Arana's back leg. He growled and clenched his jaw, squeezing our airway, making his point, but not really hurting us. Dawn seemed as stubborn as I was, so I took the reins back and the words, *'We submit,'* flowed through our bond to him.

Arana immediately let us go and roared so loud we wanted to cover our too-sensitive ears with our paws.

Rorc—who'd run to Mes's side—yelled, "What the fuck, Kali?" drawing my attention to my mate lying unmoving on the floor.

I crumbled inside as I watched my Healer's fiery-red color slowly being tainted by black.

Fear, unlike any I had experienced, gripped me as his breathing turned labored and his heartbeats got weaker with every pulse.

What have I done?

A QUEEN'S FIGHT

RORC

The ever expanding feeling in my chest was almost too much, but I was fully awake, energized, and at peace…complete for the first time ever. I glanced at my Pair-bonds to see if they were experiencing the same thing. Awestruck admiration showed on their faces.

Not wanting to break the spell, I spoke through our bond—the path unobstructed forevermore—*'I can hear you, I can feel you.'*

'Our treasure,' Mes said.

'Mate.' Arana added, before he suddenly stiffened.

Alarm bells rang through our newfound connection.

"What is it?" Kali asked.

Arana didn't answer—instead stepped back and shifted.

Our mate shivered, her skin suddenly too hot to the touch. Terror emanated from her pores as she stood up and staggered away from us.

Fur erupted from her skin and Arana pleaded with her to not fight the Change.

I had expected the shift to be fast, painless, similar to the Saberian's, but I should have known better.

Watching her bones breaking and reshaping was terrifying, but I was unable to stop it, and I couldn't make it go faster either.

Then I heard her sabertooth say, *'I will protect you. Don't be afraid. We are one.'* And her message settled the roiling in my stomach. Kali would survive.

Soon, in the place of my mate stood a magnificent sabertooth. Her silver-colored fur seemed like a solid color until I looked closer and noticed it was decorated with faint white spots and stripes. Her knifelike teeth were long and lethal, as were the claws protruding from her paws. She was smaller than Beast, but equally deadly, and breathtaking in her wild beauty.

Light-gray eyes—filled with cunning intelligence—measured Mes and me. A slight chill, accompanied by the prickling of my scalp, was my only warning before the female sabertooth attacked Mes.

Arana intercepted her, but her intent had been clear.

Our mate was rejecting us, and I was next.

Agony that had nothing to do with my physical body, but everything to do with my soul being shredded to pieces by her claws, brought me to my knees.

Our mate was rejecting us.

Mes moaned in pain. Sweat gleamed on his face, yet he remained perfectly still. Black streaks spread like the forks of a lightning across his neck. The realization made me go slack. She wasn't only rejecting us. She wanted to kill us.

The betrayal rocked me to my core, and I went on autopilot. First, I had to get my brother out of here. I'd figure out the next step later.

I rushed to his side, but try as I might, I couldn't keep my anger inside me. "What the fuck, Kali!"

Arana, who had rocked the palace with his roar, shifted and said, "She needs to heal Mes," before placing a restraining hand on my shoulder, and providing me with the perfect target to unleash my fury. Because even in my current state, I would never hurt a female—not even one that wanted to kill me—but my Pair-bond was fair game.

I sprang up, shifted my weight, and threw an uppercut at the Saberian that didn't connect because he had been expecting my rage and jumped backward.

'What have I done?' Kali's voice invaded my mind, draining my energy, stealing my fury, and leaving me bare.

She approached Mes and started licking the spot she had wounded. I stood, unmoving, a silent sentry, ready to protect the Healer if she so much as twitched a muscle the wrong way. In a few ticks, his breathing eased, and when the female sabertooth pulled back, the color on Mes's neck was back to normal.

"Shift," Arana ordered. His low voice carried the alpha order effortlessly.

Paying them no mind, I helped him get on his feet. He staggered but straightened, then opened his arms. When Kali hesitated, he closed the distance between them and folded her in his embrace.

"It's okay, my love. Don't berate yourself. It is what it is," he crooned, comforting her…unlike me.

A primal urge to destroy something rocked me. Unable to stay in the same room with them—afraid of what would come out of my mouth—I spun and left, needing to find a way to cope with what had just happened.

I sensed Arana more than heard him follow me into an empty

chamber—the newly-formed bond providing a beacon leading to my mates. "You're treading on thin ice, Saberian," I warned.

"Get your head out of your ass, Wravukian," he growled.

I crossed my arms over my chest. "Your wish was granted. If you're here to gloat, thanks, but I'll pass."

"I'd love to knock some sense into your hard head, but I don't have the time because our mate is hurting, and you're making it worse." Each word from his mouth rubbed salt into my wound.

Stomping straight into his personal space, I yelled in his face, "She rejected us! She rejected me!"

Saying it aloud brought a fresh wave of agony to the surface, and for a moment I wanted to hurt him too, to make him feel like I did, to make him understand.

I wouldn't, but it was gratifying to see his body stiffen and his jaw clench at my close proximity. The alpha didn't like challenges. Too bad for him I wasn't the beta type.

"She didn't reject you, Rorc," he said, and waited for the meaning to sink in.

"Then—"

He interrupted by dropping a bomb on me. "She needs to Change you."

Shaking my head in denial, I stepped backward and turned away from him.

It couldn't be. Changing meant I'd lose everything I had worked so hard for my whole life. Wravukians didn't allow hybrids in positions of power. I would have to step down and surrender the control of my fleet.

Kali had asked Arana what being his mates made us. He had effectively distracted her, but not me, for I knew the answer. A Queen's mate ruled alongside her. They might have lost their females, but the traditions remained. He was the King. His mates would rule by his side. Saberians, though, were a closed-community species and would never accept half-Wravukian, half-Saberian males in such roles.

"She needs to Change you, Rorc," he repeated, interrupting my thoughts. "The desire is consuming her. Are all those reasons that are crossing your mind right now enough to let your mate experience agony?"

"How would you feel if you had to become something else? If you were told you'd never be able to shift again."

The reply was immediate, but it didn't come from whom I expected. The voice was gravelly and animalistic in nature, and was in my mind. *'If I had to give my life for Arana to be with our mate, I'd do it without hesitation,'* Beast said, then Arana added solemnly, "There's nothing we wouldn't sacrifice for a life with our mate."

Was I strong enough to do this?

When she drank from the cup with my blood in it during our Mating Ceremony, she'd known it would change her.

Only now comprehending the magnitude of her sacrifice for us, my respect for her grew, along with my determination to let go of my past.

She was my present and my future. I could do no less than what I had requested of her. "Let's go back to our mate. I've got some begging to do."

He snickered and clapped my back. "That you do."

In no time we were back in our chamber. Kali was still in Mes's arms, but seeing the evidence that I'd added to the pain in her swollen eyes and pink nose was hard.

She started apologizing, but I wanted none of that. I picked her up and silenced her with a kiss. When I pulled back, her wide eyes were full of questions.

"Kali, I'm sorry. I know I'll make mistakes, and you will have to be patient with me and my overprotective nature, but I promise I'll only make them once, and I'll try to curb my dominant side," I vowed, meaning every word.

"I didn't ask you to change, Rorc. I only want you to meet me in the middle," she said, her voice raspier than usual. "I tried to stop Dawn, bu—"

Arana cut her off. "She gave you her name?"

Kali nodded, and the Saberian hunched his shoulders in defeat.

"I knew there was a possibility that this might happen, but I wasn't sure. We've never Changed anyone, monakrivimou. This is not your fault," he said.

He was still withholding information. "Explain," I demanded, and he bristled at the command, but complied.

"Beast is different. He is…as equally present as me." He hesitated, unsure how to describe the situation properly. "Most sabertooths emerge when someone is in need of protection, or when we fight. They rarely converse with our form, and are happy with whatever time they get to be in control of our body. They adopt the same wants and needs their male has. Sabertooths like Beast, like Dawn, are the exception."

His explanation hit a nerve with Kali, her body stiffened in my arms, then she straightened her spine, lifted her chin, and declared, "There's nothing wrong with her."

"No, Mate. There's nothing wrong with her. She's just different." Arana was quick to amend. "The compulsion to Change Mes and Rorc is hers. It is the way Saberian females claimed their males, by biting and embedding their DNA in them—of course your bite has other repercussions. I thought with you being a different species, the Saberian side would not be as dominant as your Human side. But I was mistaken," he chuckled darkly, "and Saberian females—even hybrid ones—need Saberian mates—even hybrid ones."

Kali defending her sabertooth, a being she hadn't known for long, was a testament to her character. Proof that she was protective of those she considered hers.

In such a short time, she had become the most important person in my life. I would do anything for her, even give my life for her. Changing would be a small price to pay, and there was no reason to delay the inevitable. I claimed her lips again, getting lost in her haven just for a moment before I pulled back. When she opened her eyes, I told her, "You hold my soul. You're my present and my future. I've chosen you, and it's my honor to have you claim me back."

"I'm sorry," she whispered, and her sorrowful tone pierced my heart.

"Nothing to be sorry for. Shift in my arms." I injected alpha command into my voice. She needed to understand this was my choice.

She obeyed, and I found myself eye to eye with Dawn. Her two front paws over my shoulders. She was heavy, but I could handle her. Her gaze was locked on mine as I explored her body. Her canines were long, strong, and could tear chunks of flesh in a flash. Her silvery hued fur was softer than the silkiest web spun by our Araneae; I ran my fingers through it, and she purred. I looked at Arana when I felt the hard surface of her skin.

"She is equipped with our invulnerable armor," he confirmed, and another weight lifted off my shoulders.

Our mate wasn't so fragile anymore. "Beautiful. Strong," I praised her.

She licked my cheek, her rough tongue scratching my skin before she pressed her pink nose on the sensitized spot. Focused on her playful antics, I didn't see her stinger coming, but I felt it. Such a light sting was deceiving because as the toxin started dispersing from my neck to the rest of my body, it was as if liquid fire flowed in my veins, consuming my power, incapacitating me. I staggered under her weight and fell on my knees, then sprawled on the floor.

All the while she kept staring at me, waiting for something.

My breathing turned labored, my lungs no longer cooperating. My chest felt as if it were caving in, the organs threatening to stop working. My eyes closed of their own accord, and yet I didn't lose my faith in her.

When darkness threatened to swallow me whole, I felt her wet tongue lapping at my neck. A cool sensation followed every lick, and as my skin absorbed the anti-venom, the relief was instantaneous.

Satisfied with her work, she soon stopped, stepped back and shifted.

She was such a beautifully alluring sight to behold, even while she fidgeted on her feet, unsure of my response. She needn't worry because one emotion ruled over all others.

I got up and approached her. "I sense your trepidation through our bond—its acrid scent is offensive. You're scared of my reaction...you shouldn't be. Feel what you do to me, little one." I took her hand, and placed it on top of my throbbing cock.

Her eyes widened and her lips parted. Desire, raw and unfiltered, coursed through me, and I would have acted on it if there hadn't been a knock on the damn door.

Instead of allowing them entrance while we were naked, Arana crossed the room—his uniform emerging from his skin and covering his body— and opened the door slightly, blocking the view into the room with his bulk.

"I'm sorry to disturb you, King Arana, but this came, requiring your immediate attention."

He accepted the holo-projector with a thank you and closed the door.

An urgent message for him could only come from one person—the warrior he'd left in charge of Saber—and I doubted it carried good news.

Both I and Mes triggered the nanites and donned our uniforms.

My other Pair-bond set the transmitter on the table and activated it. Urien's image formed. His face looked haggard, with a long, newly-healed scar marring the skin under his left eye, across his cheek, down his neck, and disappearing under his uniform.

"Arana, you need to get your mates and come back." No preambles, no fancy words, straight to the point.

The situation was serious.

My Pair-bond scrutinized the warrior's appearance, appraising the damage. He wanted to ask Urien who had hurt him, but knew the male was too proud and would be insulted, so instead he asked, "What happened?"

His gruff tone hid the true emotions—pain mixed with guilt—coursing through his mind and bleeding into our bond.

"Without you here, we've lost our anchor. I'm not sure how long we're going to last, Lethe claimed a handful of warriors already…"

"There's more," Arana guessed, when Urien stopped talking and turned his gaze downcast.

"The announcement about your mates wasn't received well. The

Western and Southern Territories have cut off all communication. I've gathered the Royal Guards and as many Elite warriors as I could in preparation for your arrival."

Arana cursed while my wheels started spinning.

Wravukians were a blessed species, most of us born with a powerful gift—some, with more than one. Mes's gift was extraordinary healing abilities, whereas mine was strategizing. A road map with the right courses of action existed in my head, and it unfolded, revealing them to me in times of need. It was the reason why I'd climbed the military ranks and had been put in charge of my own fleet at such a young age, and it was why I'd never lost a battle.

My Pair-bond had a fight on his hands, but this time he wasn't alone. He had us by his side.

"One last thing," the Saberian said, "the Elders requested a Queen's Fight." His shoulders sagged. "Your mate's sabertooth against mine."

Kali, who had activated her uniform and crept up behind Arana, circled his waist, placed a loving kiss on his chest, and looked boldly at the hologram.

"Then tell them I'll fight."

DETERMINED TO WIN

KALI

"When other women get married, they get a honeymoon. I get mated, and what do I get? A fight. Maybe I ought to rethink my decision..." I tapped my lips with my finger, pretending to be in deep thought and hoping to distract them from their foul mood.

Rorc put his foot down, though, the moment the transmission ended, as if I hadn't spoken at all. "No. Just, no."

"Your Elders requested a newborn sabertooth fight your best warrior?" Mes's scary-low voice sent chills racing down my spine. We all felt his darkness swirling, unfurling its feelers, demanding to be let out.

My attempt was an utter fail.

Arana sighed. "I'm ashamed to admit that it was our hubris that brought about our downfall. We were an undefeatable force, and we'd thought we always would be...we paid for that arrogance with our females' lives. Many believe hybrid offspring will be weaklings, that they won't have sabertooths. They are afraid of the unknown.

Kali can prove them wrong. She can give them hope. She only needs to rise to the challenge."

My Saberian mate exuded calmness, but his protective instincts ran rampant under the surface.

Arana had told me I couldn't get pregnant, and since the matter hadn't been discussed again, I'd put it aside as a moot point. Maybe he knew something his Elders didn't. Besides, we were different species, how could we possibly procreate? At the moment, we had more important issues to worry about, so I let it go.

"She evoked a Sacred Bond, for Creator's sake! Isn't that enough to convince your people?" Rorc didn't want to risk me, but he was too upset to realize there was no reward without risk. By fighting, I'd help countless males. Those warriors, even though I didn't know them yet, were my people already. If I could lighten their burdens until they found their women, I'd gladly do so.

'She will fight,' Beast declared—offended by the idea alone that his female wouldn't be brave enough to confront another warrior.

My big bad Wravukian mates were struggling with their emotions.

I'd expected the Mating Ritual to strengthen the connection that had started forming when the Sacred Line connected us. But I hadn't been prepared for the constant flow of information from the three of them. My mind used to be a quiet place and now was close to overloading, making my head ache.

"It's not to the death. The weaker one will submit to the dominant one, and the fight will end," Arana patiently explained. "Fighting Urien—an honorable male I trust with my life—will determine whether she's worthy to them. The decision will be final and no one will contest it. It will prove to them she's strong enough to protect our offspring. That she's strong enough to lead by my side."

My other two mates didn't find that answer reassuring at all.

To me it made perfect sense, but I should probably find a way to change the subject before the situation escalated further.

Rorc—at his wits end and spoiling for a fight—hit his fist on the table and sprang up, flinging the chair across the room in doing so. "There has to be another way."

Although Arana chose the diplomatic route—ignoring the Admiral's temper, for the most part—Beast wasn't as forgiving. His snarl—in direct proportion to Rorc's outburst—rattled in the warrior's chest. My Saberian mate rose from the chair slowly, but didn't bite the bait dangling in front of him. "Mes, have the results come in yet?

"Yes. My team didn't find any trace of the virus. The planet is safe," he said reluctantly, then he furrowed his brows in confusion. "What is a honeymoon, Kali?" he asked, but I waved the answer away. I wasn't serious earlier.

"It doesn't feel like nothing. Explain," he persisted.

"Married couples go on a trip to celebrate their new status and enjoy each other. It's usually a period of harmony immediately following marriage...but it's not important. We have other plans."

"We'll take you on a honeymoon, my love," Mes promised, and my heart did a back flip.

Stupid organ.

A smirk played on the Arana's lips and his eyes—full of naughtiness—sparkled when they landed on mine. "Then there are two things we need to complete before we're ready to depart."

I raised my hand in the air like a schoolkid. "Oh! Oh! I know, I know! Can I say?"

"Your warrior said there's an uproar brewing. It's one thing to have our mate going against one warrior; it's a whole other to have her defending herself against a plethora of battle-hardened Saberians."

'Party pooper,' I told Rorc through our connection, and the incredulous look he gave me had me laughing out loud, to the point my abs hurt. I heard faint chuckles coming from the other two guys as well.

My purple-skinned alien turned his brooding gaze my way. "This is not a laughing matter, Kali," he admonished.

"No, it is not. Arana was going to say that we'd have to mate for me to let your sabertooths free, but if you and Mes don't want me, I'll find someone who does." I turned to go to Arana, but before I could move an inch, I was snatched back, and Rorc's lips came crashing down on mine.

Much better.

Two growls and a chuckle were their replies to my inner thought. But I needed to make something crystal clear, and what better time than this moment?

'If you think you can stop me from fighting this time...you're wrong, Mates. These warriors are mine now, and I'll fight for them, the same way you'd do anything to protect them; the same way Mes would do anything to heal them; the same way Arana would do anything for their well-being.'

My words hit home.

Rorc broke the kiss and rested his forehead on mine. "It isn't easy, Kali, to knowingly put you in danger. I was too late to save my sister. What if I'm too late when you need me?"

Now we were boiling down to his main fear. Images of his sister's broken body filled his mind, and I felt his struggle. It took tremendous courage for him to admit what he'd just told me.

I wrapped my arms around his waist and hugged him tight, willing the ghosts of his past away. "Sweetheart, I'm not your sister—"

"I know." He was quick to assure me, hugging me back.

"I'm not helpless. I know it's not easy for you"—his body shuddered in my arms—"but you can't live your life worrying about something happening to me. Bad things happen all the time... without rhyme or reason. We can only make the best of the time we have. Enjoy the quiet, and equip ourselves as much as possible for the worse." I was about to tread dangerous waters, but if someone or three someones were worth it, it was my mates. "I don't need you to protect me." I chuckled, remembering the wee incident of being abducted. "Especially not now that I have Dawn," I clarified.

When silence followed my declaration, I felt like wilting inside. Apparently, Wravukian females didn't have my rebellious nature. Would he really be able to accept me as I am, or would we, in a year or two, end up constantly at each other's throats?

Mes remained suspiciously silent.

I guess he felt the same way as Rorc, but why didn't my own mates believe in me? Then again, my own father didn't believe in me, so how could I expect two aliens to do so?

Arana came to my rescue when my mind threatened to dive into dark memories I didn't wish to revisit. "You are strong, monakrivimou, and Dawn takes after you. I'll train with her and with my stubborn Pair-bonds, but first..." He never finished the sentence because he plucked me from Rorc's arms and took me to bed, effectively ending all conversation.

Two weeks had passed since we'd received the message from Urien, and many more had followed. Arana had decided we'd stay on Wravuk for as many days as possible so that he could prepare us, before it was absolutely necessary for us to return. Each day started with our animals training, and each night ended with us between the sheets.

I had thoroughly enjoyed the process of releasing my Wravukian mates' sabertooths, Brute—Rorc's and Savage—Mes's. As it turned out, they were as vocal as Beast and Dawn, and made Rorc and Mes's lives difficult. Unfortunately, when it came to me, they proved they could work together just fine, and I hadn't been able to win our battle for dominance. They had ganged up on me… not that I'd expected anything different. Now I carried their marks and their bites, but they carried mine as well.

Slowly, excitement for the upcoming duel filled me, and it was a great distraction from the cloud hovering over us. Since our discussion two weeks ago, doubt had started creeping in, and I had resorted to what I always did. I had begun distancing myself bit by bit. It was the only way to protect my heart, although it was possibly too late already. I knew I should tell them how I feel, but what if it didn't make a difference? I didn't think I could live the rest of my life with two males who didn't trust my judgment. Maybe I'd bring it up after we settled on Saber. I didn't want anything to divert my attention from the looming fight, and Dawn and I hadn't exactly managed to coordinate all the way. Both of us wanted to take the lead—I'd tell her I had experience, and she'd answer that she was the predator. We were at an impasse and it stressed me out, but I was determined to win.

THE ELDERS

KALI

To say the trip back to Saber was tense would be putting it mildly. Rorc was short-tempered, and his crew paid the price; Mes disappeared into the Healers' Bay, wanting to reexamine the samples from Saber, and I hadn't seen him since; and Arana became more closed off the closer we got to his home planet.

Our bond was a chaotic place during this time, and their behavior was the cherry on top. I was in a bad mood; then, after thinking about it some more, I got angry because I had given them this power over me. I felt vulnerable, raw; by loving them, I had armed them with the perfect way to hurt me. So I spent the better part of the journey sleeping, just to avoid the uncertainty that had started plaguing me, and also because I was feeling extremely tired and a bit nauseated. Dawn didn't particularly enjoy being on the ship either. Space travel it seemed, didn't agree with us. But it would soon be over, as we were fast approaching our destination.

I was glued to the viewscreen inside Rorc's quarters.

The Pyxis System had two suns—a smaller one that emitted a

turquoise color, and a bigger one that bathed the globes in a golden-yellow hue. Saber had four moons orbiting around the planet, all very close to each other. The planet's nearly spherical shape was similar to Earth's—but where our planet's seas were blue, Saber's were deep violet.

So absorbed by the view, I didn't hear Arana approach, and I started when his arms encircled my waist. He chuckled and whispered, "Welcome home, monakrivimou," before placing a kiss on top of my head.

"It's beautiful."

"It was a bleak place for countless rotations, but you're going to change that."

"No pressure there," I joked, and saw his smile reflect on the viewscreen.

Beast purred, and I pressed my back to his front to feel the vibrations. Dawn answered him, basking in our mate's warmth.

It was crazy how one minute I was seeing the colorful orb from outer space, and within the next five we'd landed on its surface. But here I was waiting—shifting from one foot to the other—for the hatch to open so I could step out onto my new home. Arana had told us Saberians were a technologically advanced species, their impenetrable planetary defense system attesting to his claim, and even impressing my Wravukian mates. Then he went on to explain that the planet was divided into five Territories, and each one had a leader who to saw to day-to-day matters but deferred to the King for major decisions. There were events that took place every rotation that brought all the males together, but for the most part, they lived apart. These people enjoyed a simpler way of life, choosing to live in harmony with nature by making caves their homes and hardly ever using technology.

I was curious to see Arana's residence, but I'd be lying if I said I wasn't a little intimidated by what I'd heard. I, along with the rest of the human race, relied heavily on technology to make our everyday lives easier. I might be a hybrid now, part-Saberian part-human, but suddenly going without it sounded a bit scary. When he'd sensed my trepidation—it was freaky how strong the mental link between us had become in such a short amount of time—he was quick to assure me that the palace was equipped with the latest gadgets, and we'd stay there as long as needed to help transition to their way of life.

Dawn was antsy too, wanting to explore, but we couldn't do that just yet. The Royal Guards would greet us, and then escort us to the palace because the Elders had requested a meeting. So as the hatch opened and the dust settled, we marched toward a new—to me —world.

My eyes widened as I took in the fifty or so Saberians waiting in formation to welcome us, and I had to do a double take because it seemed like they were naked. But on closer inspection, I noticed that their uniforms were the shade of their skin, with stripes and spots too, but thankfully no dangling bits were obvious, although most were outlined. I felt my cheeks burn. They were all similarly built, but their colors ranged, and it made for a striking sight. God had definitely been liberal in the good-looks department because they were gorgeous.

My three mates stopped in their tracks and spun to face me. *Oopsie! Was I projecting?* With flattened lips and flaring nostrils, they seemed a little bit green around the edges.

I grinned and walked around them, only to have my way blocked again.

"Really? You're going to make me say it?" My question was met with silence.

This is fun! Who would have known that my three panty-melting mates were the jealous type.

When I took too long for their liking to answer, they snarled.

I sighed dramatically and told them, in my most innocent voice, "What woman in her right mind would need more than three cavemen?" I put my hands behind my back and shook my head. "Not me…I'm not looking for any more mates." Then, to emphasize my point, I stepped backward, retreating.

My reaction seemed to satisfy them because they turned as one and got off the spaceship. I grinned, enjoying their bout of jealousy, and followed at a more leisurely pace, wanting to observe before I engaged.

I looked up at the pale minty-green color of the sky. I had been expecting a light-blue atmosphere because Mes had assured me the air was breathable for humans. So seeing this soft hue was surprising, and oddly calming. When I looked at the ground, I noticed that everyone had two shadows, which made sense given the two suns that had just risen above the horizon. My eyes wandered farther into the surrounding desert, and I was a bit disappointed that the sand was exactly like ours, when almost everything else was different. But then a deep-violet expanse, signifying a large body of water on our left, drew my gaze, making me wonder if it was safe to swim in. The palatial grounds were behind us, and according to Arana's description of the forest and cave system, the Main Territory we would call home was on our right. I refocused on the Saberians, most of whom carried fresh scars on their faces or necks, some extending beneath their clothes. They were currently stealing glances at me while they waited to embrace and greet their leader properly. I paid them no mind. I was the shiny new toy and their curiosity was endearing.

There was one male in particular, though, with eyes so dark they appeared black, who had cocked his head and furrowed his eyebrows. He wasn't sneaking peeks like the rest of them, but staring openly. Besides the menacing appearance, I wasn't getting stalker vibes, so I decided to ignore him for now.

But what I couldn't overlook was the dark-gray aura that clung to all of them. It was tinged with sadness and despair. It was denser around some and thinner around others. Was this what Arana had called Lethe? I'd have to ask him later because it broke my heart to feel the pain of these honorable males—even if they didn't acknowledge it. I vowed to myself that I would find a way to help them because the image of these males about to shatter into a thousand pieces, like they were made of glass, wound itself into my heart.

The change in my vision—the ability to see things obscured to the human eye—was Dawn's gift. It'd take me some time to get used to this new ability, but when she was close to the surface, like now, I had no choice but to adapt. My sabertooth, on the other hand, was busy cataloging all the new scents around us when another wave of nausea hit me.

'Easy with the sniffing, girl. It's making me sick.'

She didn't mind averting her attention to something else. Soon she was picturing herself jumping into the dunes decorating the desert. I laughed inwardly at her antics. Her paws had never stepped on sand, and her fur had never been wet by the sea; she longed to do both. She also hadn't met any other sabertooths besides our males. She was looking forward to her time with our body and her excitement was contagious.

I was absorbed by her shenanigans when I reached my mates, but when the conversation suddenly ceased, I looked up; the Saberians that had come here to welcome us knelt, bowed, and tilted their heads.

"Um…" Was I supposed to say or do something?

Our bond had its perks because Arana felt my unease. "Rise," he said, especially happy with the way his people welcomed me. "Warriors, when I left Saber, I hadn't expected to return. I was going on a wild chase to find an unknown alien female…and the truth is, I failed. I got captured, tortured, and was very close to dying when the Wravukians found and saved me. They didn't do only that. They found my mate as well." He paused, and scrutinized each and every male. "Some of you are hanging on by a thread. Don't let Lethe claim you, for there is hope. I want you to meet my Sacred Mates, Kali, Rorc, and Mes." Hushed tones filled the air. "The Creator hasn't forgotten us. Kali is a Human from Earth, and the place she comes from has potential mates. You only need to be patient a little while longer."

Cries of joy were accompanied by manly embraces, before everyone settled down again.

"King, the Elders are waiting," Urien reminded us. And along with the one that had been staring, and another that was even taller than my mates, he headed toward the palace. His orange uniform—dark in places, lighter in others—with the forest-green stripes and spots caught my eye as it came alive when he started walking. Urien in motion gave the false impression that he was on fire, and it was quite a sight.

"We'd better get going then," my Saberian replied, and took my hand before we followed along.

Everyone's mood changed from joyous to sober in the blink of an eye. Rorc and Mes helped form a wall around me. There was so much testosterone in the air, I could almost taste it.

'Is this really necessary?' I said through our private path of communication.

Arana chuckled. *'Urien is more overprotective than a sabertooth with offspring.'*

'I feel eyes on us, yet I can't see them.' There was an edge to Rorc's voice.

'Their darkness calls to mine,' Mes added.

My Healer was good at downplaying his emotions. In the future I'd need to keep a closer eye on him, but for now I embraced him in a one-arm hug until I felt the tension leave him. He thanked me and kissed the top of my head.

'Camouflage is one of our defense mechanisms. Our skin changes color so we can blend in. There are warriors spread out across the dunes. You'll learn in time to identify a sabertooth in hiding,' Arana explained. *'There's nothing to fear, Mates. We are stronger than them. They only want to see their new Queen.'*

'Well, they might be able to hide their bodies, but they can't hide their darknes—'

My Saberian mate cut me off by saying aloud, "You can see it?"

"If by it, you're referring to the gray shadow with feelers around it, then yes," I replied, and felt more than saw the warriors fidget uncomfortably.

"There was a single entry, a few centuries old, in the Elders' Athenaeum describing Lethe—the end for Saberians and madness for their sabertooths—with those exact words," he said.

Everybody went quiet.

Awesome. New planet, new species, and I still managed to stand out like a sore thumb. I wished the ground would open up and swallow me whole.

Arana lifted me in his arms, afraid my wish would become reality. "You were never meant to blend in, monakrivimou. You're unique. You're the gift the Creator blessed us with." His timbre was low and carried admiration. His lips, soft and warm, claimed mine before he reluctantly let me down.

He'd effectively jumbled my thoughts. It was unfair that they had such an effect on me. I'd never get anything done. But on second thought, did it even matter? It wasn't as if I had a lot of things on my plate anyway.

The palace on Saber was nothing like the one on Wravuk, except maybe in size. Both were enormous, but where one was ostentatious, the other was plain; where that one was easily accessible, this one was in a remote location.

The fortified gatehouse was the only entrance I could see across the length of the light-beige stone curtain walls surrounding the palatial grounds, and once we passed it, the area within seemed deserted.

"I remember this place bustling with life…this is where the merchants used to be," Mes said. I looked at him questioningly and he explained, "My father was on official business with Arana's parents. Callibohr and I were little ourselves, but we had been allowed to wander the market under guard."

I gaped at him when his memory replayed in my mind's eye. "I didn't know we could do that."

He smiled. "It's one of my lesser gifts, love. Although in the past I needed to touch the person I was sharing something with…our bond seems to have amplified my talents."

"What's that?" I pointed at a stadium. It reminded me of pictures I'd once seen of the Colosseum.

"That's the Pit," Urien answered, "where we'll face each other in the Queen's Fight." He sounded so serious and put off, like he found fighting a woman distasteful.

"Don't worry, Urien," I said in a sugary voice. "Dawn says she'll go easy on you, as will I."

My comment sparked guffaws around me, while Arana clapped the warrior on the shoulder.

"You're in trouble, brother," he said, and Urien cursed under his breath.

My smile remained wide up until the moment we stepped into the palace.

There, just inside the entrance, the four Elders were waiting for us.

From their title, I'd been expecting males with extremely wrinkled skin, hunched backs, and walking sticks.

I was so off base it wasn't even funny. They could have passed for my father's age.

Their hair was either white or grayish. Their faces had a few wrinkles, but nothing showing they were several hundred years old, and their bodies—without an ounce of fat—would put many twenty-year-old athletes back on Earth to shame.

They weren't wearing uniforms, but a piece of cloth was draped over one shoulder and around their waists, showcasing the unusual skin tones and markings of this species.

The Elders bowed respectfully to their King, and he began the introductions. "Elders, with pride, I present to you my mates. Kali of the Earth, whom, as you've learned, I Turned. Meskiagkasher, Prince and Second to the Throne of Wravuk. And Rorc, Admiral of the Second Fleet of Wravuk."

Then the one with the purple markings, and skin the yellow color of hyacinth, said, "Arana, the Wravukians don't belong—"

The King interrupted him. "My Sacred Mates," he emphasized in an austere tone, "belong with me. Let us move into the dining chamber and discuss matters while eating." It was an order veiled as a suggestion—nobody dared disobey.

I thought the dining room was a bizarre choice for a meeting location—who could get food down when the tension was so thick?—but at the mention of eating, I realized I was hungry. And not just a little, but rather like I could scarf down a first serving, a second, and maybe a third as well.

My mates' chuckles echoed in my mind as Arana pulled a chair out for me before he took his own at the head of the table. Rorc sat to his right side, across from me, whereas Mes sat on my left.

The Elders followed suit as the guards left. Soon, some warriors returned and placed a variety of dishes on the table before leaving again. I looked at them and my mouth watered. No one was speaking, and no one was eating.

Too embarrassed to speak aloud, I asked my mates privately, *'What are we waiting for?'*

'For you to start eating, monakrivimou. Is everything to your liking?' Arana said.

'Well nobody told me that.' I needed to have a long conversation

about the rules and customs of this society, but with everything going on, there just wasn't enough time. I eyed my options. The meat smelled scrumptious, and thank God the cutlery was familiar because I had to taste it now. I put a big chunk on my plate and took a bite. My taste buds had an orgasm as the flavors exploded in my mouth.

The others, happy with whatever they saw on my expression, started placing food on their plates as well.

Once I'd had my fill—two servings of it—the Elder with magnetizing coppery eyes focused on me.

"I'm Srah," he said. "Your arrival brings hope back to my people. For that, I'm grateful and in your debt." His soft-spoken words wrapped me in a warm embrace, making me feel welcome.

The one with the darkest coloring present spoke next. His hair matched the midnight-blue tone of his skin, and the mercurial-toned markings on his body matched his eyes. "Kali of the Earth, I'm Nurn." He bowed his head, and I noticed the dark strands were peppered with silver ones. "Welcome to Saber. Our hope lies with you."

"Thank you," I replied, moved by their words. "I'll do everything in my power to help."

The Elder who had a long-healed scar marring the left side of his face pierced me with appraising eyes, but remained quiet.

"That's all well, female, but you're one and the Saberians are many," the fourth one said, looking down his nose at me.

Thanks for the vote of confidence! I thought, not knowing exactly how to feel about the lack of respect toward me, when my mates bristled with anger.

Dawn snarled her displeasure. *Easy, girl, some of them will like us, some won't. That's life.*

He's tainted. We should end him, she suggested.

Bloodthirsty kitten! I admonished; I could understand her desire to kill the bad guy, but even though I hadn't liked his personality, that didn't mean he was evil. *I'll think about it, but not now.*

"Arana, we understand the need for alien incubators. Our species must survive after all, so we need offspring"—*did he just call me an incubator?* Okay, maybe I should rethink my sabertooth's suggestion—"but you cannot possibly think we'll accept the two Wravukians merely because you say so." He finished in a voice equal parts unpleasant and annoying.

"Actually, Sciiti, my warriors will accept my Sacred Mates ruling by my side because I say so. Do you know why? Because I'm the King, and unless this is you challenging me for the throne, I don't want to hear you questioning my Pair-bonds." My Saberian male's low voice was ice-cold, there wasn't any love lost there it seemed, and his posture radiated fury as he got up and prowled toward the Elder, who was still sitting down. Arana bent over him, making Sciiti inch backward, hitting the back of the chair. "This female…is your Queen—"

"No she isn't. Not until she wins the fight," Sciiti hissed.

Arana ignored him because he was certain about the outcome of the fight. "If you disrespect her again, I promise you it'll be the last thing you do…this meeting is over."

I hadn't noticed, up to that point, that shadows weren't surrounding the Elders the same way they had the guards.

The moment Arana had threatened Sciiti—that was a name I wouldn't be forgetting any time soon—a black shadow exploded toward my mate, trying to wrap around him, but recoiling every time it made contact, until it finally dissipated.

What the heck was that?

YOU DON'T KNOW?

ARANA

He's challenged us one time too many! Beast snarled, pacing furiously within my mind's confines. *We need to punish him.*

Not yet. We need to keep it civil. I argued. Although I was eager to give my sabertooth the reins, I had to get Kali through the fight first. Afterward, I would deal with the warriors planning to usurp the throne.

As I stood over the Elder, the acrid scent of fear filled my nostrils. He was afraid. *Good.* "If you disrespect her again, I promise you it'll be the last thing you do." The threat was loud and clear in my voice, for I didn't want any misunderstandings. "This meeting is over," I said, and pulled back. The faster he was out of my sight, the better.

Suddenly, I felt Kali recoil. Had I scared her? She wasn't focused on me, though, but on Sciiti. *'Monakrivimou?'*

Unchdryd rose first. He hadn't spoken so far, but that wasn't unusual for the scarred Saberian. "The Queen's Fight begins the tick the big sun sets for this circle," he said.

"The Queens' Fights were between females, but now you expect one to fight your best male warrior?" Rorc pinned the Elder with his stare.

My Pair-bonds were still struggling to accept that Kali would be nothing like the docile and submissive Wravukian mates. I understood where they were coming from, but she didn't.

Kali kicked his shin under the table to grab his attention. "Rorc, I've accepted the challenge. I'm not backing out."

"We're going to be Second and Third Kings. We should be the ones to fight," Mes suggested, earning a death stare from our mate before she got up and stomped toward the windows.

Sciiti laughed. "Funny how you believe a Wravukian has a chance against a sabertooth…Second King." The sarcasm dripping from his voice made me want to throttle him.

And it seemed it was too much for Rorc too because the next moment, his uniform was in tattered pieces on the floor and Brute —lips pulled back, snarling—was prowling toward the surprised Elder. The sabertooth stopped a hairbreadth away from Sciiti's face and roared at him.

"Who said a Wravukian would be fighting a sabertooth?" Mes asked, but the Elders were locked on the purple-furred animal with the Wravukian markings.

"I'm sure you will be in your fair share of challenges before everyone has adapted to your existence, and our new reality," Nurn said, before he bowed and exited the chamber.

"It's the only way she'll earn the warriors' respect," Srah added, and walked out of the room.

"May the strongest win," Unchdryd wished, and followed the other two.

"Creating hybrids…" Sciiti mumbled under his breath as he

walked out of the room, "...you will be the end of us." He was about to close the door when he looked at me and said, "An-Her was right."

I froze. He believed the person responsible for the death of our females was right? This was the drop that spilled the glass. "Sciiti," I yelled, and ran after him—fully intending to beat some sense into him, only to find Urien had beat me to it.

The Elder was lying unconscious by his feet, whereas my brother was shaking with anger.

I clapped him on the shoulder, and we returned to my mates, leaving the disrespectful fool behind. He'd wake up soon enough.

"I felt your fear spike, love. What is it?" Mes asked as we entered.

Kali looked at me, then at the warriors.

"These males, I trust with my life, monakrivimou," I told her before I turned to my Pair-bond. "Rorc, please shift. I want you to meet Urien, Aux, Pirhanh, Djoser, Mok, and Dagoner."

"Um, Admiral, are we going commando?" Kali chuckled.

"I'm not going anywhere, what are you talking about, Mate?" he asked, and Kali burst out laughing.

The Human language seemed to have a lot of expressions that said one thing, yet meant another, and our translators weren't able to translate correctly.

"It means you're naked," she replied between giggles.

I'd forgotten he'd torn his uniform. We made ours using fibers from a local plant. Sirh was one of the few semi-sentient organisms belonging to the vegetable kingdom on our planet. It could adapt to most environments in order to sustain itself. It also had a unique defense mechanism that made it virtually indestructible. My ancestors had formed a symbiotic relationship with it, and since then it was the material we used for our garments. What made it so special was the fact that when worn it shifted with us. It could also withdraw beneath our epidermis and reappear when needed.

Aux went to retrieve three uniforms for my mates. He returned, and said, "This uniform will shift with you," before giving each of my mates one. I saw him discreetly sniffing Kali before he cocked his head and furrowed his brows.

"Thank you," she replied. "How do I put this on?"

"Take off your garments and step into this one. It will adjust itself on your body." His voice was thick with emotion, and I didn't like it at all.

Neither did Beast, whose snarl rattled in my chest, making my warriors' heads snap my way.

Aux stepped away from our mate, and tilted his head—revealing his throat and effectively appeasing us.

"Are we changing here?" Kali asked, looking at Mes and Rorc putting theirs on in front of everyone. "Yeah, swinging your dicks in front of everyone might be all right, but I don't know about swinging my tits...." Her tone was contemplative, and the image of her taking her garment off in front of all of us popped into my head, making every muscle in my body tense.

"You're not changing in front of anyone but your mates." I added a growl at the end for good measure.

"Did you just growl at me? That's what I said, you buffoon," she replied, and unsuccessfully suppressed bursts of laughter filled the room.

"Turn around," I barked, and my warriors spun the other way. "Come here, Mate."

She took her sweet time—testing my patience—and then stopped out of my reach.

I narrowed my eyes, then smirked. It was time she learned there were consequences to disobeying the Kings. Placing my body between the males and her, I closed the gap separating us and pressed the deactivation point on her suit. In a few ticks she was standing in my palace naked. Blood pooled low, making me as hard as a rock. The sweet scent of her arousal filled the air, and I groaned, but first things first.

Unsuspecting, she held the garment out in front of her—letting it unfold. "Do I step into it or place it on me?"

Placing my hands on her shoulders, I applied pressure until she turned around. Seeing the now prominent spots and stripes on her sides and the fainter ones spread on her back mixing with all the badges of courage painted on her skin had warmth spreading in my chest. I leaned over her—making her bend at the waist. My fingers followed the wet trail my tongue created as I licked across her spine. Her breath hitched when I nipped the spot between her shoulder and neck, right before I fisted her hair. I straightened, and she tried to do the same. She couldn't.

"Arana?" her voice trembled.

The sound of my palm coming down on her firm cheeks echoed in the room.

She gasped, then struggled. I tightened my hold on her strands, unyielding, and she stilled. Her alluring aroma intensified and invaded my sensitive nose. Unable to resist the calling, I pulled her up, and crushed her lips with mine. I was staking my claim, consuming her essence, and yet she wasn't a passive participant. Her lips moved under my lips, and her tongue dueled as fervently as mine.

'You're killing us, Arana.' I heard—as if from afar—Mes's pained voice in my head.

'Send your warriors away, Pair-bond,' Rorc ordered in a husky, tortured tone.

I reluctantly broke our kiss. Kali blinked—eyes dazed, slightly unfocused—and her rapid breathing sounded loud in the quiet of the room.

"Actions have consequences," I purred, pulling her out of the sexual haze that had shrouded her mind.

Her neck and face flushed bright red. "I'll remember that," she said.

The promise of retaliation lay under her words.

Our mate had fire and I couldn't wait to play with it.

I helped her put on the Saberian uniform, and as the Sirh adjusted and molded to her body, I admired the creature the Creator had blessed us with.

'You're beautiful, little one.'

Upon hearing Rorc's compliment, she ducked her head, but not before I noticed the beautiful pink flush on her face.

"Let's go home. You need to rest, monakrivimou."

"Arana, we need to discuss the Western and Southern Territories' activities," Mok said. His eyes were the green color of his sabertooth, betraying his agitation.

I weighed the situation. Greber and Mador, the two territory leaders, had a lot to answer for, but Kali took priority over them. I could feel her body fighting the exhaustion. She needed to get some sleep before the sun set. I'd deal with the other mess after the fight. "Not now, Mok. We'll deal with that problem tomorrow."

"As you wish," he acquiesced.

Soon we were standing outside the palatial gates. "Do you want to take the speeder or let your sabertooths run?" I asked my mates while I scanned the surrounding area. We were alone.

Their excitement was palpable. "Run," they said at the same time —making my warriors chuckle—and shifted. Like little cubs, they galloped toward the dunes. Dawn hopped from spot to spot, catching imaginary prey and sending sand particles in the air. Brute and Savage, wrestled playfully for a bit before they focused on our mate, then they stalked her and attacked the moment she landed after one of her jumps. Our observant mate saw them coming and evaded at the last moment, making them chase after her.

I looked at my warriors. Their eyes were locked on my mates while they fidgeted in place, broadcasting their eagerness loud and clear. I decided to spare them. "Go," I ordered, and watched them as they shifted and joined my mates. All but one. I arched an eyebrow at him.

"Maybe you should cancel the fight," Aux said. Straight to the point, as always.

Something had been bothering him from the moment he'd laid eyes on Kali. "Why?"

The crease on his forehead deepened. "You don't know?" he asked.

"Spit it out, Aux."

"She's with offspring," he said, but I must have misheard.

"Offspring?" I repeated, momentarily too stunned to form a coherent sentence.

"Yes. Her scent is…ripe…but infused with scents that don't belong to her," he explained. "I wasn't sure in the beginning. It's been so long since our own females…" His voice trailed off and pain emanated from the invisible thread uniting us.

While I'd been away—searching for my female—the intangible threads that had connected my warriors' life forces to mine the day I had unknowingly claimed the throne more than a hundred rotations ago hadn't been severed. Distance had dulled the power of the connection, but I'd still felt the loss of every single warrior Lethe had claimed.

Even though the air was heavy with a sense of foreboding, I felt an overall weightlessness, and heat radiated through my chest upon hearing the news. *Our mate is with offspring, Beast.*

My sabertooth, satisfied with the unexpected development, purred happily.

I had long since discovered that my extreme emotions had an immediate effect on my people, so I let my joy spill into them. Hoping this time to offer a smidgen of relief from the constant burden they carried, needing to give them hope.

"Arana, you must cancel it," Aux insisted.

Dawn is strong enough to fight, Beast affirmed, and I trusted him.

"I can't." He took a step toward me, fists balled, so I explained, "She won't accept it. She doesn't know you, but she has claimed all of you already. I can't take away her rights, nor do I want to."

He cursed under his breath and walked away from me, shifting mid-stride to join the others.

Beast was anxious to meet those under his protective wing again, so I retreated, giving over control of our body to him.

YOU LEAVE ME NO CHOICE

MES

Being in this form felt foreign…unnatural in a way.

Savage growled in response to my thoughts and attacked my consciousness, landing a mental blow that resulted in pain for both of us. But he didn't care as long as I was punished.

Dawn stood up on her back paws and placed her front ones on our ribs. He could hold her weight, but chose to fall sideways, so we ended up under our mate. She rubbed the length of her slick body across our own before she licked our muzzle affectionately.

'He doesn't know you yet, Savage. He's not your enemy. Let him in,' she ordered, and I felt him ease off on the aggression, trying to obey to make her happy. *'He's going to love you, like I do,'* she said, shocking us both before she nipped our shoulder playfully and jumped away, laughing.

Lying on the sandy surface, Savage tracked her movements, basking under her light and playing her words on repeat.

My sabertooth's name was apt. He was volatile…dangerous… dark, yet he was putty in her hands. Thirsty for her affection, he'd do anything to satisfy our mate, even if that meant meeting me in the middle.

Truce? I suggested.

Yes, he agreed, and as a gesture of faith, I loosened the tight leash I had on him.

He sprang up and trotted toward her, tongue lolling out the side of his mouth.

Small steps.

Kali's enthusiasm was contagious, and it brought out his playfulness—something I thought he didn't possess. But we weren't the only one that held her attention. When she'd noticed the warrior sabertooths hesitating to approach us, she'd invited them to play. When tempers had risen she'd stepped in, stopping the fights before they started. She'd challenged all of us to let go, for just a moment, to appreciate the miracle of being alive, of being here with those who mattered.

She'd offered us a priceless gift, as for the first time I could remember I shed my responsibilities. I let go of what was expected of me and just experienced Savage's joy in being present, in being able to feel his paws hit the soft granules and the plethora of scents tickle his nose. His devotion to the one who had given him life was all-encompassing. He'd do anything for her; he'd gladly give his life for hers, and he'd kill to protect her.

She had us wrapped around her little fingers, and as I scanned the area, opening myself to the emotions around me, I realized she had everyone else under her spell as well.

I'd lost track of time when Beast let out a short, low chuff, ordering everyone to gather so we could head to our new home. He'd been herding us toward the forest all along and now that we'd reached the woodland edge, new scents permeated the air, beckoning us. They intensified the deeper we went, and Savage wanted to explore every single one, but Arana had a specific destination in mind, and we had no choice but to obey our Pair-bond. So we kept trotting between the wide trunks of the trees and through the colorful flowers scattered on the forest floor.

When Kali had released my and Rorc's sabertooths, the foolish animals had taken one look at Arana and, wanting to impress our mate, they'd attacked. Before they'd taken a single step, though, the Saberian King had shifted, and Beast had put them in their place, making them submit to his authority. The fight had been unfair—two against one; it had been violent and swift; it had also ended with us losing.

The temporary chaos wreaking havoc on our bond, which had been created by the disturbance in the hierarchy the addition of two new dominant predators caused, had been settled, and only one thing had remained for our Union's balance to once again be restored. As one we'd turned and advanced on Dawn. Even though Arana training with her had exponentially improved her fighting skill, Kali still needed to work on relinquishing control to Dawn. Their internal battle for dominance over the reins had cost them any chance they might have had against three males. The fight was over soon after it started with the female sabertooth lying on her back, exposing her belly.

Thinking about what had followed after we'd shifted, made desire flow through my veins. Savage approached Dawn from the side and bumped her with his shoulder blade. She purred her affection—then suddenly her hackles raised, her ears went flat on her head, and she started growling. The vibrations of the deep, menacing cadence strong enough that I could feel them going through me.

Her reaction stopped everyone in their tracks.

We formed a protective circle around her, and she swatted angrily on the ground sending leaves and soil onto Beast, who turned his big head to look at her and lift his upper lip in displeasure.

'What is it, Mate?' Arana asked, calmer than his animal counterpart.

'Don't you feel it?' Kali replied, her attention on something behind my Pair-bond.

I scanned the surrounding area, opening up all my senses, expecting and gearing up for the battering of emotions those around me would cause. A whine escaped Savage, who was experiencing the repercussions of my gifts for the first time. Everything in this form was more...the influx of information more detailed, and in turn the cost on us heavier. I was having trouble shifting through it all when raw power invigorated me, allowing me to take a big breath and center myself.

Once calmer and steadier with the help of my mates, processing became easier. I couldn't detect any Saberians or other predators near. The green oasis was full of smaller animals, but nothing that presented a threat. *'We're alone.'*

A shudder racked Dawn's body and she stumbled.

If I could sweat in this body, I would have been drenched. I had run every test possible. Had I been wrong in thinking the planet was safe for her? Had the virus infected my mate?

Catching on to my train of thought, she replied, *'No, I'm okay...*

this place isn't, and it's targeting Arana and us.' She shook her head and got her body under control. *'It's killing everything it touches,'* she gasped.

'I see the dead vegetation, but nothing else. Where's the threat, little one?' Rorc asked.

Then Arana said, *'We're nearing the entrance to the Forest of the Fallen, monakrivimou. The warriors there have long crossed the Vaults of No Return. They can't harm anyone.'*

Utilizing more than just our sight, I let my senses wander, and that's when I noticed what everyone else but Kali was oblivious to. My instinctual reaction was to recoil from such a vile entity. It was inconspicuous, barely more than a shadow, but an oil-like substance covered the ground ahead of us, suffocating the vegetation it lingered on. When I followed the trail to see where it was coming from, I discovered a skeleton suspended in the air, securely using the branches of two snags. What kind of crime justified such punishment?

'Who is this, Arana?'

'A traitor.' His clipped tone demanded I drop the subject, but he didn't know the damage being done.

'What did he do that earned him eternal unrest?' I insisted while Savage growled at the shadowy feelers coming our way.

Dawn swatted the soil, her claws leaving deep furrows, in her effort to push it away from her. But it kept coming and she jumped backward, thinking some distance from this entity that suddenly seemed obsessed with her would help. Brute sidled up to her in his effort to protect her from the invisible enemy. Unfortunately, more feelers slithered their way.

'He is the one responsible for the deaths of the Saberian females.' His words gradually deepened and roughened into a definite growl.

'It's high time you allowed his soul to rest.' I rarely chose to use the authority I carried, having inherited it from a long line of dominant males, but this was important. He needed to yield.

'No.'

'You leave me no choice,' I warned, and shifted.

In a tick I was on him. Beast, annoyed at my interference, tried to push me aside with his head, nicking my forearm with his knife-like canines in the process.

The cut burned and drops of my life-providing liquid spattered on the fallen leaves. I paid no mind to them—the wound would soon heal.

Placing my palms on the sides above his muzzle, I thrust what I was seeing in his mind's eye. Making him understand, since he didn't want to. *'You need to allow him rest. It is poisoning your home... our home. We've been here for less than half a circle and it's already targeting our mate.'* Sensing his struggle to reconcile with his past, I continued, *'I won't let anyone risk our mate. I chose to follow you, Pair-bond, but if you steer us wrong, you will find out you're not the only alpha capable of leading.'*

I hadn't disguised the threat in my voice, but my goal hadn't been to challenge him at this point, only to make him understand. So I dropped my hands, stepped backward, and tilted my head to reveal my neck.

The move appeased him and the quiet but deep, aggressive rumble in his chest stopped. He shook his head, and then his entire body, shedding the remains of his anger.

'Then give your first order and arrange for the Farewell Ritual, Pair-bond,' he said, testing my resolve.

Straightening my pose, I turned toward the warriors who had been watching us intently. "Urien, this fallen warrior has paid enough for his sins. It's time for his soul to be put to rest. Make the needed arrangements to bring down his remains and organize the Farewell Ritual."

To the warrior's credit, he didn't turn to his King for confirmation. His sabertooth nodded once in acceptance of my order.

Arana's joy seeped through our bond, and it mirrored my own. Maybe it wouldn't be so hard for the Saberians to accept us after all.

IT WAS TOO LATE

RORC

Dawn opened her muzzle wide in a loud yawn, and swayed from side to side.

I'd caught glimpses of what Mes had shared with Arana, and it seemed this darkness had drained our mate's energy.

'Take us home, Saberian.' My tone was gruffer than usual because I was worried. In less than half a circle she'd face a warrior in his prime, and in her tired state she'd make mistakes.

Arana—like the cat that ate the canary—said smugly, *'You're a Saberian now too, Pair-bond.'* Then started for our new home.

'As if I'd forget,' I huffed, letting mock-insult color my voice.

In actuality, I didn't mind it as much as I'd thought I would. Brute had the same temperament as me. We understood each other, and having him in my head wasn't that bad. We were both equally stubborn, but we had the same goals—protect our mate at all costs and keep our Pair-bonds safe—and they made navigating this new reality a tad easier.

By the time we reached Arana's cave, Dawn was dragging her paws. He shifted, and we followed suit.

Kali covered another yawn with a palm over her mouth.

I stepped to her side, placed an arm behind her back and another behind her knees, and picked her up.

"Rorc, let me down," she complained, but snuggled closer.

"No. You're too tired to walk," I said in a tone that brooked no argument, before calling out to Arana, who was disagreeing with Urien, to hurry up.

My Pair-bond's hackles rose when Aux sided with his fellow warrior. "Did my absence make you forget who the King is?" he growled.

"Did your absence make you forget our rules?" Urien asked mockingly, before he growled, "In case of threat the Royal Guards have the right to act as they see fit in order to protect the royal family."

"Fine," Arana snarled, "but you're going to get some rest before the fight. That's not negotiable." Then he turned and headed inside the cave's mouth.

I didn't much care either way. We were capable enough to protect our mate, and if the Saberians got out of hand, the Nur was a few ticks away and the rest of my fleet in orbit. What I did care about was putting the sleeping beauty in my arms on a bed.

"Arana, where is the sleeping chamber?" I asked, wrinkling my brows. There was something wrong with her. "Mes, what was that earlier? Did it hurt Kali?"

"Nothing's wrong with her. Put her down first, and then we'll talk," Arana answered before Mes.

I briefly gazed at the space as I followed my Pair-bond. The cave had high ceilings decorated with gems that resembled scattered stars, and I could hear water lapping on rocks somewhere not too far. Our mate would want to explore every nook and cranny.

"Lay her over here."

She didn't even stir as I placed her on the bed, but when Arana placed the furs on her body, she burrowed deeper.

By the time we returned to the main area of the cave, I was one tick away from shouting at my Pair-bond to tell us what the hell was going on with our mate. He gestured for us to sit, but I chose to pace.

"Talk," I ordered.

He cocked his head but didn't comment on my tone. "There's nothing wrong with Kali."

He repeated what he'd said earlier, which was totally unnecessary since I'd heard him the first time. He should get on with it—

"She's pregnant," he added, interrupting my inner thoughts.

"Pregnant?" Mes echoed.

I must have misheard. "What?" I asked.

"She's carrying our offspring, and even though it's still too early for her to know, her body is adapting to prepare for the cubs."

Nope, I hadn't heard wrong.

"Are you sure?" Mes asked.

Arana nodded. "Aux could always tell when females were fertile or pregnant by their scents. I'm not exactly sure how his gift works," he explained.

Our mate was pregnant, and soon she'd have to face Urien in a match for dominance. "We're fucking canceling the fight," I exploded.

Seeing the storm brewing in my Pair-bond's eyes, and knowing what he was about to say, was more than I could handle. I didn't want to hear his excuses. I barreled toward him, and he shot to his feet. Our bodies collided, knocking over the furniture around us. It felt good when my fist connected with his ribs, but he was equally strong and gave as good as he got.

I wasn't sure how much time had passed, but when we ceased fighting, both of us lay sprawled on the surprisingly soft ground. Breathing hurt, Arana had a split lip, and I had blood dripping from a cut above my eye.

Mes, who had left the moment we started brawling, returned, and stood between us with his arms crossed over his chest. "Are you two going to make this a habit?" He shook his head in exasperation, then knelt and hovered his hands above our ribs and heads, alleviating the pain instantly.

Arana thanked him while I snickered—having a Healer for a Pair-bond had its uses.

He punched my shoulder and threatened, "Next time, I'll let you stew."

"Aw, don't be like that." I chuckled, and got up.

"She has to fight." Arana picked up our earlier argument. "The Saberian society's structure is based on hierarchy. My people won't accept her otherwise." What he said made sense, but he continued, and there lay my problem. "Dawn will keep our cubs safe."

I had to blink rapidly to bring the room back into focus.

On second thought, maybe sitting down is a better option. I plopped on the nearest chair.

"Cubs…as in…more than one?" I echoed, my voice small and distant even to my own ears.

"Three, actually," Mes answered. "While you two had fun beating each other up, I checked on our mate. There are three amniotic sacks with three embryos." If his words were meant to be reassuring, the worry in his voice ruined it.

Both I and Arana asked at the same time, "What's wrong?"

"Were multiple offspring common in your species? Because it isn't for Wravukians, and I don't know if it's usual for Earthlings either—" He hesitated, gathering his thoughts, reining in his worry. "I'm not sure what effect Kali's DNA concoction will have on our offspring. We might need to bring a Human Healer here."

If Mes thought a Healer from Earth was needed, the situation was serious. "The Intergalactic Enosis has forbidden contact with primitive species. Earthlings belong to that category," I said, because getting the Healer to Saber would be an issue.

We steal her. Brute chipped in.

"We'll appeal to the Council," Arana said.

"And what if they deny us?" I countered.

"One step at a time," the Saberian replied the moment Kali stepped into the room.

"What step?" she asked in a chirpy voice.

I scanned her from top to bottom. Her skin glowed, she looked reenergized and steady on her feet. Then my eyes landed on her flat belly.

Unbelievable.

"Quit staring," she snapped. "You aren't going to intimidate me out of the match." She'd completely misunderstood the look I was giving her, and that was fine for now because this wasn't the right moment to tell her.

Footsteps heralded Elder Srah's presence, and we all turned toward the entrance to watch him enter the room and tilt his head to the side—a clear show of submission.

"I'm glad to hear you say so because the warriors need a strong Queen, one that doesn't get scared easily." His voice, which ebbed and flowed like the waves of a placid sea, was hypnotizing; The copper-colored spots and stripes on his deep, dark skin were soothing to the eyes. He was calm personified, lulling me into a false sense of safety. "It is time," he said, bringing me out of my trance—driving home how dangerous he actually was.

Standing on the slightly raised platform, where the tent for us was set up, I scrutinized the rowdy crowd.

The air was buzzing with excitement and anticipation. Arana told us that a small number of the Saberians fit in here and that the rest would watch the fight on the holo-projectors set up in each Territory. Yet it was loud, and the Pit was full. So when silence blanketed the area, I zeroed in on the being with the midnight-blue hair in the middle of the arena.

"Warriors, you were called here to witness our King's mate vie for the Queen's place," Elder Nurn said, and the males' boisterous voices—some supportive and some discouraging—drowned out all other noises. When they quieted, the Elder continued, "Kali of the Earth and Saberian hybrid, will have to challenge Urien, Leader of the Main Territory and Royal Guard, for the right to the title."

Our mate, who'd been standing quietly watching everyone, straightened her spine and walked confidently into the arena at the same time the Saberian warrior stepped in across from her.

"Shift to your sabertooths," Nurn ordered, and moved out of the way. When he was standing on our platform, he said, "May the Queen's Fight commence."

Our silver-furred female stood still, seemingly mesmerized by the other sabertooth's appearance. He was bigger than Dawn, and his orange-colored fur with the forest-green stripes and spots gave the impression of fire moving, devouring everything in its path, as he prowled toward her. It screamed danger, yet our mate remained oblivious.

'He's beautiful, isn't he?' Kali's voice was soft and breathless.

Her comment wrenched a reaction from all of us. The growls rattling in our chests, had the Elders looking our way questioningly.

'I acknowledged that he was beautiful, not that I wanted him.' She huffed in indignation, then continued, *'For example, if you saw another woman who is more beautiful than me and you said so, should I assume that you would want her instead of me?'* Her reasoning made it even worse, and it was evident in the roars that shook the platform we were standing on.

'Yeesh! You are total cavemen.' Her indignation vibrated through our bond.

The time she had taken to admire the warrior, he had used to measure her, form a plan of attack, and begin its execution. Urien's sabertooth was only a few paces away from her, when he covered the short distance with a jump she barely evaded because she hadn't been paying attention.

Cold sweat drenched my body and my pulse quickened. I tried to tone down the rising anger lest my emotion bled through our bond and distracted her further.

At least his attack made her focus on the male who kept coming at her, and who didn't let up at all, forcing her to retreat toward the far side of the arena.

The ferocious fight soon turned vicious and it was dangerously one-sided.

I cringed with every failed attempt at coordination between my mate and her sabertooth. I felt every slash she failed to dodge, like it was my skin being ripped in two.

Blood was matting Dawn's silver fur, turning the white spots crimson, because the warrior had managed to rake her flanks with his claws three times already, thanks to her clumsy moves.

My Pair-bonds' accelerated breathing was overly loud next to me. Their anxiety fed my worry to the point I doubted I could keep watching—without interfering—for long.

We stayed firmly entrenched in Kali's mind—monitoring the toll her injuries took in case we needed to intervene for the sake of our offspring—and we could hear her fighting with Dawn over who should have the control of their body. Kali insisted they needed to strategize to win whereas her sabertooth maintained they needed strength and agility. She was losing because she couldn't align herself with her other half.

The crowd didn't want to be led by a weak Queen and was very vocal about it, as they goaded Urien to end the fight.

It seemed he'd had enough as well—tired of toying with our mate—when he charged her head-on. Dawn sidestepped to avoid a direct hit to her dorsal side but failed to evade his front paw before it connected to her soft underbelly.

Blood spattered in a wide arc, painting the soil a dark crimson.

I charged into the arena, or tried to, but both Arana and Mes had wrapped their arms around me in their effort to hold me in place.

"Take your fucking hands off me, before I rip them off you." The guttural words were hard to understand because Brute had initiated the shift.

"You will not shift," Arana's cruel command reverberated in my head, its power binding my sabertooth and rendering him useless. "She needs to finish this herself."

Letting all the venom I felt toward my Pair-bond for getting our female hurt show, I asked him, "When will it be enough? When her guts are sprawled on the ground?"

Kali's groan of pain echoing in our minds drew our focus back on the fight.

'Let her lead!' Arana ordered—*not as unaffected as he'd wanted me to believe. 'Give up the control to your sabertooth.'*

Mes, as always, being calm enough to detect the source of the problem, told her gently, *'My love, you won't get lost. She's one with you. Let her have the reins, her instincts are strong and will tilt the tide in your favor.'*

I wanted to be tender with her, but I couldn't, not when her life and that of our offspring were on the line. *'Focus. Embrace her,'* I barked at her.

My vision blurred, my breath caught, and my heartbeats stuttered.

It took me a moment to realize I wasn't experiencing my body's reactions, but Kali's, through our bond.

Fuck. Allowing this had been a mistake and now it was too late.

I NEEDED TO HAVE NO REGRETS

KALI

Shit! That hurt like a bitch.

Urien used the fact that we were momentarily stunned to his advantage, and he sunk his teeth where our shoulder met our neck.

Dawn struggled and, in addition to the pain his bite caused, we both felt the wound he'd just inflicted gape open.

The world around us turned fuzzy.

'Let her lead! Give up the control to your sabertooth.'

'My love, you won't get lost. She's one with you. Let her have the reins, her instincts are strong and will tilt the tide in your favor.'

'Focus. Embrace her.'

My mates' booming voices bounced around the walls in my head at the same time. Gee! They were relentless, and if I ended up not being able to take back control of myself, it would be on them.

Okay Dawn, you win. Knock 'em dead.

Suddenly, it was like time stood still. I was no longer on the earthly plane, and everyone else faded to the background but the furry creature—a wild feline—coming slowly toward me, purring.

She rubbed her body all over my sides and settled around me. Her love warmed me; her primordial instinct to protect me rocked me to my core, and the ferocious need to destroy everyone who stood in our way of becoming the Queen, surprised me. I hesitantly delved my hand into her fur, it was soft like velvet. Then I pressed my face to her neck, and wrapped my arms around her thick torso, hugging her tight. I wasn't alone anymore. What I always felt was missing clicked into place and, like a stretched elastic band that was finally released, we were thrown back into our body.

As reality set in, a wide variety of smells, colors, and sounds assaulted me. The rich scent of the soil was overwhelming, clouding my senses, until I felt Dawn shifting through every minuscule detail and cataloging it. The roars coming from the crowd were deafening, reminding me of the time I had gone to watch an NBA final with my teammates. Our ears hurt, but I let her go through every sound as well and discern friend from enemy.

Her mind was racing at unbelievable speeds, analyzing and calculating the odds. She measured our foes, sniffing out their weakest points, then went over plans of attack, forming and discarding the ones that wouldn't work as fast.

Finally, her gaze fell on our mates. They were magnificent in both their forms, but at the moment their terrified looks upset her because they should trust in us more.

With a sinking heart, I realized my mistake. From the beginning she was thinking in us terms, whereas I was holding us back. Well, not anymore.

I'm sorry I was holding us back. You are amazing, I praised her.

We are amazing, she purred, and I laughed. That was translated into a humph that rattled in my sabertooth's throat.

The sound startled Urien and his hold loosened slightly.

That was all we needed. With a calculated move, knowing we couldn't get away from under him unscathed, we turned, grinding our shoulder bone on his teeth—making him open his mouth wide —and pulled. His long canines tore the side of our neck, but the injury was not fatal.

My mates' fear leaked into our bond upon seeing more blood matting our fur.

We spared a second to turn and snarl at them.

'Infuriating males,' Dawn growled. We were a female warrior, the best there was and they doubted us.

Well we haven't exactly earned their trust, I told her.

It's time we showed them, she icily replied, and turned—all her focus on the warrior.

He'd sensed a change and was cautiously approaching us.

We exaggerated our limp and whined, trying to provoke him into attacking. He was a great warrior—he was fast, too, but he had nothing on us.

The change in his stance was infinitesimally small, but we noticed he'd lowered his body just a bit. He was about to pounce and we let him.

He was mid-jump when we sprang in action and attacked. Having a smaller body gave us an advantage; utilizing our agile spine, we spun mid-air and we managed to grab onto his underbelly, as our unexpected weight caused him to lose balance.

It was a bold move, but it paid off.

We landed in a heap of fur and paws, each vying for the dominant position, but we already had the upper hand as we immobilized his most dangerous weapon with one of our paws. Another furrowed deep in his back leg, putting a stop to the fight for dominance altogether.

Urien's sabertooth was lying on his side, panting, when we felt his muscles bunch, and his claws touch our underbelly in his effort to throw us off him.

Dawn, in the blink of an eye, sliced his flank open with her thick claws, brought her muzzle closer to his neck, letting her knifelike teeth graze him, and growled before he had the chance to rip us apart. We could not risk our cubs.

Wait, what? I asked, but she was intent on the warrior who was trying to dislodge us, and was ignoring me.

She clamped her mouth on his neck, piercing his skin with her long canines.

Dawn! Are we pregnant? I asked again. Wouldn't I feel different if I was? I mean, Arana had told me I wouldn't get pregnant. We were different species, for God's sake, how was that even possible?

Yes, we have three cubs, she answered, putting me out of my misery and sending me straight into a panic attack.

I wasn't ready to be a mother…and on top of that to not one, but three children. How would it even work? I mean she'd said cubs, did that mean that I'd have three little sabertooths in me? Every horror sci-fi movie I had ever seen, flashed before my eyes making me hyperventilate.

Thankfully, while I was falling apart, Dawn held the fort for both of us, allowing me to digest everything.

The male sabertooth was still struggling to get free, and she clamped her mouth tighter, feeling his blood trickling on her tongue.

None of that mattered to me, but what she did next brought me out of the news-induced trance.

'Surrender, you fool,' her husky voice warned him.

I had no idea we could communicate telepathically with anyone but our mates. Then I realized everyone had gone silent. Not even their breathing was heard. The warrior was surprised too because I saw his eyes dilate in wonder. He shifted while we had our teeth clamped on his neck and we instantly released him, lest we fatally wounded the great warrior. His neck, his thigh, and his shoulder blade were bleeding. He had other minor cuts and scratches too that were already healing.

He got up, then knelt and bowed in front of us. "My Queen."

Two words uttered reverently brought about havoc. Everyone, or to be more accurate, almost everyone, Dawn noted, had started cheering, whooping, and yelling in joy, for they now had a new Queen.

Our roar joined their voices—it was heard above all sounds—and it was a celebratory one. Our chest swelled with happiness—we had made our mates proud.

We turned to focus on the most important people in our life.

Do they know they will be fathers? I asked my sabertooth, and she admitted they did.

That raised my hackles, and adrenaline rushed through my body. The pounding in my ears muffled all other noise, and my vision tunneled to the point only my males were visible. They'd known but said nothing.

The sudden anger streaking through me propelled me forward. The snarl starting low in our chest rumbled like lightning and grew in strength.

The crowd, upon hearing the menacing sound, quieted. They didn't know what was going on.

My mates, who had been walking toward me, stopped in their tracks, and their sabertooths—answering my challenge—burst from their skins.

Dawn purred in delight at seeing the powerful predators.

Down, kitty, they lied to us.

Our audience gasped, for it wasn't widely known that the Wravukians could shift too.

I didn't give a shit.

My males had kept the truth from me.

'You lying bastards!' I was furious at them, but as I opened myself to our connection fully, I realized they were furious at me too, for daring to snarl at them in front of everyone. Disrespecting them by reducing them to weaklings.

Oh fuck. I was mad at them for the whole pregnancy thing. I hadn't meant to insult them.

With everything going on I hadn't had time to familiarize myself with their customs, but I was aware that hierarchy carried weight, and knowing they would never hurt me, I'd just thrown the gauntlet.

They didn't dignify my outburst with an answer, but they did react to my challenge by pouncing on me.

All three at once.

United, exerting their dominance in front of everyone, and taking back what I'd cost them with my thoughtless reaction.

We had found out that we were a great warrior only moments ago, yet now we didn't stand a chance because these males were our mates to whom we had already submitted. So our baser instincts that were supposed to give us an advantage, prevented us from fully attacking.

They had us on the ground in less than a minute. Their roars were deafening.

Arana shifted first, looking so regal and so…so mad.

Rorc and Mes followed—their expressions equally livid.

Darn it. I was in deep trouble, but maybe I could play it off as accidental…

'Oopsie,' I told them in a sugary sweet, dripping with honey voice.

'Are you going to hide inside Dawn all day?' Mes asked, and his teasing tone took me by surprise.

Rorc snickered, and Arana's pride spread through our bond and warmed my heart.

Okay, so despite outside appearances, they weren't actually mad.

'Why would we be mad at you, monakrivimou? No Saberian female with self-respect would accept her mates without a challenge.'

Dawn got up, purred, and rubbed her fur on our mates' legs—marking them with her scent. As our muscles slowly relaxed and relief swept away my reservations, I remembered why I had been angry in the first place. But before I could bring up the subject of the three new lives growing in me, the Elders called us to them.

I was planning to shift, but the sudden tension riding my males made me reconsider. So I followed them on all fours, sacrificing my ability to converse in favor of the protection of my mates.

Elder Srah opened his mouth to speak, but Elder Sciiti cut him off by addressing Arana, "You can't possibly expect us to accept the hybrids as our rulers."

His tone was rude, and the way he'd spat the word 'hybrids' had my hackles rising.

"How many of you share Sciiti's concerns?" Arana's calm demeanor betrayed nothing, and his voice remained neutral. On the inside, though, where they could not see, a terrible storm was brewing.

"I do. We stood by your side when you proposed we take

females from other species to procreate. We defended you to the warriors that insisted you'd destroy what was left of our species." Elder Unchdryd stopped and looked at me and my two Wravukians with contempt before he continued, "But we're not going to stand by and let hybrids from inferior species rule us."

I felt as if I had been bitten by a snake—its venom flowing through my veins.

They had asked me to fight. I'd agreed and won. Yet it was becoming abundantly clear that I'd never be accepted, and neither would two of my mates. My insecurities came back with a vengeance—maybe it was a human thing because my mates didn't have any. They'd never accept me, the hybrid they'd called me.

How will they react when they learn I'm pregnant? Will my babies be safe?

That thought stopped me short. I had to think about others besides myself now. Fuck, I needed to get out of here. This place was too crowded, I had to find a place where I'd be alone so I could think.

'Do you want me to go too?' Dawn's voice sounded forlorn in my head.

'No, kitty kat. You and I are a packaged deal,' I reassured her, but my focus returned on the males.

If the other warriors shared this Elder's feelings, which based on his words seemed to be the case, Saber would not be a safe place for my children.

"These hybrids," Arana growled menacingly, "are my mates. We formed a Sacred Union, so be careful of your next words, Elder."

I heard the words as if from afar, while I retreated both physically from them and mentally by raising thick walls and breaking our connection. My males could deal with the Elders without me just fine.

There was a very important decision I had to make all on my own. I couldn't allow them to influence me. With such high stakes, I needed to have no regrets.

YOU'RE KILLING US

ARANA

"These hybrids are my mates. We formed a Sacred Union, so be careful of your next words, Elder," I growled, frustrated with their reaction.

They should have been happy I formed such a bond because it spoke of the power we had together.

Finding females that we were not only compatible with, but could also Change, and thus ensure our offspring would have sabertooths, should have them rejoicing.

Rorc and Mes's anger at being referred to as inferior was growing by the tick, and Kali's emotions were a messy jumble. I hated that the wisest of my people were hurting them. But they were letting me handle it, and I wouldn't disappoint them.

I saw, from the periphery of my vision, Dawn retreating toward the exit. Unchdryd's words had cut her deep and doubts were rearing their ugly heads. I was about to reassure her, when suddenly, the mental link connecting us since she'd evoked the Sacred Bond, broke.

Beast howled in agony. Was she rejecting me and my sabertooth?

I looked at my Pair-bonds. As our pained stares met, a wave of nausea hit me, and the air exploded out of my lungs as if I had been dealt a physical blow.

She had rejected our Union.

"…you gave them their beasts…" An Elder was speaking, but I couldn't grasp his words.

The Wravukians and I turned to go after our mate. We were ready to beg and plead, to do everything in our power to get her to accept us back.

"Don't you dare walk away from us, youngling." Sciiti's yelled words finally pierced through my foggy brain. "Your hybrid female has put a spell on you, and you've fallen into her trap."

"What did you call me?" The temperature around us seemed to drop in direct proportion to my rising fury.

He's accusing our female. Beast was equally enraged.

I spun and prowled toward him.

"She's evil. How else could she speak in everyone's mind?" he continued oblivious to the danger he was in.

Elder Srah, recognizing the danger, nudged him to stop, but Sciiti didn't.

"She will taint us all, and her offspring will bring about our destruction," he said right before I slammed into him.

His body flew and hit the wall. I was there before he dropped on the floor, hand wrapped around his throat.

"Kali is not evil. You are," I spat, squeezing my palm tight. "She decided to fight for the Saberian warriors, and find a way to save them before she even met them," I growled, and let Beast's claws spring from my fingers, drawing his blood.

Sciiti's eyes widened, as he realized the mortal danger he was in.

"Our offspring will bring hope, but you won't be here to witness it," I said, ready to end his life, when Srah came into my field of vision.

The Elder stood far enough as to not challenge my personal space, with his head tilted to the side, revealing his neck—recognizing my dominance.

"King, Sciiti hasn't committed a fatal crime that deserves death," he said, giving me the opportunity to consider all the things he hadn't uttered.

Killing an Elder because he was disrespectful and made false accusations would cause unrest among my people. It would undermine my authority as I would be deemed unfit to rule. But I couldn't allow him to remain here anymore. "You will leave the Main Territory, and are forbidden from entering the rest," I decreed, and multiple gasps met my statement. "I exile you to the Rahk'a Mountains." I unclenched my hand from his throat and let it drop.

I wouldn't kill him, but nature would.

"You can't exile me," he yelled.

"I am the King, and it is my right." Having made the right decision, a weight lifted off of my shoulders and allowed me calmness. "You have one circle to gather what you think you'll need, then the Royal Guard will escort you out of my Territory." Nothing else needed to be said, and I could no longer ignore the chasm Kali created when she left us, so I turned away from him toward my Pair-bonds. "Let's go find our mate," I told them, and we left the Elders behind.

We remained quiet, lost in our own pain and our own regrets, while we looked for her.

I couldn't sense her through our connection, but I could still hear the thoughts and feel my Pair-bonds' emotions. It struck me as odd, but I couldn't focus on the why of it. The awful realization that if I had told her how much I loved her and what she meant to me, she wouldn't have believed the Elders' words and wouldn't have left us, was playing on repeat in my head.

Initially, we'd gone to the Palace, thinking she'd be somewhere there, but no one had seen her. Next, we searched the Pit and the palatial grounds but she wasn't there either. Then at the gated entrance, we picked up her scent leading toward the forest and we followed it.

We finally found her.

She was standing outside of the Forest of the Fallen, near where An-Her's bones used to be. She heard our approach and turned slowly to face us.

She had wrapped her arms around her middle, over our cubs, and tears were streaking her beautiful face. She was deeply hurt, yet not even the slightest sound slipped from her lips.

Seeing her like this broke my hearts…all of our hearts, and we rushed to surround her with our warmth.

"Don't cry, my love," Mes pleaded, "you're killing us."

"We're here now, little one," Rorc added and swiped up her tears with his thumbs.

I couldn't touch her, not yet, not before I knew she'd forgiven us and would let us back into her heart. "We're sorry, monakrivimou. We hurt you," I said, and waited with bated breath.

"After the fight, I felt everyone's pain. They've nearly given up hope. These warriors who fought hard to protect others most of their lives had no one else but you, Arana, to protect them. Then and there I decided to help them, whether they wanted me to or not," she said, looking me in the eyes. "They might only accept me because I won, and I could live with that. But then the Elder confirmed what I didn't want to see." She stopped and closed her eyes, gathering strength for what she would say next. "So I had to reconsider and decide, based on what would be best for my children. I should leave you"—her breath hitched, while her words sliced our souls. I pressed a fist to my chest, trying to keep the pain at bay—"but I can't. I need you—all three of you—to love me, always, because I've fallen in love with all of you." She rushed the words out as if afraid we'd turn her down.

Divine relief filled my every pore as our connection was restored and I could feel her through our bond again. It was like the suns rose in the horizon, chasing away the darkness and bathing everything in their cool light.

She felt about us the way we felt about her.

When she pulled back, we realized we'd taken too long to answer her.

We caged her in, and my hands fisted her hair, before I tilted her head to the side and whispered in her ear. "I've loved you since the first vision I had of you." Then I pulled back.

Mes, standing on her left, kissed the side of her neck. "That day in the Human flying contraption, you stole a piece of my heart, and I've been yours ever since. I love you."

Rorc applied pressure under her chin until she turned and looked up at him. "There's no one else like you, little one. I love you, always," he said before he claimed her lips.

Her eyes closed and the happiness, along with the unconditional love that spilled into our bond, nearly brought to me my knees.

Beast and I were so absorbed in our own emotions that we failed to notice the sabertooths coming until it was too late.

Brute was the first to detect the threat, and Rorc exploded into action. He shifted and jumped between us and danger. Mes and Savage did the same to our rear.

I let my senses flare, allowing the power that was bestowed upon me when I became king unfurl and seek the threads that united my warriors' life force to mine; it revealed their positions to me in spite of their camouflaged appearance.

I felt the disturbance in the air when Dawn took Kali's place before moving a few paces away from me to give both of us some fighting room.

I spread my arms and turned a full circle, daring the insurgents to make the first move, surprised by the big number of sabertooths closing in on us. "This is how you welcome your Queen and the Second Kings?" Disappointment in my warriors, and scathing fury at the insult, roughened my voice.

Snarls and growls accompanied my question, before the one who'd become the bane of my existence the moment I had declined his granddaughter's advances more than a hundred rotations ago—and who I'd earlier banished from our Territories—stepped to the side, revealing himself.

"We see no Kings and no Queen. Take the abominations you call mates, and leave while you can, or stay and die with them," Sciiti warned.

This time, we kill him, Beast decreed, and I was in agreement because to blatantly defy my ruling showed he chose death instead of a life in exile.

His actions sealed his fate, so instead of dignifying his request with a verbal answer, I rushed head-on, shifting mid-stride, with only one goal in mind.

To grant his wish.

My sudden movement had everyone exploding into action. The forest filled with sounds of violence, of teeth ripping flesh and of blood spattering on the soil. Growls and pained chuffs created a macabre symphony that overpowered all other noises coming from the animals scampering to escape the fray. Adding my snarl of impatience to the chorus, I jumped onto the closest sabertooth, uncaring about who was who, only that they were standing between me and my target—the arrogant Elder who stood in his biped form, thinking himself safe, smirking at me, assuming he'd finally outwitted the King.

Well, he had another thing coming because even though for every warrior we defeated, two new took their place, neither Beast nor I would rest until he lay dead at our feet.

The number of warriors circling us meant this wasn't some hastily put together plan, but a coordinated one. It was what Urien had warned me about.

At the edge of my vision, I saw more than a dozen sabertooths closing in on each of my mates, who stood strong and deflected most of the offensive moves. But this battle wasn't equal in numbers and the insurgents seemed to enjoy toying with them, attacking, but not yet inflicting maximum damage, only enough to weaken them.

I'd been so focused on getting to Sciiti, that I had closed myself off to our mental link. I braced for the onslaught of their emotions and opened up to our connection, silently berating myself for such a crucial mistake.

'Kali, the green sabertooth on your left is the weakest, and your open-

ing. You need to maneuver closer to me,' Rorc instructed without losing focus on his own opponents. *'Mes,'* he barked, *'get your ass here. We need to form a triangle and guard each other's backs.'*

'Easier said than done, Rorc. They keep coming,' Mes said, but tried to do as asked.

With my attention divided between my mates and my own battle, I didn't react in time to avoid the sabertooth barreling into my side. The cracks of two of my ribs were overly loud in my ears as the added weight of the male pushed me harder on the unyielding soil. Beast, ignoring the fire on our dorsal side, lifted his head, opened his jaw wide and latched on to the offender's neck. Then he clenched his jaw tight, severing the spine and killing another warrior.

We got up on our feet, wheezing, trying to breathe through the pain, when two sabertooths bit Brute's hind leg and pulled in opposite directions, breaking it—the open fracture revealing the bone. My Pair-bond roared in pain, and fell under the weight of the other three that took the opportunity to bring down a wounded foe.

The sharp, stabbing agony was broadcasted through our bond, disorienting us and causing black spots to blur our vision, giving our enemy the opening they were looking for.

I saw a warrior jump on Savage's back and latch on my Pair-bond's neck. I felt fire spread through my underbelly as another raked his claws on Dawn's soft flesh, spilling my mate's blood on the soil.

Beast inhaled deeply and let out an emotion-choked roar—calling for help—for our own arrogance had put our mates, the ones we ought to protect above all others, in grave danger.

Sciiti, seeing my state of discombobulation, shifted and charged me. We were a tick too late to react and he managed to slash our shoulder before we gathered our wits. His need to get one over us, would be what would cost him his life, for he had brought our target to us.

He realized his mistake, but was unable to retreat because the other insurgents—in their haste to get a piece of me—had caged him in.

Beast curled his lips, his version of an ironic smile, when something shockingly unexpected happened.

We heard Kali through our bond hiss the word "enough". Her command froze everyone in place, rendering them unable to move a muscle.

Her order, though, had no effect on us—her mates, because in our Union, we had established our dominance.

I gazed around me and saw confusion. When my eyes landed on the Elder, I witnessed his fight to break her spell. Then when he failed to do so, I felt his anger rise like a tidal wave. I gave him a few more ticks to understand the reality of his situation until terror rocked him as he understood he couldn't escape Kali's hold, and he couldn't flee from the wrath to come.

NEXT, MATE, IS OUR HONEYMOON

KALI

Hearing my mates say they loved me, but more importantly feeling the depth of their emotions, settled my turbulent soul, and put my insecurities to rest like nothing else could. Happiness that was hard to contain filled me. I didn't try to hold it in, but closed my eyes and I shared it with my males.

One moment I was safely in my mates' arms, and the next, all hell broke loose.

I was the most unlucky person in the entire universe, but also the most determined. The moment I had spoken telepathically to Urien, something had clicked into place, changing me irrevocably. A connection between myself and the warriors, who desperately needed hope, had been forged and I couldn't explain it. But I was determined to do everything in my power to offer it to them, and I would start by standing beside my mates and presenting a united front.

So I shifted and fought alongside my males. These sabertooths that were attacking us didn't represent the whole. Their scents were unfamiliar to Dawn, so I was certain they hadn't watched the Queen's Fight. That meant we needed to convince them that we were worthy anew, their numbers, though, were overpowering.

'Kali, the green sabertooth on your left is the weakest, and your opening. You need to maneuver closer to me,' Rorc said, making me roll my eyes, although the gesture went to waste since he couldn't actually see it.

Of course I knew who the weakest was, I just had a different plan.

'Mes, get your ass here,' he continued, *'we need to form a triangle and guard each other's backs.'*

'Easier said than done, Rorc. They keep coming,' my other mate replied.

What we needed was backup. Mindful of the position of the hostiles, but trusting Dawn to protect us, I turned inwardly and searched for my link to Urien—not really sure if it'd still be there. I did a mental backflip when I found the intangible line I was looking for. As I spared a few seconds to study it—because it was different from the one I had with my mates—I realized the connection was one sided.

It was time to test it. *'Urien, we're under attack at the Forest of the Fallen. Bring help,'* I sent my thoughts to him and hoped for the best.

As I refocused on our surroundings, I saw a huge sabertooth collide with Beast's side before taking him down. Then Rorc was overpowered, and the pain from the wound they inflicted on him made the world tilt on its axis and us lose our balance. I turned to Mes, needing him to be all right, only to witness another sabertooth jump on top of Savage and clamp his mouth over the back of his neck.

I wanted to scream at the injustice. I couldn't lose my mates right when I allowed myself to need them, to love them.

A paw with huge claws coming our way reminded me that I didn't have time for a pity party. Dawn moved out of the way, but not fast enough, and the male's razor-sharp tips raked our underbelly.

Fear that my babies had been harmed made me freeze in place, and the sabertooths surrounding me decided to pounce on us, creating a mountain of bodies with us in its base.

Dawn, are our babies harmed? I trusted she would know, and wouldn't lie. The longer she took to answer, the more I felt life drain from us.

They are safe, she said, and I would have taken a big breath if the bodies above me weren't squeezing the heck out of me.

The pounding in my ears drowned out all other sounds.

Adrenaline rushed through my body, suspending the pain.

An edgy, twitchy feeling started growing, morphing into ice-cold fury.

When I couldn't hold it bottled up any longer, I let it explode out of me as I thought, *'Enough!'*

The sabertooths that were on me and on my mates jerked away from us, but they moved as if they weren't the ones with motor control of their bodies. Then they froze.

I didn't care. At this very moment I was only interested in the well-being of my mates.

Savage shifted, and the moment Mes's feet touched the ground, he rushed to us. He pressed his palm on our underbelly, and we felt warmth spreading as the torn edges of our skin were glued back together. The moment he healed that one, he started examining the rest of my injuries, but I shooed him away.

'Rorc needs you more. I'm fine.'

He looked into our eyes, hesitating, but he must have found what he'd been looking for because he raced to his Pair-bond to start healing the open fracture.

We turned our attention to Arana, who had shifted and was looking at me with an emotion I couldn't decipher.

'What?' I asked, suddenly embarrassed, unsure whether I had done something wrong again.

'No one has ever done what you can do.' Arana's voice in my head was full of awe. *'Do you know how powerful you are?'*

Dawn shook her head negatively, making our mate chuckle.

But as he turned to the warriors, all traces of mirth disappeared from his face. "You considered my mate, who won the fight against Urien, and earned her place as your Queen, weak," he said out loud, and stepped in front of the Elder. "The hybrid female, as you called her, is the one who's stopping you from moving, so who is weak? Her or you?" He let them digest his announcement while I felt warriors fighting my hold in vain.

"Shift," he ordered Sciiti, and the Elder had no choice but to obey.

I also released the hold I had on him.

The moment he stood on two feet, Arana wrapped his fingers around Sciiti's throat.

"I gave you a chance at a life away from us, and you threw my courtesy at my face." The baritone depth of my mate's voice lent an ominous tone to his words, and the Elder started struggling in his vain attempt to escape my warrior's hold. "Your disobedience revealed your true desire. So be it. I will grant you your wish."

The hollow crack sounded loudly in the quiet of the forest, and Sciiti's arms fell limp on his sides.

Arana laid the body respectfully on the ground and turned to look at me, his posture rigid. His mind was open wide to me, and his hearts were in his eyes. He was expecting me to condemn him.

'Silly male,' I huffed. *'If you hadn't killed him, I would have,'* I said, giving him the raw truth, for I wasn't one to pretend to be someone else.

The tension left him in a rush, and I felt his love radiate through our bond. *'Wicked female, release the warriors. You punished them enough.'*

I did as he asked, and not too long after, a bewildered Urien, followed by a whole brigade of sabertooths, rushed into the fray to protect us. Only to stop short when they saw the Saberian warriors kneeling before their royals.

As I looked over as many of them as I could, I realized with a sinking heart we weren't the only ones who had been fighting.

Mes's innate healing ability came to life with a vengeance just by being in the presence of so many wounded individuals. He only managed to stay put by Rorc's side because his Pair-bond's injury was too serious to even consider stopping for a second.

"It is over," Arana announced.

"We would have reached you sooner…but we had to fight…then we couldn't move…I don't know how…" Urien stuttered, at a loss for words.

My mate spared him. "It was Kali's doing. She prohibited your movements."

I could almost hear the jaws dropping on the floor.

"Be proud, for your Queen is stronger than any before her." Arana's deep voice carried the message to most. "I know you are afraid of change, but it has already found us. We had been so sure we could protect our own, and our precious females were the ones to pay the price. We won't make the same mistake twice. The Creator has given us another chance. We need to grab it with both hands."

The warriors erupted into celebratory yells, and hoots, and whistles, and I rejoiced with them.

When Arana stretched his hand and beckoned us to him, Dawn trotted to his side.

I took control of our body and shifted at the last second, but as soon as I did, he slipped his arm around my tummy, and pulled my back flush against his chest to watch the warriors surrounding us with him.

Arana gave them the chance to settle, while he waited for Mes—whose color had paled dangerously—and Rorc, who was limping, but had no bones protruding, to flank our sides.

As the crowd quieted, he addressed them again. "We were worried that even if we found compatible mates, we wouldn't get offspring out of those Unions, or that the cubs wouldn't have sabertooths. With great joy, I announce to you that the Creator has blessed us again. Your Queen is expecting three cubs, and they each have the ability to shift."

If reverence was something tangible, it would be what I was experiencing at that moment as the warriors knelt as one and tilted their heads, revealing their necks respectfully to me. Even the ones that had been determined to kill us not too long ago.

Slowly, with Urien at the helm, they approached and started congratulating us.

I might have been standing there for hours, I might have been standing there for days. The only thing I knew was that I was too tired, and very relieved to see that the long line of Saberians had finally come to an end.

My three mates had alternated holding me while we conversed with the warriors, and I was currently in Mes's arms. I pressed back against him, burrowing deeper into his warmth.

"So what's next?" I asked, not really caring what that would actually be, as long as we were all together.

Mes pulled my hair to the side and kissed my neck. "Next, Mate —" he started.

"Is our honeymoon," Rorc finished, managing to knock my socks off.

"Excuse me?" I asked, because there was no way they knew what that was.

"We promised to take you on a honeymoon, and that's what we're planning to do," Arana purred, his smoky voice full of seductive promises.

"Okay, I'll bite. What's our destination?" I asked, certain I'd call their bluff this time.

My males snickered in response to my thoughts.

"Earth," Mes whispered, his lips caressing the shell of my ear, causing shivers to race down my spine.

They were serious. "Well in that case, I guess...we're going on a honeymoon. I call shotgun!" I yelled and ran, knowing they'd come after me, and that soon the chase would turn to much more enjoyable endeavors.

Damn, I was one lucky gal.

Thank you for reading Saved Warriors!

Turn the page for an **excerpt** from **DIVIDED WARRIORS**, book 3 in The Pyxis System series.

DIVIDED WARRIORS—THE ROYALS OF SABER

Kali

I should have been dreaming, yet sleep evaded.

Snuggled as I was between Rorc, who was lying on his stomach, and Mes, who had his arm draped over me, I should have been able to rest.

Instead, I lay wet, dissatisfied, and aching. Deep and fervent longing filled me as I traced my mates' naked bodies in our reflection in the mirrored ceiling.

All of them had loved this feature when we'd stayed at the Wravukian palace, so Arana had warriors install them in our palatial chambers too.

It had its advantages...I loved to watch their muscles ripple and their faces strain while they did everything in their power to make me orgasm as many times as possible before they reached their peaks.

I trailed my fingers along Mes's forearm.

He didn't even stir.

Argh, I swear they do it on purpose.

Let's punish them. Then they'll realize they've been neglecting your needs, Dawn—my occasionally bloodthirsty sabertooth, and willing conspirator—said.

A sigh escaped my lips. Unfortunately, drawing orgasms from me wasn't something they did anymore. As my pregnancy progressed and my belly grew, they became more distant.

Oh, they were still doting on me, the perfect mates really... unless it came to sex. Then they turned into guardians, like I was a fragile being about to break if they touched me intimately.

It frustrated me to no end. My mood had soured, and my patience was wearing thin.

I freely admitted that the first trimester hadn't been easy.

Morning sickness should be named differently because it didn't just occur during mornings, but all freaking day long. Trying to keep food down had proved to be a challenge, and I'd ended up vomiting at least twice a day. I still did.

My hormones were all over the place, and my sex drive, the same one that had been non-existent until recently, had skyrocketed.

I was just going through what many women on Earth experienced while pregnant. My symptoms were nothing out of the ordinary.

Was it fun? Definitely not.

Was it scary? A little bit.

I was certain, though, all first-time mothers felt similarly. Unfortunately, it drove my mates' protective instincts through the roof. Especially since there'd never been another one like me, and they had no information on Humans.

Telling my mates that what was happening was normal was not enough for Mes—who wanted scientific evidence. And until he got it, he'd decreed that we wouldn't be mating, lest they hurt me or the babies.

Well, if I have to lie awake, they should too.

Having decided on their punishment for now, I was about to wake them up when suddenly an acute pain zinged through my lower abdomen and I felt liquid gush out of me. My eyes were still glued to the mirror, and I watched the color drain from my face and stain the sheet underneath my thighs. The room spun and became blurry.

Dawn leaped to the surface. Her claws sprang through my fingers, but it was too late. Everything turned black.

Mes

Kali's panic brought us out of our slumber. Was she having another nightmare?

Rorc turned sideways and raised his head. "Wake up, little one. It's just a dream."

A metallic scent permeated the air, and Arana gasped, "Kali."

Pain seared through my forearm—Dawn's claws had burst from Kali's hand and raked me.

What had me ignoring the pain, and all of us scrambling to our feet, though, was the red circle widening under her body.

Our bond radiated with fear.

"Mes, what's happening?" Rorc's first instinct was to act, yet he refrained from doing so because he trusted I'd do everything to help our mate, to fix whatever was wrong.

Arana pushed him out of the way and was about to lift Kali's body when a growl from Savage—my sabertooth—stopped him. "She's still bleeding. I need to stop it before we move her to the Healer's Hall," I explained.

Images of his mother's last moments blinded me for a moment, and his fear that the same virus was now claiming our mate had me in its grips.

"Arana, look at Kali. What happened to your females isn't being repeated." I did my best to reassure him before I called forth my healing light and placed one palm over our mate's heart and the other over her lower abdomen. Closing my eyes, I let everything else but our female disappear.

Her heart rate kept increasing, and her breathing was loud and labored.

Time was running out.

I concentrated on her lower half. Her body transformed into a map of muscle, tissue, veins, bones and organs inside my mind. I saw our babies and heard their fast-beating hearts. They were aware something was wrong with their mother, but they were nestled safely in her uterus. I released the breath I'd been holding when I found the blood was coming from Kali's cervix. I could temporarily fix that.

Carefully targeting the problematic area with my healing light, I stopped the flow and repaired the damage. But our mate wasn't out of danger yet.

Picking her up in my arms, I secured her close to my chest so as not to jostle her, and raced to the Healers' Hall where the med-pod was.

"She needs a transfusion, immediately," I informed my Pair-bonds, who trailed behind us.

Both of them remained silent while I laid her down, retrieved neutral blood and plasma units, inserted them in the med-pod's transfusion portal, and activated the machine that would help her recover.

Its adaptable protective capsule soon enfolded Kali. It stretched all over her, then shrank to mold around her body.

Our offspring moved inside her swollen belly, and I clenched my fingers where I was holding on to the control panel, then closed my eyes and hung my head. My entire body shivered as the reality of how close we'd been to losing her—and them—sunk in. "She has a fucking fragment embedded in her cervix." The sudden lump in my throat made speaking difficult. "I can't remove it alone, and my Healers aren't familiar with her physiology…we need to bring a Human Healer here."

Desperation filled me because it'd been a close call, and I wasn't willing to risk her. The darkness in me reared its ugly head, and Savage fought for control over our body. He wanted to expel its energy before it overpowered us and we ended up hurting those we loved.

My Pair-bonds sensed my inner turmoil and placed their hands on my back, lending me their strength, allowing me to rein in my dark side once again. But I couldn't stand still, so I started pacing.

"How are we going to get the Earthling to come here?" Arana asked.

Unbelievable. He was putting another's life over our female's. I exploded. "I. Don't. Care."

Let's challenge him. It's time we took the reins. Savage snarled in my mind, equally furious.

Maybe my sabertooth was right. I advanced on Arana. "No one is more important than Kali. We'll do whatever the fuck it takes."

Rorc laughed out loud, and we zeroed in on him.

"I'm really enjoying the role reversal we've got going on." Grinning like a fool, he added, "Usually I'm the hot-headed Pair-bond."

Noticing the death stare I was giving him, he raised his arms up in surrender. He'd only been trying to lighten my mood to keep me from spiraling.

"Of course Kali takes precedence over everyone else, Mes," Arana interjected. "But our warriors need Human females. We can't mess this up. Our request needs to go through the Intergalactic Enosis first."

"We can't spare that much time—"

The door opened and Grim—Urien's sabertooth—burst in, followed by many sabertooths.

Having my Pair-bonds with me usually lessened the impact others' emotions had on me, but they caught us by surprise, and without Kali's shield that kept external feelings at bay, their panic hit me all at once. A thousand needles pierced my skull—the pain blinded me and muddled my thoughts. It would have brought me to my knees, if it weren't for Savage's strength.

Arana, experiencing my feelings through our Sacred Bond and needing to protect me, ordered them to shift at the same time with a furious Rorc.

The combined command blasted through the warriors, whose pained groans from the forced change echoed in the hall and around us.

Urien, like those behind him, kneeled on the floor in front of us, panting. All of their faces were etched with worry. "Is the Queen all right? We all felt her terror," he asked while scanning the chamber.

We knew he saw her when he swiftly sucked in a deep breath and staggered to his feet, trying to go to her.

"What do you mean you all felt her?" Arana asked, taken aback by the new development.

The tension in his body had both me and Rorc paying our undivided attention to their discussion.

"Her terror…it woke us up." He was shaken. "The same way she spoke in our minds at the Queen's Fight."

"I'd hoped that was a one-time thing." My Pair-bond rubbed his bottom lip with his thumb, lost in thought. "Did Dawn make those?" He pointed to the four angry pink lines decorating my forearm. The edges of where the skin melded together, jagged and bumpy.

"Yes."

"She shouldn't have been able to shift partially yet. It takes many rotations to achieve such a feat. Her powers are growing," Arana commented.

An ominous cloud settled over us. We didn't know whether there would be any repercussions to her gifts. Many were easy to control, but the stronger they were, the heavier the toll on the individual.

Protect our mate. Savage paced within the confines of my mind, every few paces pushing against my boundaries, trying to take our body over, but we didn't need his aggression. We needed a level head and a plan.

"Is our Queen all right?" The pain was clear in Urien's voice, who was standing next to the med-pod.

"She will be. We'll allow no other outcome," I declared, and stared pointedly at Arana.

"Is she stable now?" he asked, and I nodded. The Saberian then turned toward the crowd and ordered, "Gwyr, stay with Kali. If anything changes, inform us immediately. Urien, come with us. Let's move to the Communications Chamber."

"I want Zoltor to stay as well," the Saberian Healer asked, and I accepted his request. The more looking after our mate, the better.

A commotion had Rorc running outside, Urien, Dag, and Aux right on his heels.

I chuckled when I heard him cursing under his breath. Having others shadowing him annoyed my Pair-bond to no end. He was used to being the one doing the protecting, but he was now the Third King of Saber, and he had no choice but to allow the warriors to do their duty.

After checking the updated report on the med-pod and making sure Kali was safe and comfortable, I joined the others outside.

"Return to your posts, warriors," the King ordered, and the crowd started dispersing. "Admiral," Rorc turned to Thora, "put your weapon away. No one will hurt the females here."

The Admiral's emotions were like an angry volcano erupting—its spewing lava swallowing everything it came into contact with. The hatred and distrust emanating from him burned me with their intensity, but his expression revealed nothing. His hand holding the blaster steadied as he lowered it to his side.

"Kings," he acknowledged and briefly bowed his head. "I came to deliver the Mardonians per your Queen's request."

One circle ago, my father had insisted on shipping the females back to their planet, but our stubborn mate would hear none of that. She had proclaimed them citizens of Saber and had demanded they'd be brought here immediately. I hadn't expected him to accept. The last time I'd seen the King of Wravuk acquiesce so easily was when my mother was still alive.

Kali's uncanny ability to wrap those she met around her little finger kept surprising me. She was extraordinary.

The older female was shifting from one foot to the other, and there were scratches across her forearm where the youngling was clutching her.

"Of course, they are welcome to stay here." Arana was quick to say, wanting to put the fidgeting females at ease. "Tris, Kas," he addressed the mother and then the daughter, "Ewen will accompany you to the guest chamber, and once Kali is up, we'll find you a permanent dwelling."

"Thank you, my Kings." If her verbal acknowledgment of our authority hadn't been proof enough of where she stood, tilting her head to the side, declaring her submission, made it very clear before the females followed the Royal Guard, leaving my Pairbonds and me alone with Thora and Urien, who'd stayed even though everyone was ordered to return to their positions.

A rumble vibrated in Rorc's chest, sounding loud in the quiet of the night. Brute didn't like disobedience any more than his biped counterpart did.

The leader of the Main Territory revealed his neck. "I need to help." His tone was demanding, insistent.

Arana's eyes snapped the warrior's way. A subconscious current of worry zinged from him through to our bond, alerting both me and Rorc that there was something we were unaware of. In the short time I'd known the Saberians, I came to care for them, to claim them as mine—Kali was solely to blame for that. So I let my walls fall, wanting to get a feel for Urien's emotions and see if there was any way I could help him.

What I sensed shook me, and abruptly, I turned away from everyone.

Arana's brother—in all ways but blood—was hanging on by a thread. Grim's blood-thirst was almost out of control. The warrior's sheer will seemed to be the only thing controlling the dangerous sabertooth.

Lethe, the bane of every unmated Saberian's existence, would claim him soon and end his life, unless he found his mate.

I shared what I discovered with my Pair-bonds, and it was as if I could see the gears turning in Rorc's mind, already forming a plan.

"First, we contact the Enosis," Arana reiterated.

"Yes, but we need a contingency plan, and I happen to have found the perfect one," Rorc said, arms crossed and a look of superiority adorning his face.

I doubted these two would stop antagonizing each other, no matter how much time passed.

"I'll leave you to it, then," Thora interjected. "I'm just asking for permission to stay on the surface tonight, so my crew can rest."

"You aren't dismissed, Admiral," Rorc replied, and since my father hadn't stripped him of his rank yet—a hybrid in a position of power was a first—the Wravukian had to obey his superior. "Your assistance will be needed."

"Let's take this meeting to the War Chamber. Urien, you're coming too," Arana said, turning on his heels to head to our destination with us behind him.

DIVIDED WARRIORS—EXCITEMENT FOR THE HUNT

URIEN

It was a fifty-fifty chance when I demanded to help that one of my Kings would tear my head off, but despite the dire situation with our Queen in danger, I'd been lucky. So I trailed after them, ignoring Grim's attempts to take over our body and attack the Wravukian trailing behind us. My sabertooth hated placing ourselves in vulnerable positions. And usually I agreed, but I couldn't let him influence me now. We were safe, and Kali needed all the assistance we could provide. So I followed them, ready to volunteer for whatever the males I'd give my life for had planned.

Once we were all seated at the round table, Arana initiated the virtual call.

All the species participating in the Intergalactic Enosis appointed a Senator to represent them and take part in the Committees responsible for different matters and for creating laws and procedures the Enosis members abided by.

Every ten rotations, the Senators would elect sixteen beings who would act as Ambassadors—usually in charge of everything the Committees couldn't handle. The Ambassador with the most votes was appointed the title of Cardinal Prime and had the final say in all escalated issues.

I didn't know how crazy my Royals' plan was, but I was in nonetheless. No matter what the Enosis would decree.

The Delegates from the Preliminary Committee would be the ones answering Arana's call and cataloging the request, but it would be at least a couple of circles before our issue was escalated, and we heard back from the Core Committee—who handled the affairs regarding primitive planets—about whether we were allowed to proceed or not.

Slowly, a figure taller than me, with a strong broad back dressed in partial armor, appeared through the holo-projector in the middle of the table, and my mouth fell open. "King Arana." The helmet covering this being's face didn't muffle his deep voice. "What a pleasant surprise. Have you reconsidered my proposition?"

Fuck. The situation must have been worse than I assumed because my warrior brother bypassed the Intergalactic Enosis' established procedure and called the Cardinal Prime—Lord Mo'dta.

"I wish I could say the same." Arana's grim tone had the imposing being straightening his shoulders. "This isn't a social call. I'm here to collect one of the favors you owe me."

Everyone held their breath. My King's move was bold.

The head of the Intergalactic Enosis lifted his clawed fingers and took off his helmet. He retracted the white membrane that covered his narrowed eyes and locked his bright-orange gaze on Arana. "What is this about?"

Mine widened, partly because I was surprised and partly because the sight was terrifying. I'd never seen a Shartja, commonly known as Apex Hunters, without his armor's mask. Even though our physiques were similarly built, his head with the horns where brows should have been, the protective membrane over his big round eyes, the lack of lips over his rows of sharp teeth, and the three mandibles on each side—like the ones our arachnids had—made for a dread-inducing sight.

Arana didn't seem disturbed at all, so I schooled my features and paid attention to their discussion.

"We ask for permission to access a primitive planet and acquire one of their Healers." My brother wasn't in a mood to beat around the bush.

Mo'dta crossed his arms, waiting, appraising my King silently. When he divulged no more information, the Cardinal Prime heaved a sigh. "Why would you need one from a primitive world? My Healers are at your disposal, you know that."

"My mate," Arana started, but a loud growl—coming from Rorc—reverberated in the room, interrupting him and making Admiral Thora tense. "Our mate," he corrected, "is in danger."

The image of the holo-projector went completely still, and I wondered whether it was a glitch or if the Head of the Enosis was just speechless. "Our?" he asked as his mandibles went slack and his jaw dropped.

Ha. He was stunned.

I grinned.

Arana's hand hovered above the holo-projector before tapping a key that allowed the whole chamber to be viewed through the projection. "Mo'dta, allow me to introduce my Pair-bonds—Second and Third King of Saber—Mes and Rorc."

The Hunter's head jerked back. "Your female evoked an inter-species Sacred Union?" he asked, but before my brother could speak, he continued in a rush, "Which planet?"

"Earth. We need to acquire one of their Healers as soon as possible," Arana reiterated, drawing his mouth into a straight line, unease leaking through the connection we all had with our King.

He wasn't amused by the fact that the Cardinal Prime had ignored the introduction to his Pair-bonds, both of which had gone rigid while he'd focused on the Queen.

I didn't like it either. We'd never warred against the Shartja, but if the Apex Hunter got any funny ideas in his big head regarding our most prized female, he had another thing coming. Every single Saberian warrior would protect her until his last breath.

Mo'dta leaned forward, his eyes practically glowing orange. "Earth..." he trailed off, his gaze turning inward for a moment before he caught himself and continued, "I allow you to request one of their Healers to assist you. You will offer your protection with no strings attached, and return him unharmed once his knowledge is no longer required."

"Of course," Arana promised, in a rush to wrap up their meeting.

"Expect my presence on Saber in a cycle's time. I'm looking forward to making the acquaintance of your female," he said, and it was like a dark cloud entered our chamber, lowering the temperature and causing chills to erupt on our skin. "Kings." He nodded and his image disappeared as the connection was terminated.

"That went well..." I let my voice trail off in a failed attempt to lighten the mood.

Foolish male, Grim—who'd remained silent thus far—told me. *How does lightening the mood help? Our Queen needs our help, let's go pick up the Healer.*

Arana finding his mates was an event almost all Saberians rejoiced in. I was truly happy for my brother, but at the same time, the joyful event dredged up a deep pain I thought I'd put to rest.

It had been more than a hundred rotations since all the male warriors had left to defend the Zirgnoln, but I remembered the events as if it were yesterday because earlier that day I'd found my mate.

She'd come to the Main Territory from the South to protect Queen Aenthear and Caeleah while all the males were off-planet. I was so certain that she'd be there the moment we returned that I'd barely spoken to her. Wanting to remain focused on the upcoming battle, I didn't allow the bond to strengthen when I knew we'd be apart for a while and the distance would have only brought us pain.

Little did I know that Yenoctonia—the day we lost all our females—would rob me of the opportunity to get to know her…to cherish her…to create a family with her.

I was devastated, but since the bond hadn't been established, I could still function. Helping Arana rebuild our society had further softened the loss. Being needed by so many others had taken my mind off my own troubles until at some point the pain faded completely.

From the moment Arana had found his mates, Grim's mood had gradually but steadily deteriorated. I had chalked it up to the new reality we had to get used to. He was still our brother, but he now had two Pair-bonds who were there to assist him, so he no longer needed our help.

Hope we'd still be useful had bloomed when I'd seen the size of the Human female. Then we'd fought the Queen's Fight and lost. Kali had demonstrated how strong she was, not only by establishing a mind-link with every Saberian alive, but by asserting her dominance over everyone but her mates.

She definitely didn't need us. She was powerful, and she'd proved just how much when she stopped the Southern and Western

Territories' rebellion…the one we, the Royal Guards, and the Elite warriors had failed to prevent.

Observing the Sacred Mates together was like rubbing salt in wounds I thought had been healed. I was wrong, and my sabertooth started slipping slowly down the path to Lethe, and I didn't know how to stop him. The Creator had blessed us with a Sacred Mate, but we'd lost her. There was nothing on the horizon for us, and it fucking tore me apart.

So Grim suggesting to help now was a big deal. It meant he hadn't given up completely, and maybe we'd escape Lethe—the madness that would end us both—for a little while longer.

The sound of Mes's fist connecting with the table pulled me back to the present. "We have the Intergalactic Enosis' permission. We need to act now," the usually calm Arch-healer said.

Arana turned to his other Pair-bond. "Rorc, what's the plan?" he asked.

"We'll lure a Healer to us." The Second King started pacing around the chamber, breathing evenly and exuding tranquility as he shared his idea. "We'll need to be near Earth's orbit, but we'll advertise that a hefty payment will be given to the Earthling who is willing to travel to an unknown destination to assist with a Queen's difficult pregnancy." He stopped as if considering what he had just proposed, then continued, "Yes, and we won't divulge any other information until the Human has arrived on Saber for privacy reasons."

"I'll go fetch the Earthling," Thora volunteered.

Why would he want to help us? A Wravukian Admiral with his own fleet was the last person I'd expect to step forward for such a mission.

"No need. I'll bring the Healer here," I declared.

"And how familiar are you with intergalactic travel, Saberian?" His condescending tone grated my nerves.

I opened my mouth to tell him exactly what I thought when Rorc said, "It's not a one-male job. Both of you will go, and you'll be rewarded upon your return."

The mistrust was a knife slicing me deeply. "Arana, I will not fail my Queen," I appealed. "I don't require a reward, and there's no reason to involve an outsider."

Something passed between the Sacred Mates that I couldn't decipher.

"You'll both go," my brother decreed, and I could not deny him. I nodded my assent.

"I do not require a material reward either, but I wish for something in return," the Wravukian said, and locked gazes with Rorc.

"What is it you want, Admiral?" Arana asked.

When he remained silent, Rorc nudged him. "It's not my story to tell. Go on, Thora. This might be the only chance you'll ever get."

These two had a history, and it made me curious. What was so important that the Wravukian would give up a financial reward for?

The older male squared his shoulders and planted his feet wide apart. "I demand Ivar Al-Jurjani be punished for his crime." He clenched and unclenched his fists before continuing in a tart tone, "He killed my Chosen Mate."

Curling my upper lip at him, I let the snarl brewing in my chest out. Simultaneously, I stepped back, putting more distance between us because I wanted to punch him for accusing a Saberian warrior of such a serious crime.

"That old male has no tact," Rorc mumbled under his breath, but thanks to our enhanced senses, I heard him just fine.

And maybe in any other instance, I'd have found his comment funny, but not now.

"Do you have proof?" Arana asked.

Thora furrowed his brows and ground his teeth. "I don't. But I was the one who cost him his right eye." Volunteering no more details, he simply waited for the Saberian King's reaction.

Arana let the silence stretch, measuring the Wravukian, and I could tell by the tightness on Thora's face that he expected his request to be declined. "Your accusation is of a despicable crime. Before we pass judgment, we will set up a hearing with both of you present, Admiral," my brother said.

"That is acceptable, thank you." The Wravukian bowed respectfully, then added, "I'm also to inform you of what we found during the prisoner's interrogation."

"Go on," Rorc ordered.

"A new group that calls themselves the Order of the Prime hired the Crootan. Their orders were to capture a Saberian male and deliver him to them—in one piece or many, it didn't matter. They want to finish the job they started so many rotations ago when they had your females killed."

My guttural roar joined Arana's and drowned all other noises. The desire for vengeance, the need to hurt those responsible, to see their blood spill was amplified by my King's emotions, and overpowered my other senses. "Do you have their location?" I growled, my voice less intelligible than normal due to Grim rising to the surface.

"No. He was more afraid of betraying this Order than he was of our interrogator," Thora said.

I stomped to him, ready to grab him by the collar and demand he take me to the prisoner, when Arana stopped me.

"Urien, stand down," he said, then addressed the Admiral, "Where is the pirate?"

"He was murdered in his cell."

Rorc's lips pulled back in disgust. "That means there's a fucking traitor high in the Wravukian ranks."

Thora's posture was stiff, his jaw set. "An investigation is being conducted according to King Nathraichean's orders." His clipped words indicated he wasn't willing to discuss the matter further.

Arana clapped Rorc's shoulder in camaraderie. "We'll contact him, to let him know he has our support if he needs it."

The Second King of Saber nodded, then told Thora, "As soon as the sun rises on the horizon, Urien will come get you, so make the needed arrangements for your departure. You'll travel with the S-970, as time is of the essence and that's the fastest ship at our disposal." Then he turned to me. "Inform Mok to add Thora's biometrics to the navigational system before you depart."

I agreed, and when no one had anything else to add, the Third King of Saber said, "That is all for now. We'll be in constant communication for anything else that may come up," wrapping up our meeting.

And for the first time in a while, lightness replaced the hollowness that had been dragging my chest down as excitement for the hunt filled both me and Grim.

If you enjoyed this excerpt from DIVIDED WARRIORS, ask for a copy at your favorite bookstore.

GLOSSARY

Astronomical Unit (AU): AU is the distance between Earth and the sun.

Biska: Explorer.

Circle: A full circle is the Saberian day and is equivalent to twenty-eight hours.

Cycle: A full cycle is the Saberian month and is equivalent to thirty-eight circles.

Monakrivimou: My precious, my one and only.

Pallium: A rectangular length of cloth, worn around the waist and over one shoulder. The Saberians used it as a cloak.

Psehimou: My soul.

Pneuma: Soul.

Rotation: A full rotation is the Saberian year and is equivalent to eighteen cycles.

Scaths: Weight measurement equivalent to kilos/pounds.

Sharacval: A venomous snake-like species.

Spires: Equivalent to one hour.

Stridulate: To produce a shrill, grating sound, as a cricket does, by rubbing together certain parts of the body; shrill.

Tick: Second, moment.

Torsek: A domesticated species that looks like a four-legged phoenix and are excellent companions.

Vackal: Asshole.

ABOUT THE AUTHOR

Aurora Welkin is a sci-fi and paranormal romance author. She lives in Sydney, Australia. She enjoys reading a little too much, and her loved ones usually find her with her nose in a book. In her free time, you'll find her strolling along the beach with her husband, savoring a cup of cocoa and watching their little prince explore the world.

www.aurorawelkin.com

Aurora loves to hear from readers! The best way to connect with her online is via her newsletter. You can sign up here: www.aurorawelkin.com/mailing-list

www.ingramcontent.com/pod-product-compliance
Lightning Source LLC
Chambersburg PA
CBHW020458310726
48979CB00016B/2703/J
* 9 7 8 0 6 4 8 9 7 7 4 9 0 *